Don't
Embarrass
the Bureau

BY THE SAME AUTHOR

Dancehall

Don't Embarrass the Bureau

BERNARD F CONNERS

W.H. ALLEN · LONDON
A Howard & Wyndham Company
1984

To CCC

With all our most holy illusions
Knocked higher than Gilderoy's kite,
We have had a jolly good lesson,
And serves us jolly well right!

—KIPLING

Contents

PART ONE

Harvey Tucker

'United Airlines Flight 274 to New York now boarding at gate 7B.'

Harvey picked up the bag from the seat next to him and started toward the glass doors that led to the planes. He was only a few yards from the exit when a hand gently but firmly closed on his upper arm. 'Agent Tucker?' said a voice softly.

Harvey turned quickly and found himself confronted with a pleasant oval face belonging to a man about forty-five years old. The man was wearing a nondescript raincoat and a grey snap-brim hat. From under the hat curled blond, rather frizzy hair into sideburns that were just a trifle long. Crow's-feet at the corners of the eyes and lines near the mouth suggested the face was probably most relaxed when it was smiling. It was an agreeable, honest-looking countenance.

'Yes?' said Harvey, surprised. 'I'm Tucker.'

'FBI, Tucker.' The man popped open and shut his credential case with his left hand, demonstrating a facility for the manœuvre that came with years of experience. 'Would you come with us, please?'

'What?' said Harvey, looking at the man askance. 'But my plane's leaving and—'

'Sorry, Tucker,' said the man with a slight shrug. 'We were told to bring you to the office.' He placed his arm about Harvey's shoulders and started to guide him toward a door that led to the street.

'But what about my luggage?'

'We've already got it. Just come along and don't worry.'

'Je-sus Christ!' exclaimed Harvey. 'Don't they ever let up?

My folks will be waiting at the train station.'

'You can make a call from the office. We'll be there in a few minutes.'

As they neared the door to the street, a second man, who apparently had been waiting nearby, fell into step alongside Harvey. 'Hi,' he said, smiling pleasantly. He was younger than the other man, possibly thirty-five or so, fair, good-looking, conservatively dressed.

'Huh—oh, hello,' responded Harvey glumly. 'How come they had to send two guys to get me?'

'Two nothing,' said the younger man as they pushed through the door out onto a ramp. 'Three!' He nodded toward the kerb, where a third figure sat in the darkness behind the wheel of a grey sedan. 'You're apparently more important than you take credit for.'

'What's it all about, anyway?'

'Beats me,' replied the man, opening the rear door of the car and getting in.

The older man motioned Harvey into the centre seat and got in behind him. 'All we know is our orders were to pick you up before you boarded that plane.'

'Hell, I feel like a subject sitting here between you two.'

'Sorry, fella,' said the older agent in the same kind tone. 'You can appreciate our position, though. We're just handling an assignment. You know the procedure.' As the car pulled away from the ramp, he reached inside Harvey's coat and withdrew the service revolver. 'Procedure, you know,' he added apologetically.

Harvey pursed his lips but said nothing. He had a rather good idea why he was being taken back to the office. He had stumbled onto some sensitive facts, the significance of which he could only guess. The Bureau undoubtedly wanted to question him about how much he knew and just how he had secured his information. Well, he would tell them. Everything! And while he was at it, he'd tell them what he thought about their crackpot organisation. He'd had enough. Their egocentric Director! Their bugged rooms! Their plants! Their fruity girls!

* * *

4

Nine months previously the life of Harvey Tucker had been less complicated. The day he received notice of his appointment to the FBI had started in a particularly relaxing fashion. He was lying in bed watching the formation of bundles of grey clouds through the window just over his bunk. He had become fairly proficient as a forecaster. Because the forecast was important. If it rained or was unpleasant, he was not needed on the dock downstairs to perform as lifeguard. Hence, a few extra hours of sleep, which was always welcome to a bachelor twenty-seven years old.

But on that particular morning his hopes for a few more hours in the bunk faded with the appearance on the horizon of an ever-widening patch of blue. It was regrettable. He had had just two hours' sleep. Finally he knew it was hopeless. It would not be long before the ladies came drifting down to the beach. Rolling into a sitting position, he reached for his bathing suit, which hung from a peg on the wall just above the bed. 'All right, you guys, your leader is on his feet!'

'Screw the leader,' came a sleepy voice from somewhere in the room.

'Yeah,' responded another. 'First time the leader's been off his dead ass in a week.'

Harvey, ignoring the comments, demonstrated extraordinary dexterity as he pulled on his bathing suit while striding across the room. He stopped next to a large mound of dirty grey sheets rising and falling rhythmically on a bed in a corner. 'LOUIE!'

The form jumped, and a shaggy dark head appeared from under the covers. Louie Alimonti rubbed his eyes and looked up at his boss. 'Why can't you just wake somebody up in a civilised manner?'

'Let's go, Louie. Get your ass downstairs and unlock that gate. And that goes for the rest of you. When the leader works, everybody works.'

Harvey descended the stairs and walked out onto the canvas-covered deck. As was his usual procedure, he walked toward the guard tower. While guests were rarely on the dock that early, he had found it a good practice to sit on the tower as early as possible. The guard tower could be seen from the

5

office of Mr Piper, the club secretary, whose responsibilities included overseeing the waterfront. Harvey liked to give the secretary a look at him the first thing each morning.

He felt the sun starting to burn through the overcast as he climbed the ladder. It would be another hot day. Stretching his long legs out, he leaned his head back against the tower and gazed out over the water. He delighted in these peaceful moments which followed a morning rain—the lake still and mirror-like, the occasional ponderous creaking of the dock, the far shoreline taking shape and seeming to move toward him through the mist, which slowly rose to dissipate in the high mountains that ringed Lake Placid. It was as though he were ensconced in the crow's-nest of a ship moving silently through a fog.

But soon his vessel would come alive as the middle-aged women who comprised the club's beach set came fluttering down. There would be the usual exchange of 'oohs' and 'ahhs' as they commented on each other's seemingly inexhaustible wardrobe of beach regalia—outfits calculated to focus attention on what might better have gone unnoticed. The gentle slap of the water against the dock and the comfortable creaking of the piers would be replaced by the incessant chatter of banal conversation, voices vying for dominance as fuzzy thoughts tumbled forth at the moment of their inception. The cacophony would rise and fall on the summer air until it all merged into one continuous drone, interrupted occasionally by the cackle of one struck by her own wit, or an infrequent splash followed by a squeal, as a tired old form was immersed in ageless Lake Placid.

For Harvey Tucker it was a languid existence, stretching out his six-foot one-inch frame on the guard tower, leisurely sunning himself and only occasionally peering from beneath his sunglasses at the faded shapes that covered the waterfront like lumpy sacks of grain awaiting shipment. He had spent the previous five summers at the club while attending college and then law school. Each summer had seen the implementation of new procedures designed to simplify his job to provide a maximum of leisure and a minimum of effort. It was doubtful if the members of the club who paid upwards of fifty dollars

6

per day enjoyed more ease and relaxation than the incumbent lifeguard.

He was a tall but otherwise average-looking young man with pleasant if somewhat angular features. He had brownish blond hair complete with cowlick bleached white from the sun, eyes that matched the washed-out blue of his denim shirts, an easy smile, and features that readily folded into a glad-to-see-you expression. It was the kind of appearance that was an immediate success with older women.

Over the years he had developed a certain confidence with the members, and his familiarity of expression, which might have been considered excessive in a less attractive young man, could awaken the dormant coquetry in the most dour of the ladies who frequented the beach.

Few arrived who were not favoured with a cordial, if sometimes indelicate, remark from the tower, and while the comments themselves on occasion may have been considered unpropitious by some, always they were delivered with an abundance of goodwill from which it was difficult to take offence.

'Good morning, Mrs Hepple. New bathing suit? Smart! Smart, indeed.' One hundred and seventy pounds of sixty-year-old flesh sagging from a black tank suit with latticed sides.

Or, 'Lovely! Just splendid!' to Mrs Green, who once every hour executed her swan dive, flopping onto the water with the poise of a stricken bird.

Or, commenting on Mrs Allen's efforts to tan a body the colour of frozen french fries, 'Why, it's coming along just beautifully. Say, why don't you try a bit more iodine in the olive oil? Ah . . . as a matter of fact, Madam, why don't we just put a touch of this olive oil in the iodine?'

And to Mrs Wilson and Mrs Carraway, a couple of regulars arriving in tent-sized bikinis, 'Good afternoon, ladies. Airing your differences, I see!'

Yes, of course, it was too much, but he was able to carry it off, and of those women who regularly availed themselves of the Lake Placid Club beach facilities there was hardly one who did not consider Harvey Tucker a charmer.

'Mr Tucker! Mr Tucker! Wake up, Mr Tucker!'

'Oh! What? Yes! What is it?' said Harvey, awakening with a start. Shielding his eyes from the sun he gazed down to see Mr Piper standing next to the guard tower.

'You've done it again, Mr Tucker. You've fallen asleep on the watchtower.' His voice was not unkind in spite of his concern.

'Oh, no, sir. Not at all, sir,' said Harvey, groping for his sunglasses as he tried to adjust to the sunlight. 'I wasn't asleep, Mr Piper. I was just kind of resting my eyes. It's a bit bright up here, sir.'

'No, you were asleep, Mr Tucker,' persisted the man. 'I saw you dozing from the clubhouse window. It looked as though you were going to fall off the watchtower.'

'Oh, no, sir,' responded the lifeguard, struggling to clear the cobwebs. 'Ah, Mr Piper, sir, would you please hand up those sunglasses? It's a bit bright up here, sir.'

Alvin Piper retrieved the glasses from the dock where they had fallen and handed them up to his lifeguard with a hopeless sigh. He was a mild-mannered gentleman, well regarded by members and employees alike. Probably the only stern words Harvey had ever heard him utter were those directed at the brown cocker spaniel which followed him endlessly, and then only when the animal went too near the water. For Mr Piper was afraid of the water. If it had been possible to run a lakeside resort without benefit of a lake, he would have been all for that.

He had personally hired Harvey five years previously, mostly because Harvey looked like a lifeguard. It had never occurred to him to ask for lifesaving credentials. Had he done so, Harvey never would have landed the job, for although he *looked* like a lifeguard, there any similarity ended. He never had undergone as much as one water-safety course. Instead, after landing the job, he had placed all his confidence in a battered old lifesaving ring that he kept close beside him on the guard tower. This, he reasoned, he would throw to any victim should an emergency arise. Beyond this, he gave little consideration to the plight of any poor soul who might be favoured with a poor aim.

8

'Where is your assistant, Mr Tucker? I believe you had mentioned he would be with you on the tower when things picked up.' To Mr Piper things picked up when more than one or two guests appeared on the dock.

'He just stepped up to the apartment, sir,' said Harvey, wishing almost immediately he had not mentioned the apartment. Mr Piper might amble up, and the apartment was in no shape for a visit. Also, the assistant, like as not if indeed he were in the apartment, was probably asleep. 'He should be back before long, sir. I'll have him take out the lifeboat as soon as he comes down.' He knew that would make the secretary happy.

'Oh, that's an excellent suggestion, Mr Tucker,' said Mr Piper, brightening considerably. 'I think the guests would appreciate that very much. He wouldn't have to stay out in the boat all day—only when things pick up.'

'Yes, sir, Mr Piper.'

Mr Piper ambled slowly away, trailing his pet and taking enjoyment from the pleasant summer day now that the waterfront had been started off right.

'Say, Harvey, you got any razor blades?' It was Ray, the assistant lifeguard, who emerged from behind the tower displaying a three-day growth of beard.

Harvey was immediately torn between a choice of giving up a razor blade or suffering the remote but possible criticism from some club official for permitting a scruffy-looking crew.

'No, I'm all out,' said Harvey, electing the latter choice. 'Listen, take out the lifeboat.'

'The lifeboat? Why the boat? There's no one in the water.'

'It makes Mr Piper feel better,' said Harvey, nodding wearily in the direction of the departing secretary.

'Whatever you say,' said Ray with a shrug. He started walking toward the lifeboat.

'Better put on a lifejacket while you're at it.'

'What?'

'Go ahead. It won't hurt.'

'Are you serious? Ten feet away from the dock in a lifeboat and you want me to put on a life preserver?'

'Go ahead. It'll make the old guy feel better.'

'Je-sus Christ! You sure you don't want me to take along a few flares?' The assistant walked disconsolately over to where the lifejackets were hanging from pegs on the side of the boathouse.

'Hey, Ray, tell Bob to sun himself someplace else. God, what a boatman. It's not bad enough he won't get the boats out, the members have to climb over him to get them!'

Harvey turned and started for the tower. 'Oh, Christ! Here she comes.' It was Mrs Vanderway, who at eighty-seven years of age was a serious liability on the waterfront. It made Harvey nervous when she was around. Whenever he heard a splash, his first thought was that she had tottered off the end of the dock. 'Say, Louie, keep your eye on Mrs Vanderway, OK?'

He climbed back on the watchtower. Ah, the sun felt good. Adjusting a pillow behind his back, he put on his sunglasses and stretched out his legs. With one final look around—oh, oh! 'Louie! Ask Mrs Vanderway not to wash her teeth in the drinking fountain!'—he leaned his head back against the tower. A slight breeze ruffled the blond cowlick and he was soon asleep.

'Hey, Harvey, wake up! You got a telegram!' It was Ray emerging from the locker room, a yellow envelope fluttering in his hand. Harvey was wary. He was expecting some sort of trick. Only yesterday he had hit Ray with a bucket of cold water from upstairs in the pavilion while the assistant had sat playing solitaire on the dock below. While Ray had come to no definite conclusions (it could have been any of a number of bellhops or busboys), Harvey knew that the man suspected him.

'A telegram?' said Harvey cautiously. 'Let's have it.' The sun broke through in all its brilliance reflecting sharply off the yellow paper as he opened the envelope.

HARVEY L TUCKER
LAKE PLACID CLUB
LAKE PLACID, NEW YORK

10

OFFERED PROBATIONARY APPOINTMENT SPECIAL AGENT SALARY TWELVE THOUSAND DOLLARS PER ANNUM PLUS OVERTIME COMPENSATION AMOUNTING TO SEVENTY-EIGHT DOLLARS EACH PAY PERIOD IN VIEW OF SEVEN DAY WEEK. REQUESTED REPORT TEN A.M. OCTOBER THIRTEENTH ROOM SIX NINETY TWO OLD POST OFFICE BUILDING SEVENTH AND PENNSYL-VANIA AVENUE NORTHWEST WASHINGTON, D.C. NO PUBLICITY SHOULD BE GIVEN. LETTER FOLLOWS.

> DIRECTOR
> FEDERAL BUREAU OF INVESTIGATION

'Hey, I made it!' shouted Harvey exuberantly.

'Made what?' asked Ray, who waited patiently at the foot of the ladder.

'The FBI. I got an appointment as an agent.'

'No kidding. How did you work that? Does that mean you won't have to go in the army?'

'That's what it means,' answered Harvey. 'This is essential government work which takes precedence over the military.' He reread the telegram slowly.

'How did you ever pull that off?'

'I got an FBI application a few years ago when I first started law school and sent it in.'

'It took that long to get accepted?' asked Ray.

'I had to get my law degree first. That's one of the requirements. It's pretty tough to get in. I sent the application in so I'd be on file and get the jump on the other applicants. This spring they contacted me and asked if I was still interested. *Still* interested! Can you imagine that? With Viet Nam staring me in the face?'

'Well, that's great. Congratulations,' said Ray.

'Thanks. It's goddamn lucky. Believe it or not, it all started with a babe I met right here at the club.'

'Really?'

'That's right. You've heard of David Wallingford.'

'Vaguely. Isn't he the super-rich guy? The one who gave all the dough to the club?'

'Right. That's the guy,' said Harvey, nodding his head. 'Daddy Warbucks himself. According to Piper he's one of the richest men in the world.'

'Did he get you in the FBI?'

'No, I've never even met him. But a few years ago, before you came, this babe was here for a week or so as Wallingford's guest—really gorgeous. I got talking to her on the dock a few times. She worked for some department down in Washington where they handled liaison or something with the different government agencies. You know, where they coordinate things. I told her I was going to law school, but I was worried about the army and she suggested I apply to the FBI—that I could probably avoid the service if I got an appointment.'

'Well, what happened to her?' asked Ray, after a pause. 'Did she ever come back up?'

'No. That was the last I saw her. She really wasn't that friendly. Kind of aloof—like a rich bitch who didn't have time for the help. I gave it a real shake though. Man, you've never seen a better-looking chick.' Harvey shook his head slowly from side to side. 'The first time I saw her she came through that gate over there by the lockers wearing this bikini about the size of a jock strap. Everything stopped. I mean she paralysed the whole dock. She was kind of blonde with beautiful tits—not too big, but you know the kind that sort of hung out and bounced a little when she walked—and a beautiful shape with long legs and—'

'What's going on?' It was Louie Alimonti arriving on the scene with a bundle of used towels which he dropped next to the guard tower.

'His nibs here made it in the FBI,' said Ray, nodding toward Harvey.

'The FBI?' said Louie quizzically. He reached up quickly and snatched the telegram from Harvey's hand. 'Say, this is something! You're really going to be an FBI agent, huh?' He read the telegram twice, and then looked wistfully up at the lifeguard. 'Wonder what chance I'd have of getting in?'

'You?' said Harvey with mock disdain. 'Where you been anyway? The whole idea is to put the Guineas in jail, not in the FBI!

12

'Hey! What are you doing? That thing's important!' said
Harvey, as Louie methodically folded the letter into a paper
airplane. He made a frantic grab as the towel man arched the
telegram gracefully out into the lake. 'You crazy bastard!' He
jumped from the tower, watch and all. It was the first time
he'd been in the lake in three weeks.

Special Agent Ed Timmons was a tall, broad-shouldered man
with dark hair greying slightly, brown eyes, and a swarthy
complexion. His face, although on the rugged side, was a kind
one. One of Ed's favourite comments had always been, 'You
can send a man away for 20 years, and if you handle it right,
he'll think you're the greatest guy in the world.' Ed Timmons
was a man who felt it was important to be liked by virtually
everyone.

But now as counsellor of New Agents' Class number five in
Washington, DC, he manifested a certain ambivalence as he
stood behind the lectern in the front of the classroom. To the
casual observer he seemed a relaxed, pleasant person who
was not particularly displeased with the matter at hand. But to
the more discerning viewer he might have appeared
otherwise. For although the corners of the mouth were
elevated in what purported to be a smile, a closer look would
have revealed a rigidity to the expression which could just as
well have been a grimace.

Also, upon closer scrutiny one might have noticed that
while the facial lines which ran horizontally across the
forehead were probably always pronounced, now they were
firmly etched as though a rake had been drawn across the
swarthy brow. In addition, although probably not noticeable
beyond the first row of the class, tiny beads of moisture had
begun to collect on the upper lip and just below the greying
hair at the temples.

But if there was one feature more than any other that
evidenced concern in the man at that moment, it was the large
hands which clutched each side of the speaker's table. The
fingers were white at the knuckles in a way which suggested
that were the man to relax his grip for even a second, the
lectern might blow away.

13

Approximately five weeks previously Ed had been pursuing his regular duties as a resident agent in the Waterville RA, which was attached to the New York office of the FBI. A Resident Agency was considered good duty by the agents. Much as the term implied, the agent spent a large amount of time at his residence, although obviously the Bureau officials did not have that in mind.

However, the Waterville RA was more to Ed than just another Resident Agency. It was his Office of Preference. Like other FBI agents, he had spent most of his government career being shuttled between the metropolitan areas around the country with little hope of every reaching his OP. When it came, it had been truly a gift from the heavens—a gift to be cherished, revered *and protected*.

And he had made it by the narrowest of margins. Only a month before the transfer he had closed out his most celebrated case—the Rudolph Elba espionage case. And what a case it had been. Everything had gone wrong. Each succeeding day had produced more unfavourable developments, which had threatened to blow Ed all the way to Butte, Montana. But somehow he had made it. Item four had been his salvation—a block of wood found with the subject. Following Elba's apprehension Ed had bundled up the subject's personal effects and sent them to the FBI laboratory in Washington. Included had been 'Item four—one block of wood, $6' \times 1\frac{1}{4}' \times 1\frac{1}{4}'$.' Following its examination, the laboratory had returned the property to Ed, including item four, which after careful analysis had been found to be 'one block of wood, $6' \times 1\frac{1}{4}' \times 1\frac{1}{4}'$.' It was quite by accident that a few days later Ed had knocked item four off his desk and the wood had split apart revealing the microfilm that later served as the government's case.

Elba had been swapped to Russia after that and Ed had been relieved to see him go, but his relief had been short-lived. Elba had no sooner landed home than he was writing a book in which he described FBI agents as 'bungling.' Uneasy days had followed, but it all had been labelled propaganda. Fortunately the Master Spy's rendition of his relationship with the FBI had been somewhat clouded and

14

things had returned to normal in Waterville.

However, reaching one's OP was one thing and staying there was something else again. But Ed had the formula. Like any agent who survived in the Bureau for any appreciable period, he was conservative of dress, conservative of speech, conservative in his working habits—in short, conservative. 'Conservative' was a better word than plain 'scared', but as the older agents like to say, 'In the Bureau we have *old* agents and we have *bold* agents—but we have no old bold agents.'

Well, Ed was no exception. Not only had he finally made his OP, but what was even more important, he had only three years to go until retirement, when he would be guaranteed over eight thousand dollars per year for the rest of his life. He wanted to do nothing, absolutely nothing, that might upset this pot of gold at the end of the rainbow. Thus the conservative approach to all things, not excluding the amount of work he did. 'The less you do, the less chance you have of doing something wrong,' he was fond of saying. Much as a physician practised his code—*'Primum Non Nocere'* (First, Do No Harm), so did Ed Timmons practise his—*'Primum Non Facere'* (First, Do Nothing).

When Ed first received word of his assignment as counsellor to a new agents' class, he had been like a man contemplating surgery. Actually he had done almost as much investigation during ensuing weeks trying to find out the nature of the counsellor's job as he did in almost a year as a resident agent. And the results had confirmed his worst fears. The horror stories had been incredible regarding the position. Unseasoned agents, even in the field, were unpredictable and were regarded by older agents as though they had a communicable disease.

Ed had come to Washington a few days prior to the opening of the class and stoically received his instructions. He was to counsel 23 new agent candidates through eight months of intensive training in all phases of the Bureau's work. While the actual training was to be handled by various instructors, Ed was to be completely responsible for all the new agents' activities—their performance, their whereabouts, in short everything from the time they were sworn in until the time

15

they left Washington.

It was disheartening. He had a chaplain's job without the authority to forgive and, in fact, a good chance that he probably would be condemned with any sinner.

The date was 13th October, and while Ed was not superstitious, it *would* have to be the thirteenth. He had greeted the class cordially, assigned them chairs, and was preparing for the arrival of Mr Karp, the Assistant Director in charge of the Training Division. Mr Karp was to perform the swearing-in ceremony and deliver his usual lengthy inspirational talk to new agents.

Things seemed to be going nicely. Ed considered making a remark to inject some levity into the atmosphere, but almost immediately thought better of it. Not only could he not think of such a remark, but things were going nicely, so why take any unnecessary chances?'

His eyes roved the class and came to rest on two blond-haired men sitting side by side in the front row. Immediately he was struck by their similarity in appearance. He wondered idly if they might not be brothers.

At that particular moment there came a noise from the door at the rear of the classroom. Ed's face blanched ever so slightly, the smile vanished, and the hands took an even firmer grip on the lectern. The door swung open and a tall, slender man with sandy hair entered the room and walked to the podium.

'Sorry to interrupt, Ed,' said the man, 'but I'm leaving now.'

The relief was perceptible in Ed's face as he stepped down from the podium to shake the outstretched hand. 'Christ, I thought you were Karp,' he said softly. 'He's due here any second.'

'Oh, boy. Better you than me. Say, you got a good-looking group here,' said the man, raising his voice and turning toward the class.

'Yeah, nice group,' said Ed uneasily, eying the rear door. Then turning to the class, 'Mr Karmody here is leaving the Bureau for the more lucrative field of private business.' Almost as soon as he said it, he realised it was not a very good

16

comment. He would have to be more careful.

Mr Karmody smiled good-naturedly and said, 'Good luck to you fellows. You'll need it.' And then, looking at the ceiling, 'I see they haven't installed the new sprinklers in here yet.'

'Oh, are they installing sprinklers?' said Ed, gazing at the ceiling curiously.

'Yes,' replied the man smiling. 'That way the Director can piss on you all at the same time!'

A rumble of muffled laughter spread over the class and Mr Karmody sailed from the room, leaving Ed looking as though he were undergoing an attack of the bends.

Jesus Christ, thought Ed. Here he is bulletproof, screwing around—

His thoughts were interrupted as a pair of horn-rimmed glasses adorning a pink head appeared in the window of the rear door. The counsellor stepped quickly from the platform and moved to the rear to greet the tall, heavy, stern-looking man who came through the door.

'Good morning, sir. All ready to proceed.' Ed, never at his best around the brass, could feel the perspiration in his armpits and hoped it would not show through his summer suit. If there was one thing that annoyed the Director, it was perspiration rings under an agent's arms.

Mr Karp grunted his acquiescence and brushed by Ed toward the lectern at the front of the room. A respectful hush settled over the class. Mr Karp cleared his throat, adjusted his glasses, gazed out over his audience and said, 'Gentlemen, raise your right hands.'

Assistant Director Karp administered the oath of office with profound solemnity, enunciating each syllable as though it were a transmission through enemy-jammed radio waves. After each phrase he paused, listening to the respectful, hushed echoes from the class while his eyes probed the room like spotlights on a prison tower.

Following the oath, the agents took their seats amid the sound of scraping chairs and subdued conversation when another clearing of the throat from the podium announced

17

that the traditional new-agents' talk was about to get underway.

'You are among the most select group of men in the world,' said Mr Karp. 'Only one out of 400 applicants is accepted as a special agent of the FBI.'

He's got the statistics inflated as usual, thought Ed. It was more like one out of 20 and that included all the applications from the laughing academies as well as the crackpots who wandered in off the street to volunteer their services. But it was all right. As with so many of the Bureau's statistics, no one knew the difference.

' ... the success of the FBI in the fields of espionage, law enforcement and civil rights is legendary,' continued Karp.

It was legend all right, thought Ed. And any similarity between the legend and actual fact was just like all the statistics—so much baloney. It always bugged Ed when a Bureau speaker started giving out with the party line. It was simply too much for a guy who'd seen the operation in action for 25 years.

It was moments such as these when the other Ed Timmons would appear. The other Ed was a handsome, smooth-browed man who wore a suit of armour and sat tall in the saddle on a white charger. His smile was an honest-to-goodness, wide-open smile, and the only beads of perspiration came from good, honest hard work. But the only trouble with this other Ed Timmons was that he rarely showed himself. It was mostly around the house when Ed was talking to the children that he came out. As for the other times, he would clank out rather uneasily, look nervously in each direction, and then, if all was clear, launch himself with something of a flourish into the saddle, where he would sit chin high and resolute. But the only trouble was when a dark cloud appeared on the horizon. Then this other Ed, like as not, would promptly get his charger going in the other direction, leaving Ed there to fend for himself.

But at this particular moment the other Ed was asserting himself. He was standing there in the front of the class, his helmet removed in deference to the American flag furled against the wall, telling Mr Karp what a big bullshitter he was,

18

and how the United States was considered a soft touch in the world of espionage; how the Director still thought in terms of Dillinger, Floyd and Karpis and concentrated on the statistics in the bush league while syndicated crime had the country by the balls; how investigations of civil-rights violations were a whitewash while the Bureau itself violated citizens' rights through bag jobs, wire taps, intimidation of citizens, illegal searches and seizures.

But of course Mr Karp was not listening. He was well along in his talk on Bureau rules and regulations, citing horror stories to illustrate his many points. ' . . . and for this breach of security the agent was dismissed with prejudice!' he said, slamming the lectern for emphasis.

The other Ed, startled by the whack on the hand, looked nervously down at the counsellor. Did he say 'dismissed with prejudice'? Quickly he replaced his helmet on his head and departed for wherever he went when things got tough. It was quite all right with Ed. It made him nervous with this other fellow clanking around.

A short time later Karp lumbered from the room. A good deal of the tension followed the assistant director out the door, and Ed Timmons, dabbing his brow with a handkerchief, took the podium.

'We were very fortunate to have Mr Karp here to perform the swearing-in ceremony and to deliver his spirited talk. As you probably realise, he's a very, *very* busy man.' With a slight, unintentional movement of his eyebrows that suggested, 'If you believe that one, I'll tell you another,' Ed launched into a practical introductory talk concerning his role as counsellor.

'You should feel free to consult me at any time on any problems. Remember, I'm here to be of help to you. This afternoon there will be no classes. You can use the time to get yourselves settled. It's required that you live with at least one other agent. You agents who are loners will have to make the adjustment for the next eight months. We don't want any agents living alone while they're in training school.

'Gentlemen, this is most important.' Ed paused, assuring himself of complete attention. 'Probably one of the more difficult things for you to realise as new agents is that from now on the Bureau must be kept informed of your whereabouts *at all times*. You are on call 24 hours a day. You should know right from the start that if the Bureau can't get you when you're wanted, it will result in immediate and serious administrative action.

'Now, gentlemen, certain things are academic in the FBI. Emotional stability and maturity are prerequisites to a successful career in this organisation.' (He was tempted to include the advantages of a conservative approach to the job, but that could become involved.) 'Your personal appearance is very important. If your hair is long, then cut it. If it's real short, then let it grow. If you like to talk, become a listener. Never discuss Bureau business with anyone, least of all your wife. Remember—and this is the best advice I can give you on the subject—don't ever tell the big-mouth wife anything!'

He paused momentarily to consult some notes on the lectern, rubbing the palms of his hands in his handkerchief as he did so. Then, reaching down behind the podium, he withdrew a heavy black manual with pink pages. With a slight grimace, partly from the heft of the volume but mostly because of the unpleasant memories it stimulated, he flopped the book on the lectern. 'Each of you has been assigned a briefcase, which is to the right of your chair. If you look inside, you'll find a large manual like this one. This, gentlemen, is your *Manual of Rules and Regulations*. It tells you—well, frankly, it tells you what you *can't* do.' (That was not a very good comment. He'd have to watch it.) 'The smaller leather case contains your badge. You will have that for as long as you're in the Bureau. And I mean that literally, gentlemen, for if you lose it, you won't be in the Bureau.'

His eyes roved the class significantly. The indoctrination had started; he could tell from the beleaguered expressions. Before long they would be so infused with the policy, they would be afraid to go to the men's room without advising the Bureau, except for the ones who would not be moulded, but there were very few of them. The screening and background investigations had taken care of that. The organization knew precisely what it wanted—anonymous, colourless individuals

20

who were ready to submerge their own identities into the mainstream of the Bureau, which was one method of operation, one way of thinking, one personality—really one man.

The Old Post Office, where the FBI trained its new agents, was constructed in such a way that the rooms above the main floor opened onto a loft type of corridor with the classrooms on one side and a large brass railing on the other. The corridors on each floor formed a rectangle around an immense open space, at the bottom of which was a skylight covering the main floor. It was a cavernous structure of incredible design as though conceived by a designer of Zeppelin hangars. One peering over the railing from the sixth floor down at the skylight could not help but sense the precariousness of his position as though any second the aged, granulative walls might dissolve into the huge void below.

The class had just moved into the hallway for a break following the introductory speech from the counsellor. Harvey Tucker was resting his arms on the railing, looking down at the skylight, sensing not only the insecurity of the building, but the questionable tenure of his employment, when he was joined by the tall, slender, blond-haired man who had sat beside him.

'Quite a drop, isn't it?' said the man, glancing over the railing.

Harvey looked up quickly. He was impressed again by the man's good looks. Somewhere in his early thirties, he had fine, smooth features, possibly a bit delicate for a man, with high cheekbones and deep-set eyes. The light hair and brows contrasted with a clean, tawny complexion, reminding Harvey of a figure in suntan advertisements.

'It sure is,' said Harvey. 'I guess a person should be a little cautious moving around up here.'

The man turned toward Harvey and smiled. 'After listening to those lectures in there, I rather think caution would be appropriate in most all areas around here.'

'Christ, it's like a monastery, isn't it?' said Harvey.

The man laughed and shoved his hand out abruptly. 'I'm

21

Jay Von Vlack.'

'Hi, Jay. Harvey Tucker.' They shook hands. 'Did you say Von Black?'

'Von Vlack!' The white teeth extended over his lip as he emphasised the V's. 'V as in virtuous.' He leaned his arms on the railing next to Harvey and looked down at the skylight. 'No, it doesn't sound like there will be much time for moonlighting around here.' There was a soft, resonant quality to his voice which was at once both pleasant and disturbing to Harvey—sort of an upper crust delivery which suggested that the man might have been reared under favourable circumstances.

'Kind of makes you wonder if it's worthwhile unpacking,' said Harvey, as though unpacking for him were more than a three-minute job.

'You from the East, Harvey?'

'That's right. Eagle's Notch, New York.'

'Eagle's what?' Jay looked at him quizzically as though Harvey might be kidding him.

'Eagle's Notch.' Harvey was slightly uncomfortable. 'It's upstate New York—small town.' After he said it he realised the qualification was unnecessary. 'How about you?'

'Westchester. Nayraville.'

He might have guessed it. Harvey had heard of the aristocratic little community north of New York City, and Jay Von Vlack appeared to fit the bill.

'Have you found quarters yet?' Jay peered over his shoulder at the class starting to filter back into the room.

'No, not yet. I'm in a hotel up on Avenue G, but I've got to get out of there. The tariff is pretty stiff.'

'I understand there's a fairly decent spot out on Berkshire Boulevard. We might go take a look if you'd like to.'

'Sounds great.'

'Fine. Meet you out here then after class.'

Harvey watched as the butter-coloured hair and immaculate blue suit merged with the group funnelling through the door back into the room.

After classes, Harvey found Jay waiting for him in the corridor. The prospects of having someone with whom he could talk things over lifted his spirits considerably. As they headed for the elevator, he swung his new government briefcase over his shoulder, carrying it by the handle the way a schoolboy carries strapped books. 'What a morning. Do you get the feeling we're kind of expendable?'

'Oh, I don't know. They already have quite a bit invested in us with all the clearances and all. I rather think they'll want to salvage any they can at this stage.'

'Let's hope you're right,' said Harvey. 'I wonder how many they drop from the average class. The way that Karp guy talked I don't think it would be smart to lay out too much rent in advance.'

'So what if they do let you go? Go back to Eagle's Notch and relax.'

'Hell, I couldn't go back home and tell everybody I'd been canned. I'd be mortified. You've apparently never lived in a real small town. For the rest of my life I wouldn't be called Harvey Tucker. I'd be known as 'Tucker, the guy who got bounced from the Bureau.' Besides, I'm in the Reserve, and with all that stuff going on in Viet Nam, who knows when a guy might get called up? That's why I applied to this outfit in the first place. I'd sure as hell rather be here than in some rice paddy.'

'It's bit early yet. Maybe before long you'll wish you were in the rice paddy.'

'Whatever got you to join the FBI, Jay?'

'Oh, I don't know really. It is kind of a prestigious thing, you know.' He smiled, but it was not a true smile. After a pause, he said, 'Actually I'm a bit flattered that they accepted me.' He was not interested in pursuing the subject. In fact, although he had spent less than 15 minutes with the man, Harvey already sensed a quality of reticence, a certain preoccupation.

They emerged from the Old Post Office and started down the layers of steps that rose pyramidally from Pennsylvania Avenue. It seemed awkward, the rise of the steps so gradual that one was tempted to take them two at a time only to find that each step was deceptively broad, rendering the savings a questionable, if not dangerous effort. Harvey would try it

23

both ways during ensuing weeks, but soon he would come to the conclusion that, like everything else about the place, there were no shortcuts, no canned briefs, no alternatives—there was but one way.

It was a grey stone building on Berkshire Boulevard—old, with light-blue shutters long since discoloured, and wilted English ivy clinging in patches here and there. A faded blue canopy, similar to that in front of the other buildings, extended from the doorway down three steps and along the short walk to the street. Pale-yellow letters appearing on the valance of the canvas once proudly proclaimed 'The Gaylord', but long since had been muted by the years. A small wooden tub bursting with morning glories perched gallantly at the foot of the walk, a sign of spirit in an aged mien like a flower in the lapel of a man grown old.

Harvey rested his old Gladstone bag and newly acquired government briefcase on the sidewalk next to Jay's luggage. The battered valise suffered from the comparison with the smooth beige pigskin of the other bags.

'The Gaylord looks a bit run down at the heels,' observed Jay.

Harvey drew a handkerchief from a pocket and wiped his brow. 'It's not that bad,' he said. 'Don't you think it might be a bit far out, though? There should be something available a little closer to the office.'

Jay appeared deep in thought and said nothing.

'Jay, don't you think we're a bit far from the office?' persisted Harvey.

'No, I think it will be OK, Harvey. The transportation seems pretty good.' Without waiting for a reply, Jay moved under the canopy towards the door.

As they approached the entranceway a curtain moved slightly in the front window. 'Did you catch that?' said Harvey. 'Probably the landlady checking us out. They all look out the window first to size you up and see if they want to rent to you. Things are going to be tight enough around here without some grey-haired old—'

Harvey had not time to finish as the knob rattled and the

24

door opened.

'Won't you come in?' A woman opened the door wide, turned and moved back inside. She was neither grey nor old. The two men exchanged glances and followed her inside.

The interior of the house produced little in the way of surprises. Dim lighting and faded wallpaper gave the place a gloomy, stuffy atmosphere. Oriental rugs, long since threadbare with traffic patterns leading in all directions, covered the darkly stained floors, and various pieces of Victorian furniture, showing the effects of years of performance for which they had not been intended, rested in feeble groups about the room. But, in spite of the infirmities imposed by time, there was an orderliness about the place.

'You *are* FBI, I presume?' The woman spoke with a very slight accent which had not been noticeable at the door.

'Yes, how did you know?' asked Harvey, surprised.

'Oh, it is very easy. I can recognise you people immediately. Almost everyone in Washington can. You all look the same. Look, you two are almost twins. I believe they have some strange device down there in which they create you.' She withdrew a guest register from a dresser drawer and dropped it on the office table near Jay.

'We'd like a double room,' said Harvey.

The woman turned and delivered a cool, analytical gaze at Harvey that made him uncomfortable. 'That is very nice. You have come to the right place. Won't you please sit down?' She motioned toward some chairs as she sat down.

'I am Alberta Gunther.' As she crossed her legs and lit up a cigarette, the pink housecoat she was wearing fell open above her knee revealing the most thigh Harvey had seen since leaving Lake Placid. With a nonchalance which suggested that a thigh was of little interest, she adjusted the garment, and, exhaling slowly, added in a casual tone, 'The other boys call me Alberta.' If Harvey were to draw any inference thus far, it was that there were plenty of callers.

Alberta Gunther seemed to be a woman in her early thirties. Upon closer scrutiny she was not as good looking as Harvey had thought when he first saw her in the doorway. She was attractive, but probably her most prepossessing feature

25

was her completely relaxed, self-assured manner—that of a woman who looked for and was accustomed to a good deal of attention from men.

'My Aunt Frieda, Mrs Butler, is the landlady,' she said, as though perceiving the question in Harvey's mind. 'She is quite elderly, however, so I take care of most of the transactions.'

After exhaling in a way that suggested more interest in her cigarette than the company, Alberta indicated that there were four other agents living in the house and that agents-in-training had been staying there for the past three years. 'We have one room with two beds. The fee is fifty dollars a month—apiece,' she added, in a take-it-or-leave-it tone.

'That sounds very fair,' said Jay, reaching for the guest book.

'Just a second,' said Harvey. 'Don't you think we should have a look at the room first?'

Jay looked at him sharply. 'I rather think we've seen enough, don't you?'

Harvey was surprised by the man's assertiveness. 'OK. Sure. Whatever you think. I always look at a room first.'

'Of course. Come this way,' said Alberta, rolling out of the chair easily and piloting cigarette, body, and housecoat, in that order, to the stairway at the other end of the room.

The room was made to order. Much like the average college fraternity room, it had twin beds, two small desks with reading lamps, and an easy chair. Two windows offered the perfect view for one interested in studying—a side alley with a brick wall 20 feet away.

'This is fine,' said Jay.

'Yes,' agreed Harvey, anxious to recover whatever graciousness he might have lost in questioning the room. 'It's just great.'

Alberta counted two weeks' rent in advance and, with a few comments to the effect that she hoped they were comfortable and quiet after 10:00 P.M., she was gone, leaving behind a faint aroma of perfume.

'My God, what a gorgeous creature,' said Harvey. 'Did you kind of get the idea she might be on the make?'

'Remember what Mr Karp said about forgetting everything

26

but the Bureau?' Jay turned and gave a knowing look.

'Well, I don't think Mr Karp had that in mind. Anyone who could keep his mind on the Bureau when Alberta was around probably shouldn't be in the Bureau. Man, she sure had a lot packed into that bathrobe.'

The comment drew no answer from Jay.

'And a lot that wasn't packed in,' continued Harvey. He pulled open a drawer of one of the dressers, preparing to put away some shirts.

'Why don't you take that dresser over there, Harvey?' suggested Jay. 'That way you could have that bed and dresser next to each other.'

Harvey looked at the other bed and dresser. They seemed the same. He shrugged good-naturedly. 'Sure, what's the difference?' He carried his shirts to the other dresser a few feet away. Kind of odd, he thought. What was it going to be like rooming with this guy for eight months?

Black woollen dress, a string of pearls, autumn-haze mink jacket, beautiful slanting eyes (her eyes had not been that noticeable earlier), Alberta Gunther was stunning. Harvey paused on the stairs, momentarily fascinated at the metamorphosis which had taken place in the woman since that afternoon.

Alberta moved toward the front door, pulling on a long tan glove. 'Going out?' she asked, as Jay and Harvey descended the stairs into the room. 'Don't forget to call the office and tell them where you are going.' There was a maternal note in her voice which Harvey might have found irksome were she not so attractive. She looked back and smiled at the agents as she moved into the hallway.

Near the doorway there were sounds of conversation as Alberta spoke to someone entering the building. After a few seconds, a tall man bearing a special agent's briefcase entered the living room. He smiled and nodded when he saw Harvey and Jay. 'Are you fellows in the new agents' class?'

'Yes, I'm Jay Von Vlack. This is Harvey Tucker.'

'I'm Bob Chidsey. Glad to know you. I'm in the class ahead of you.'

27

They shook hands.

'How do you like that?' said Bob. He motioned with his head toward the door through which Alberta had departed. 'Don't get any ideas, though. They've got a whole chapter in the manual devoted to how you shouldn't try to make the landlady.'

'Care to join us for dinner?' said Harvey. He liked the man immediately.

'Sure, let me drop my bag in the room. I'll be right down.'

Within a few minutes they were three abreast in a taxi heading downtown.

'There's a pretty good seafood spot down on H Street,' said Bob Chidsey. He was a big man with dark hair and a round, almost cherubic face who could have taken up the back seat of the cab very comfortably by himself. His manner was sociable and it was soon apparent that he was not averse to talking about the training activities. He was quick to affirm that the school was every bit as difficult as they had been led to believe and that with a month to go his class had already lost six out of 27 agents. They were warming up to the subject when the cab came to a stop in front of the restaurant.

'Well, is it tougher than law school?' asked Harvey as they were seated inside.

'Oh, no comparison with law school or OCS or any of that other stuff. In law school all you had to do was attend classes and get some canned briefs. Here, you don't even know when you're being graded. That's the worst part.'

'I hear we spend some time at the Bureau Academy down in Virginia,' said Jay.

'That's right. It's just as tough down there. They'll work your ass off seven days a week. Incidentally,' he moved forward over the table, his fist alongside his mouth, 'When you're down at the Academy be careful what you say. A guy in our class was down in the basement where the gym is and he wandered into one of the rear rooms which are ordinarily locked and saw these wires. He checked them out and found the rooms were all bugged. The real weird part of it, though, was that the Joint Chiefs of Staff had just had a meeting there. They apparently asked for the place because they wanted top

28

security—and there they were being bugged by the Bureau.'

After a short pause, Jay said, 'I thought they had to get a court order or something to bug places.'

'Hell, no,' said Bob. 'They're supposed to get approval from the Justice Department, but from what the older guys say, they by-pass the Justice Department on most stuff.'

'But what about the Attorney General?' said Jay. 'He's the Director's boss, isn't he?'

'That's a laugh. The Director says openly that the Attorney General is the worst Justice Department head in 40 years. Of course, he said the same thing about the AG who had the job before this one. No, they tell me the Director acts like he owns the whole thing. In case nobody told you guys, this outfit operates pretty much the way it wants.'

'How about the Gaylord?' Jay paused to take a sip of coffee and replaced the cup gently on the saucer. 'Maybe they've got the rooms bugged there.'

'I doubt that,' replied Bob. 'None of us would still be here if they were. Alberta runs kind of a wide-open shop. She doesn't give a damn about the place. If it weren't for her aunt, no one would even collect the rent.'

'She's terrific,' said Harvey.

'Aunt Frieda?' said Bob, a startled expression on his face.

'No, no. Alberta.'

'You should see her girl friend.'

'Girl friend?'

'Absolutely the most gorgeous thing you've ever laid your eyes on.' The man rolled his eyes back in his head and leaned back in his chair. 'Blonde ... beautiful ... everything! Nobody ever gets to see her though.'

'You seem to be doing all right,' observed Jay quietly.

'No, what I mean is, they spend all their time in that back room near the rear stairs. They'll spend a couple of hours back there, and all you can hear is the music from the radio. I think they're lesbians.'

'No kidding,' said Harvey. 'That's awful!'

'Yeah, what a waste. A couple of times I've been tempted to creep down the back stairs and conduct a little physical surveillance on what goes on in there.'

29

'Why don't you?' asked Jay.

'Why don't *you*?' replied Bob. 'I'm just about through with this place. It would be just my luck to fall through the goddamn keyhole.'

After dinner was served, a silence descended on the table and the three ate pensively. Bob's comments about the listening devices in the rooms and the other training activities had done little to engender confidence in Harvey. Also, he had found the conversation about Alberta and her girl friend had aroused him sexually. It was a frustrating feeling.

He gazed at the candles burning brightly on the table. Their light, flickering against the wall, created shadows which hovered phantomlike over the table. The stuffed profile of a large mounted fish peered down at him from the wall, its one eye catching the wavering light from the candle and focusing on him intently.

'Do you think any of these fellows bothered to leave last night?' whispered Harvey. He and Jay peered in at the expanse of heads buried in the pink manuals. Although it was only 8:10 A.M., it looked as if most of the class had already assembled. All were studying intently. They walked quietly past the lowered heads to the front of the room where the register was located, and signed in.

At precisely 8:30, Ed Timmons appeared at the lectern. He looked down at his notes, dabbing at his brow with his handkerchief. 'In respect to the curriculum, you will find posted each Monday morning on the bulletin board on my left a schedule of the week's training programme. This schedule is not all inclusive and you will find that examinations, as well as other unannounced training activities, will be included from time to time.'

With a few final comments on the importance of taking good notes, he picked up his papers from the lectern and started to leave. He had taken only a few steps from the podium when he stopped suddenly and stared at the coatrack at the other side of the room. 'My God! Who owns that?'

The heads in the class turned as though following a tennis volley and riveted on the shelf above the coatrack, where a

30

light-coloured straw hat bearing a multicoloured band stood out brightly like a rainbow in a dark sky.

'Now really, fellows, you've got to get into the spirit of this thing.' He walked to the coatrack and covered the offending hat with several others. 'Whoever owns that thing, dump it at lunchtime.' With a final dab at his forehead, he was gone.

The class was exposed to a myriad of subjects that day, from federal criminal procedure (of which Harvey had received a smattering in law school) to some brief introductions to Marxist-Leninist ideology and the Bureau work in the counterespionage field. A stream of instructors flowed to the podium, tall, good-looking men, each a specialist in his field endeavouring to capsulise careers of experience into 50-minute lectures.

But regardless of what the course or topic of discussion, from the very first, the basic philosophy of the Bureau was becoming impregnated in Harvey's mind—the underlying code, like a strong, unrelenting conscience, which guided the agent in all things, whether making an apprehension of a dangerous fugitive, conducting a surveillance on a Russian agent, or merely engaging in cocktails with a neighbour—the main rule, indeed the one that seemed to prevail over all others was, 'Don't embarrass the Bureau!'

BRRRRRRRR! It was like a long burst from a Thompson submachine gun, shattering the soft hours of the dawn. Harvey awoke with a start and reached for Jay's alarm, jangling on the small table between the beds.

'My God!' exclaimed Harvey. 'Jay! Jay! Wake up!'

Instead of 6:30, it was almost 7:15. It was the second week of training, and they had already had a similar experience the preceding week when the clock had run late.

Peeling off his pyjama top, Harvey headed for the bathroom. He had lathered his chin, preparing to shave, when Jay came trooping in dragging his bathrobe behind him like a security blanket. Reaching into the shower, he turned the hot-water handle.

'Oh, no,' murmured Harvey, watching his reflection in the mirror slowly fade into the steam billowing from the bathtub.

'Can't you wait just a few more minutes, Jay? You're going to fog up the whole place.'

'Sorry. It's late. I won't be but a minute.'

'Well, leave the door open.'

'It's quite chilly in here,' said Jay, ignoring the request and closing the door firmly. He stepped into the tub and drew across the shower curtain.

In an effort to hasten the shower, Harvey reached over and flushed the commode. A sharp exclamation came from the tub. As soon as the tank filled, he flipped the handle again.

'Harvey, must you continue flushing that blasted thing?' said Jay. 'You know damn well it changes the water temperature in here 50 degrees.'

'Sorry, you know how this head works. You've got to flush the thing a few times to get everything down.'

The flushing ruse helped little and, if anything, it created more steam. Soon it was as though a small cloud had moved into the Gaylord and settled in the bathroom.

Harvey waited a few seconds and then opened the door quietly. He thought he had brought it off until a breath of cold air went through the room.

'Harvey,' came a constrained voice from the bathtub, 'I believe someone opened the door.' Pulling the shower curtain back slightly, Jay leaned out and stretched his left arm out, grasping the top of the bathroom door.

'Come on, Jay,' said Harvey, turning around and holding the door, preventing his roommate from closing it. 'I can't see my face in the mirror.'

'Consider the advantages,' said Jay airily. 'Now I suggest you let go of that door before I have a very wet roommate. With just a flick of the wrist I can turn this shower nozzle your way.'

Harvey was not listening. He was absorbed by the underside of his roommate's arm which was extended directly in front of Harvey's face.

The shower curtain hid from Jay the quizzical look on Harvey's face. 'That's better,' he said as Harvey released the knob. 'After all, our Director wants freshly scrubbed bodies, you know. You wouldn't want me to have BO and embarrass the Bureau, would you?'

Harvey turned to the mirror and slowly resumed shaving. In Jay's armpit, where they never would have been seen were it not for the unique circumstance and the hair being matted from the shower, barely discernible, but unmistakably imprinted in the skin, were several tiny digits.

The training school was the Bureau mould, meticulously developed through the years to the point where it could digest a heterogeneous group of new agents and within six months turn out the same men as look-alikes with remarkably similar personality traits. The finished products invariably had been brave, loyal, hardworking special agents. The mould was the bedrock of the organisation and it had always been most proficient. But it was a lot to expect of a man-made apparatus, and eventually, like everything else in the organisation, it also began to yield to Bureau pressure. The end result was that it was now turning out brave, loyal, hardworking special agents who would never embarrass the Bureau, and the latter trait seemed to be dominating all the others.

Great care was exercised in selecting material for the mould, since obviously just anything could not be popped in without affecting the quality of the product. Certain basic requirements were essential in a new agent. Naturally, he had to be physically sound. Next, he had to be the right size and shape. This was relatively easy. Either he fit or did not. True, there were some on the fringe who by stretching a little or adding or losing some weight were able to squeeze in, but generally the cast was quite inflexible.

Then came the more subtle aspects: the way he dressed, his features, the way he combed his hair, his general grooming, all were considered before he was fed to the mould. But the physiological part of the selection was relatively easy. It was in the psychological area that things could become tricky.

The paramount requirement in a new agent, if the mould was to perform its job as intended, was that the mental framework of the embryo agent was one that lent itself to the shaping process. Above all else he must be ready to have the Bureau mind subrogated for his own. If not, then the whole

33

thing was for naught, since the finished product could be a
bogus special agent—one who looked, talked, and acted like
all the others, but who had a mind of his own. Nothing
worried the Bureau more. Careful examination of an
applicant's background was a great help in ascertaining his
way of thinking, but it was not infallible. No one could ever be
certain that the minds that went into the mould could be
tailored to Bureau requirements. And had the Bureau the
insight into a few of the minds in New Agents Class number
five which had just been placed in the mould, the crank never
would have been turned.

To Harvey the moulding process was an ordeal every bit as
difficult as reputed. His day began at 6:30, a maximum effort
for one who rarely turned the study lamp off before one in the
morning. The day inched by, each one promising its own
unique, if traumatic, experience. Virtually every subject
pertaining to crime detection, law enforcement and
counterespionage was covered. It was a seven-day week.
While there were no classes on Sunday, that day was spent
trying to catch up, always trying to catch up.

Tours of the FBI laboratory and the local field office, as
well as trips to remote sections of Washington where
surveillance techniques or double-agent contacts were
practised, helped to break the monotony, but mostly it was
long, tedious hours of classroom lectures and note-taking.

Harvey's roommate remained a puzzle to him. He had to be
some kind of blue blood. Just the way he held his head was
different from the others in the class. There were times when
he appeared relaxed and friendly, exhibiting a light if
somewhat dry sense of humour, but invariably such moments
proved fleeting, yielding to the more reserved personality
when the man became distant and preoccupied. There was
rarely the relaxed exchange which had characterised
Harvey's relationship with roommates in the past. For the
most part, the man exhibited a dignified, aloof manner that
gave the feeling that Harvey was really of very little
importance in the world of Jay Von Vlack.

Harvey had given up trying to figure out the significance of
the digits under his arm. They could be anything, he

34

reasoned—a college fraternity, a joke, some kind of secret club. He had been tempted to ask Jay about them a couple of times, but had refrained from doing so. The whole place was pretty spooky. One could never be sure of anyone. There was always the possibility that Jay was a plant—a 'submarine,' the agents called them—someone placed by the Bureau in a situation where he could inform on the other agents. No, it was best if he kept the information about the numbers to himself. Besides, Jay was cool. He had seen him under pressure a few times. He would have a ready answer for anything Harvey might ask.

With the passing weeks Harvey felt the pressure mounting. By the third month four agents had been rejected by the mould. No reason was ever given. One morning there would be an empty desk and Ed Timmons would simply say 'All right, men, everyone move over one seat,' and that would be that. Those close to the departed could offer no explanation other than the man said he was leaving and declined to give a reason. Such departures had obvious effects, and the study lamps at the Gaylord would burn longer and brighter.

Thoughts of impending interviews with Bureau officials were particularly disquieting to Harvey. He would be listening to a lecture when the door in the rear room would squeak open, a man would enter and whisper to the instructor, and an agent would gather his things for the unenviable trek to the Justice Building, where the Bureau executive offices were located. Generally, but not always, the agent came back. It seemed to Harvey that they should stand and shake his hand when an agent returned.

The daily format was unpredictable. The class might be engrossed in some problem when suddenly in would come two men distributing blue booklets. Mimeographed sheets would soon follow containing questions requiring comprehensive answers on almost any subject. There would be an hour or so of intense silence, broken only by the sound of scribbling pencils as elusive answers were cornered in weary minds and quickly tumbled into the blue booklets.

Most of the questions dealt with material which had been presented in lectures or textbooks, but there were always the

35

others. 'Describe in detail the man who was contacted by the double agent in the mock surveillance Tuesday morning,' or, 'Write everything you can recall about the room and personnel in which the lecture on admissibility of evidence took place on Mondy afternoon.'

One of the few diversions for Harvey in the onerous grind of the classroom came in the form of 'interesting case write-ups,' which were read to the new agents periodically. These consisted of Bureau cases that had been solved in some unusual manner or had some distinctive characteristics that made them of particular interest. Invariably the announcement that a case write-up was to be read was met with audible sighs of relief as pencils were put down, legs stretched, and sounds of men becoming comfortable settled over the class.

Typical of the training-school system was an incident that took place one afternoon when an instructor named Scott closed a textbook on federal criminal procedure, indicating it was time for a break. Harvey leaned back in his chair, stretching appreciatively, preparing to go into the corridor, when the instructor said, 'Instead of going out in the hall, why don't you stay at your desks and those of you who want to may light up. I thought I'd read one of these case write-ups.' He proceeded to read from a file about a rather involved espionage case in which a female employee in the Department of Justice had been developed as a Soviet contact and had been transmitting classified data to Russian agents. Many of the elements of the case were complex, requiring careful concentration by the listening agents for a proper understanding of its solution.

Concluding the case write-up, the instructor picked up the textbook from which he had been reading before the break. 'We'll resume where we left off on the filing of information.'

Almost an hour had passed when two men entered and began to distribute the blue booklets. 'Gentlemen,' said Mr Scott, 'you will write everything you can recall about the case write-up read to you during your break.'

Judging from the scribbling sounds, few agents had been caught napping. There were no patsies left. The 22 desks in the room still in use were occupied by suspicious, sensitive, deadly serious men. The mould was at work.

'Spit it out! Spit it out!'

'I can't spit it out,' said Harvey, an expression somewhere between perplexity and dismay on his face. 'I just swallowed it.'

'My God, you swallowed it?' Had Harvey just swallowed hemlock, Jay could not have appeared more horrified. 'Are you sure?'

'Of course I'm sure. I've never been so sure of anything in my whole life.' They started to leave their room for class, and Jay had been pocketing some personal objects from the top of his dresser, including a comb, his wallet, and some change, when he turned away briefly. Harvey, who had been in the embryo stages of a headache, had been waiting by the door when he had noticed a small box of aspirin with the other personal items on the dresser. Jay had turned back just in time to see Harvey popping one of the tablets into his mouth.

'Well, can you cough it up? Try to cough it up!' said Jay.

'What's the matter with you? It's only an aspirin. It *is* only an aspirin, isn't it?'

'You sure you can't cough it up?' said Jay, ignoring the question. 'Here, try sticking your finger down your throat.'

'Get away from me! What's the matter with you, Jay, anyway?' It was soon apparent that nothing was going to dislodge the pill.

'Would you kindly ask before you take things the next time?' mumbled Jay. Pocketing the box of aspirin and the other personal items, he stalked from the room.

Harvey quietly closed the door and followed, uncertain that what was now dissolving in his stomach was indeed aspirin.

It was during a session on the collection and preservation of evidence when Harvey was summoned. A tall, swarthy individual entered the room and handed a slip of paper to the instructor. Harvey immediately made mental notes of the man's description. Height—6' 2"; Weight—195 to 200; Hair—black (wiry); Eyes—dark?; Peculiarities—low fore-

37

head, erect bearing, heavy brows; Attire—grey suit, rep tie, cordovan shoes.

'Mr Tucker, would you please take your things and go with the gentleman.'

'Oh, no,' murmured Harvey. He started collecting his things. Gabriels, one of the agents nearby, leaned over about to say something. 'I know,' said Harvey before he could speak. 'I'll give it to Von Vlack if I don't see you.' (He owed Gabriels ten dollars.)

The swarthy-looking man who led Harvey out of the Old Post Office over to the Justice Building displayed all the pleasantry of one who had been just asked to step out in the alley. After an initial nervous comment on the weather drew no reply whatsoever, Harvey was silent.

The interior of the Justice Building was an impressive sight to one who had spent several weeks in the cave-like interior of the Old Post Office. The floors were immaculately polished, the elevators smooth and quiet, the people brisk and businesslike.

Harvey was motioned through a door on the fourth floor into a secretary's office, where the leader held up his hand. His one-man command came to a halt.

The man disappeared inside the inner office. Almost immediately he reappeared pointing an authoritative finger toward the door. Presumably Harvey was to enter. Realising the danger of flippancy but irked by the man's silence, Harvey pointed a finger at his chest, then at the office, mocking his guide's gestures.

The man looked at him solemnly with steady eyes, his face impassive, and then slowly raised his chin, drawing his neck out of the collar. A large, ugly scar appeared where apparently the man's voice box had once been.

Whatever flippancy was not dissipated by that scar immediately left Harvey when he went through the door. It was as though he had stepped into a chamber where few were permitted and fewer ever returned. In spite of windows on a far wall, the room seemed unusually dark. Sunlight sifting through the Venetian blinds sent shafts of light through the office casting bar-like shadows on the opposite wall. Heavy

38

metallic-looking draperies, the colour of diluted sherry, swung ponderously in the breeze which came at irregular intervals through the thick garrison-like window sashes. A rectangular-shaped bookcase near the windows sagged uncomfortably from the weight of the heavily bound legal library peering judiciously from its shelves. Several chairs, attended by squat ugly cigar stands, stood rigidly in rank seating invisible witnesses, while the Director of the Bureau peered balefully down from a large black frame. A red carpet spread across the room, and sitting in the centre at the headman's block, a spiral of cigarette smoke curling to hide his face like an executioner's veil, was the Bureau hatchet man, Avery Hawkins.

Hawkins had climbed unmercifully over the bodies of his fellow agents to his eminent position as Assistant Director in charge of the Administrative Division. His reputation as a vicious bureaucrat had earned for him the title, 'the Barracuda'—a name known even to new agents such as Harvey. At twenty-nine he had attained a position that few men could have achieved in a lifetime. In spite of his age he was a trusted confidant of the Director (who, in fact, had been younger than Hawkins when he took command of the Bureau), and generally it was thought that the Director was grooming Hawkins for his own job.

Harvey noted the name on the door and immediately sensed the extraordinary nature of the interview. None of the new agents to his knowledge had ever been summoned by Mr Hawkins. As he stepped into the room, an arm slowly uncoiled through the veil of smoke and a slender hand, seemingly disjointed, pointed in the direction of a chair near the door. Clearly the agent was to be permitted no farther than just beyond the threshold of that office.

Not a word was spoken and the lack of conversation which Harvey had found almost amusing during the trip over was now oppressive. Before seeing the scar he had attributed the silence to Bureau psychology intended to heighten the tension, thereby making the interview a more impressionable one. But one could sense immediately that there was no sham in that office to impress new agents. Rather, there seemed a

39

tomb-like quality about the place which inhibited talk, as though, once spoken, the words would reverberate about the room as a hollow echo. The only sound was the light rustling of the draperies which fluttered in the breeze.

The figure leaned forward through the curtain of smoke and sunlight pressing out a cigarette in an ashtray. He squashed the remnants thoroughly and finally, reflecting the purpose of one who always did things with thoroughness and finality. Harvey caught but a brief look at the blond hair, strange blue eyes, and seemingly perfect, almost girlish features before they retreated behind the veil.

It seemed that the man was about to speak when a telephone rang from somewhere behind the desk—one sharp, sustained ring. The figure stiffened slightly, and then out of the depths of the smoke the Assistant Director summoned the guide from the outer office.

'Gotty!'

Harvey had assumed the Barracuda's voice would be heavy wheels crunching on gravel. Instead, it was a light bell floating down choir-like, a full octave above the average man—a euphonic sound made even more singular by the oppressive silence. Only one word but unforgettable.

As though he had been hovering just beyond the door, the guide reappeared. With his articulate forefinger he motioned Harvey from the office. Although he had been in the chamber no more than ten seconds, Harvey sensed he had been carefully measured for Bureau execution.

'Sure, it sounds ridiculous, but that's exactly what happened.' 'How do you know it was Hawkins?'

'Because I read his name on the door.'

Jay applied the finishing touches to a plaster cast of a footprint he had made at a classroom crime scene that afternoon. They had received a prodigious assignment for the evening. The class had been presented a theoretical kidnapping case that day in which two ransom notes had been received for the safe return of an infant. By the following morning Jay and Harvey had to deliver to the rest of the class the results of their preliminary investigation.

'I'm telling you, it was something,' continued Harvey, disappointed that his account of the meeting with the Assistant Director had not elicited more interest from his roommate. 'It sounds stupid, I know, but it really got to me, him sitting there behind the smoke watching me. I think he was just about to say something to me when the phone rang.'

'Are you sure you saw him?' said Jay indifferently. 'They say no one ever sees him.'

'I saw him all right. He sure doesn't look like a heavy. I mean he looked awful young to me. And his voice—Christ, I never heard anything like it. I don't know, kind of like—well, like he was a fag or something. Of course, the way the sunlight came over his shoulder and with the cigarette smoke and all I couldn't see him very clearly. I wonder why they play it that way? You know, behind the smoke and all.'

'Oh, the usual Bureau psychology. He's the Bureau hatchet man. They probably figure if no one ever sees him, it makes him more sinister. You should know how the operation works by this time.'

'But why did he send for me? I never heard of any other new agents having to see him. In fact, just like you say, *nobody* sees the guy. According to Ed Timmons, even the rest of the brass rarely have any contact with him except on the phone. Everything's done through that guy Gotty who can't talk. Christ, I wish someone had told me. There I was mimicking the poor bastard.'

'Do you plan to help out on this thing at all tomorrow?' said Jay abruptly.

'Look, I'm trying to read the statute here. We've got to be sure we've got a kidnapping case. Maybe it's just a child-molesting case. Say, that's an idea. Let's try to pin a child-molestation case on Ed Timmons. We'll throw in a witness who said they saw him near a school with a bag of candy. That'll break the class up.'

'Try to be serious, will you please? We have two ransom notes and the instructor's footprint.'

'Jay, you've got two ransom notes which Ed Timmons wrote left-handed, and Gabriels' footprint. Ed had a hole in his shoe and didn't want us to make a plaster cast of it, so he

41

had Gabriels step in that box of dirt. Gabriels told me and made me promise not to tell.'

'Well, that does make it easier.'

'Say, did you notice anything peculiar today when those two instructors were presenting the Soviet espionage case?' asked Harvey, rolling his body into a sitting position on the bed.

'No,' said Jay. He picked up a manual from the floor and started to leaf through it. 'Why, what was it?'

'Well, the shorter one, who was handling the projector, made some comment about the Soviet KGB and the "who case" or something like that and the other guy just about dropped his teeth.'

'Yes, now that you mention it, I do recall that,' said Jay.

'And the other guy looked at him as though he'd just called the Director a dirty name. It will probably be on some test tomorrow, checking our powers of observation.' Harvey held his forehead with his left hand. It had been an enervating day and the first stages of a headache were beginning to take hold. 'Say, Jay, you have any . . .?' He caught himself abruptly, but his roommate looked up quickly. It was the briefest exchange, but he could see in the other man's eyes that he knew Harvey had been about to ask for some aspirin.

Jay looked away immediately, and then, as though nothing had happened, said, 'I saw Alberta's girl friend.'

'No kidding? Honest?' Harvey stood up abruptly. 'Where? How was she?'

'I couldn't really see her. She was standing in the living room near the piano when I came in last night. She turned the other way when I walked past.'

'How could you be sure it was Alberta's friend?'

'I figured it must be from the way Chidsey described her. Even from the back you could tell she was super. Tall, beautiful legs—'

'Why didn't you tell me about it sooner?'

'I only saw her last night. Besides, I forgot about it.'

'You forgot! How could anyone forget something like that? Here I've been waiting for weeks to get a look at this doll, and you forget to tell me she's downstairs. Maybe I could have done something. A pretext conversation. You know, *anything*! Christ, with all the subterfuge we're learning we could at least use some of it for our own benefit.'

'What difference does it make? Chidsey said she's a lesbian. She's not going to be interested in you.'

'How does Chidsey know? He hasn't been any closer to her than you. So they spend some time in the back room together. So what? Maybe they're doing crossword puzzles or something. There *are* legitimate things people can do in a room together. Besides, Chidsey's evil-minded. I don't believe everything that guy says.'

'I don't either, but I agree with you on one point. I think he's evil-minded, too. And if he's as evil-minded as I think he is, he's probably been down that back stairs checking out the keyhole pretty regularly. So what you're getting is probably firsthand evidence.'

'My God, what kind of world have I gotten myself into!' Harvey slapped the papers he was holding onto the bed in mock despair. 'A hundred-hour work week! Crazy tests! Queer girls!'

'Well,' said Jay laconically, 'there's always the rice paddy.'

'Gentlemen, you are about to undergo a vital phase of your training. What you learn here today might very well save your life someday.' The speaker was Harry Fry, otherwise known as the Coach, the man in charge of the defensive-tactics course at the FBI Academy.

New Agents Class number five had been at the Academy for almost three weeks. The Academy was a four-brick building located on a Marine base in Virginia, several miles from Washington. It was here new agents received their training in firearms, defensive tactics, and other practical field work, and where agents from the field returned for in-service training.

Harvey's class had been funnelled from one weapons course to the next, each of which promised a unique method for annihilating a fugitive. They were now preparing to undergo intensive training in hand-to-hand combat.

Harvey and Jay were seated in bleachers with the rest of the

43

class at one of the ranges listening to the Coach's opening remarks. The Coach was standing with his assistant on one of the mats that had been drawn up in front of the bleachers for the occasion.

Harvey's first impression of the man was disappointing. The Coach was a balding, fragile-featured man in his early forties with horn-rimmed glasses that magnified a pronounced tic, and bandy legs that stemmed from oversized shorts. To Harvey, the man presented the picture of an ageing, atrophying jockey.

The Coach's assistant was something else, and it was on him Harvey was focusing his attention. 'Can you imagine being in the ring with that guy?' he whispered to Jay. 'You might just as well be in a cage with a gorilla.'

First on the agenda was a vivid description of the vital parts of the body that might easily be maimed, rent asunder, or at least partially paralysed by the right kind of kick, jab or blow.

'Now for some practical demonstration. First of all, gentlemen, the on-guard position.' The Coach assumed what appeared to be a relaxed, nonchalant stance in front of the hulking figure. 'You will notice I am holding the lapels of my jacket,' he said, simulating with his hands. 'In this way, even though I am not overtly ready to defend, I am, nevertheless, prepared to immediately ward off any blows to my face, chest, or midsection. Also, you will notice that I am standing at a slight angle from my opponent. In this way I am prepared, by turning by body slightly, to avoid a kick in the vital organs.'

'Can you imagine if that ape kicked him?' whispered Harvey. 'It wouldn't make a helluva difference if he caught him in the vital organs or the ass.'

'Now,' continued the Coach, 'I'm ready to snap immediately into my action position.' He snapped into his action position. His legs spread stiffly apart, his head pulled sharply back, and his hands with fingers extended rigidly in front of his face, the Coach resembled a man who had just stuck his finger into an electric socket. A ripple of muffled laughter ran through the class, but the Coach was too engrossed in his action position to notice.

'From this position I am now ready to deliver any number

44

of blows. Now, you will notice my left hand is extended slightly with the outside edge ready to deliver one of the elementary strokes. This is called "the edge of hand to nose striking upwards." This, my friends, is a crackerjack and could come in very handy some day. It can cause an instantaneous massive brain hemorrhage.' With a lightening motion the Coach thrust his hand up and outward, checking the stroke a scant inch from his assistant's upper lip. The assistant, with an apathy that suggested either tremendous confidence in the Coach's precision or an indifference toward brain hemorrhages, flinched nary a muscle. 'That,' repeated the Coach, 'is a dandy.'

'Well, it'd at least give a guy an awful fat lip.' Harvey made little effort to conceal his disappointment in the instruction.

The edge of hand to nose striking upwards was but the beginning. The Coach had a repertory of kicks, digs, punches, slaps and thumps covering just about every way of attacking a person short of pulling his hair. Each manœuvre bore a precise title composed by its inventor, parts of which seemed culled from a medical dictionary.

The day passed quickly, with the Coach meticulously explaining the nomenclature of each manœuvre and then following up with an electrifying demonstration on the assistant, who had an uncanny knack for propelling himself aloft and landing with a resounding whack. The agents would then pair off among themselves, gingerly practising the procedures as the Coach scurried among them shouting corrections.

It was getting on toward 5:30 when the Coach assembled the class in front of him. 'Now we'll finish off with a few demonstrations of some "come-along holds". These holds are designed to take a resisting subject into custody without disabling him as the other material is liable to do.'

After a look at a few of the 'come-along holds,' which at best seemed designed to assist along a sick or very weary fugitive, Harvey and Jay agreed it would be far better to chance the disabling techniques. In the first place, the few 'come-along holds' which looked as if they might work were so elaborately contrived that it required substantial cooperation from a fellow trainee, to say nothing of a fugitive, to obtain the proper grip. Secondly, and far more important as far as the agent was concerned, once the felon was so ensnared, it took a good deal of togetherness to untangle without disabling both the agent and the person with whom he was coming along.

But the Coach and his assistant were a symphony of movement, falling in and out of the grips with all the grace of a veteran dance team, each grunt and anguished expression a convincing testimony from the assistant as to the effectiveness of the 'come-along holds.'

The last few minutes of the day were devoted to the Director's weight chart. The agents had been given notice that each man's weight must conform to the chart and failure to make the weight resulted in swift punishment—usually taking the form of disciplinary transfers.

Following the presentation of the weight chart, Harvey and Jay climbed down from the stands.

'I can think of a perfect name for the Coach's course,' said Harvey. 'Harry's Carries.'

'I can think of a better one if you ever try any of that stuff on a fugitive,' replied Jay. 'Hari-Kari!'

As they rounded the corner of a building at the base of the bleachers, Harvey caught a slight motion out of the corner of his eye. Turning, he saw a figure facing the building with his hands to his face as though lighting a cigarette. There was a certain familiarity about the individual's build, and while he could not be certain, it occurred to him that it might be the voiceless man who had taken him to see Hawkins.

'Did you notice that guy?' said Harvey casually, as they continued walking.

'Where?'

'The man by the building. Don't look back, though.'

Jay looked anyway. 'What man? There's no one there.'

Harvey turned quickly. Nothing. 'Well, there *was* a man there. He was standing about halfway down that building. It looked like the guy who took me over to Hawkins' office.'

'I think maybe your imagination is working a little overtime. There couldn't have been anyone there. Where

46

would he go?'

'He could have gone straight up as far as I know. But there *was* a man right over there.' There was a defiant tone in Harvey's voice now.

'OK, OK. So there was a man there. Take it easy.' Jay looked at him uneasily and they continued walking in silence.

It was dusk by the time the class climbed into the bus that ferried them between the ranges. Harvey and Jay sat quietly side by side. Harvey was the first to break the silence. 'When are we supposed to meet the Director, do you know?'

'Right after the first, according to Ed Timmons,' replied Jay.

'I understand it's pretty quick. We just file by and shake his hand,' said Harvey. 'I wonder if there's anything to that stuff about his standing there with his finger on a button.'

'What button?'

'You mean you haven't heard about the button?' Harvey brightened considerably. 'When you file past the Director to shake his hand, he keeps his left hand on a button. If he doesn't like the looks of you, ZAP!'

'Oh, I don't know. I find that a little hard to believe.'

'Did you hear about the class several months ago who had just about finished their training and went to see the Man?'

'Probably not,' replied Jay with a sigh.

'They all filed past the Director and after they'd gone, he said he didn't like the looks of the last man. So there's a big rush to bounce the last man and guess who it is?'

'Who?'

'The counsellor,' said Harvey.

Jay leaned his head back against the seat and laughed. It was rare that Harvey saw him genuinely laugh. It gave him a good feeling.

As the days passed and the training gradually drew to a close, the meeting with the Director loomed as the biggest hurdle to the class. It seemed any type of meeting with 'the Man' was at best a calculated risk, not only for the new agents but just about anyone in the organisation, for virtually anything could result. It was not difficult to obtain an audience. Any agent

47

could ask to see the Director and his wish was fulfilled forthwith. Because of the possible consequences, however, there was never an abundance of requests.

Yet agents from the field occasionally would ask to see him for one reason or another. Before an agent entered his office the Director reviewed a brief statement that summarised the man's background. Following the interview, he jotted down on the memorandum in black ink his personal impressions of the agent and other information he deemed pertinent. If it was favourable, the visiting agent's future in the organisation might be bright, indeed, but if it was unfavourable. . . .

The black ink was treated as the will of a sovereign, and there was little delay in its implementation. Stories abounded in Harvey's class concerning the results. Typical of such tales was the one about a memorandum that had been sent to the Director's office concerning an important fugitive who was reported to be somewhere in the Southwest. The memo reappeared with the words scratched in the black ink, 'Watch the border!' Immediately 50 agents were dispatched south of the Rio Grande. The Director, when informed, was infuriated. He had merely intended the note for his secretary, who had typed too far over the edge of the memo page.

Such stories were told with tongue in cheek, but they did, nevertheless, create respect for the power of the black ink.

Harvey had heard most of the stories and was fully aware of the dangers inherent in the forthcoming meeting. When he talked of it, he did so jokingly, but always uneasily. It was clearly to be the supreme test—the magnum opus of the training activities.

It was Monday, the last week of the training programme, when a succession of events began that were to have great significance for Harvey Tucker.

Harvey dined alone that evening. Jay had disappeared at 6:00 following the last class, with a hurried explanation about some shopping chores.

After dinner Harvey called the Gaylord to see if there had been any calls for him. Aunt Frieda answered. After a terse exchange, Aunt Frieda—a frosty, whiskered lady in her late

48

seventies who was not overly fond of answering the phone—abruptly hung up. Harvey left the restaurant in no way confident that, should the office call, Aunt Frieda would relay the message that he had gone to do some shopping and would return before ten o'clock.

It was a damp, misty evening, cold and very dark. The headlights of passing vehicles reflected dully off the wet pavement, while streetlights glowed ineffectively like old gas lamps in the thin fog. It was the kind of evening in which it was pleasant, if somewhat forlorn, to walk. Whether it was raining or not was impossible to tell unless one held one's hand out for a few seconds. Then ever so lightly one could feel it, droplets so tiny they did not appear to be falling, but seemed suspended colloidally in the air.

The closest shopping place open at that time of evening was several blocks from the Gaylord. It was a poor section, inhabited mostly by blacks.

The weather seemed to have cleared somewhat by the time he arrived in the area. He saw what appeared to be a stationery store in the distance and with long strides moved that way. Within a few minutes he was standing in front of a counter making purchases of some notebook folders and paper. He determined from the proprietor that a drugstore was located just three blocks farther down, and after paying for the supplies, he left the store and headed in that direction.

As he walked, it seemed the neighbourhood deteriorated considerably. Small, ill-kempt stores, many of them basement shops, interlaced with small stoops in front of indigent residences, gradually faded into an even more improverished tenement section. Solid banks of crumbling buildings were separated by entrances to pitch-black alleys. Soggy heaps of refuse lined the sidewalks, and garbage cans amid the debris looked as if they had been targets for inaccurate aims from windows above. Looking the length of the block through the dimly lighted, misty atmosphere, it seemed as though the inhabitants of the stark dwellings had emptied the contents of their households onto the street.

He saw the outline of what he supposed to be the drugstore on the next block. As he walked toward it, he noticed two

49

figures approaching from the opposite direction. When the men strode under the light of a streetlamp, Harvey recognised the clean, handsome features of Jay. The other man, tall, a bit heavier than Jay, was indistinguishable, but there was something familiar about him.

Certain that they had not seen him, Harvey moved into the shadows close to the buildings. There was something strange about the pair. While walking together, they seemed almost oblivious of each other. There was an alley a few yards away and Harvey stepped into the dark entranceway. He listened to the sharp click of the heels against the pavement in unison as the men approached the entranceway. It would be terribly awkward if they should happen to see him. Within a few seconds they drew abreast of the alley and passed on. It was only a fleeting glimpse, but Harvey had seen him. The dark, Slavic features, the heavy brow—there was no question: it was the voiceless man, the man who had taken him to Hawkins.

After waiting a few minutes to ensure that they were out of sight, Harvey stepped from the alley and headed in the opposite direction, toward the next block. Within minutes, his heart pounding and thoughts racing confusedly through his mind, he was walking rapidly toward a lighted thoroughfare heavy with traffic.

'It looks like tomorrow's the day.' Ed Timmons paused and looked at the class significantly. Yes, tomorrow was the day. The day when the Director would personally inspect the class and render his impressions of the 19 men who remained. If he liked what he saw, everything would be just dandy. If he did not, well, the repercussions would be great.

Ed had been thinking about the new agents' class that had preceded his. Things had gone remarkably well for the group right up to the minute they had met the Director, and then—'They look like a bunch of truck drivers!'

In the ensuing purge everyone in the training and inspection division from Mr Karp on down had been blamed, but the counsellor who was at the bottom of the chain had borne most of the criticism. It was, after all, *his* class.

The tips of Ed's fingernails dug into the lectern as he gazed out over the class. 'Make sure you wear your best suit, and it wouldn't be a bad idea to have it pressed tonight. Also bring an extra white handkerchief for your breast pocket. Needless to say, your shoes should be signed.' Ed swallowed hard, 'Shined, that is.' God, he needed a rest. If only he could get through the next day, it would be all over—then back to the Resident Agency. It would be good to be home. He would take a couple of weeks annual leave, then maybe a few days' sick leave, then ease back into the case load gently. Less than three years to go . . . very gently.

Harvey listened intently as Ed continued with detailed instructions pertaining to the meeting. Had someone told him six months previously that an audience with the Director would have entailed such planning, he would have found it incredible. But now it seemed logical that the greatest test of all should entail some preliminary training.

'The main thing to keep in mind,' Ed was saying, 'is the sooner we're out of that office, the better. That line has to keep moving. Just file past, state your name, and shake his hand. Don't stop what ever you do . . .that is, of your *own* volition,' he added darkly.

If one could judge from the expression on the faces, the Director would see little more than a blur as 19 figures swept by him.

'All right, let's line up for a practice run,' said the counsellor. 'I'll be the Man and you fellows line up there by the window.'

Scraping of chairs and light conversation followed as the class grouped on the far side of the room. 'No, John, you get toward the centre,' said Ed. 'Everyone try to line up by size. No sense in having him meet Clarence right after Bob. No offence, Clarence. I mean there's no point in his seeing a real tall man and then a shorter one. That's it. That's the idea. The whole thing is to try and look as much alike as possible. That way you've got less chance of being singled out for any reason. OK, let's see, now. Harvey, why don't you be first?'

Harvey was less than enthusiastic about the assignment. He would have preferred the anonymity that might come with

51

being sandwiched between two other agents.

'OK, now when you shake his hand, make sure you give it a good, firm clasp and look him right in the eye. Even though the palms of your hands probably will be sweating like hell, act as though you're not afraid. Now let's start. Remember, just your name and "How do you do, sir?" Nothing else. Jesus, *nothing* else! OK, Harvey, let's start.'

'Harvey Tucker. How do you do, sir?'

'James Von Vlack. How do you do, sir?'

'George Davis. How do you do, sir?'

As the class quickly shuffled past, Ed offered appropriate comments. 'Don't shake quite so hard. . . That's good. . . A little firmer, Lennie. . . Jesus! Easy does it, Nick, you'll bust every bone in his hand!' Generally he seemed quite pleased with the group. That is, with all but one shorter agent named Maynard Emmons.

'That's some handle you got there, Maynard. Maybe you'd better just say your initials and last name, OK!'

'OK, Ed. Ahem . . . M M Emmons. How do you do, sir?' He looked up hopefully at Ed, who grimaced slightly.

'Gee, I don't know, Maynard. "M M Emmons" sounds kind of like you were stuttering—as though you were scared.'

'Well, I am,' answered Maynard candidly. 'Who isn't?'

'Oh, I guess it's probably OK," said Ed, bending his head and rubbing the back of his neck. 'I'm probably getting a little neurotic about this thing. All right, everybody, let's line up and go through it once more. Dick, see if you can't drop your voice a bit more this time, OK?'

Again the class moved smartly past Ed, who seemed satisfied with it all, except for M M Emmons. As the shorter agent passed, Ed shook his head grimly. 'I don't know. Maybe you should go back to "Maynard" again.'

Harvey avoided Jay that evening. The events of the preceding night had dispelled any doubts that he had concerning his roommate's position in the new agent's class. He was now convinced that the man with whom he had been training for eight months had been masquerading as a new agent. Jay Von Vlack had to be a Bureau plant.

It was almost ten o'clock when he arrived back at the Gaylord, a sharply pressed suit beneath his grey raincoat. The house was still and dark. As he crossed the living room towards the stairs, he heard a soft laugh from the room beyond the backstairs. From the exhilarant quality of the sound, he judged Alberta was not visiting with Aunt Frieda. He considered the liabilities involved in going to the rear to listen, but almost immediately discounted the venture as too risky.

His feet made soft brushing noises on the carpet as he mounted the stairs, and almost before he reached the floor on which his room was located, he sensed the upstairs was empty. He wondered where Jay was. Bob Chidsey and the other agents who shared the third floor had long since left, and the absence of any sound or movement in the house was disturbing.

After snapping on the overhead light in his room he took off his raincoat and draped it over one of the chairs. Thoughts of Alberta in the back room had stimulated his imagination, and he had difficulty putting the matter out of mind. He felt certain the landlady must be entertaining her friend. He thought once again about a trip to the rear of the house. It was a perfect opportunity. Probably Jay was right about Bob Chidsey making a few trips down the backstairs. Maybe they were lesbians.

It was an exciting thought. Beyond an occasional glance at a good-looking girl, Harvey had had little sexual release during the preceding months. He thought of the magazine his crew had had back at Lake Placid which showed pictures of two nude girls in various positions making love to one another. These recollections together with the presumption that something similar might be taking place at that moment between Alberta and her friend were proving difficult to ignore. Finally he reached down and pulled off his shoes. It wouldn't hurt to take a walk down the hall. Maybe he could hear something from the top of the stairs.

As he moved through the darkness down the corridor, conflicting emotions began to form in his mind.

Here he was in the last few days of training, taking a stupid

53

chance. The Bureau was an antisex league. How could he look the Director in the eye the next day after peeping through a keyhole—he, a Special Agent of the FBI? And what if he got caught? What if Alberta suddenly pulled open the door and there he was, crouched over like some poor deformed creature? What if she called the Bureau? What would Ed Timmons do? How about the people back in Eagle's Notch? His mother and sister! 'Harvey Tucker, the guy who got bounced from the Bureau for peeping at his landlady.' Man!

Still, what an opportunity. No one in the house. The two of them down there. Beautiful girls, kissing, and fondling each other's hot, moist vaginas.

He came to the end of the hall and peered down into the empty blackness of the rear stairwell. Except for a strong breeze that buffeted the back of the house at intervals, it was completely quiet.

Again the inhibitions. He'd almost made it through the training school. One out of 500. Hand-picked, investigated, trained, abused, surveilled, tested, and finally—graduated! And here he was blowing it all the last week. Again the image he had conjured up in his mind—a configuration of plump breasts, soft pink tits, blonde matted vaginas, intertwined with long graceful legs—just beyond the door!

It was worth it. Besides, if he was caught, he was only trying to contact the landlady. 'What? With no shoes on? Sneaking down the backstairs?' He considered going back to the room to get his shoes. But what purpose would the shoes have in his hand? 'He took his shoes off so he could get down the stairs quietly,' that's what they'd say. They'd have him cold. He'd never be able to stand up under a polygraph.

No, best he forget the shoes. He could say he was just relaxing. Everybody relaxes with his shoes off. 'But his suit coat! He had his suit coat *on!* How could he be relaxing with his suit coat *on* and his shoes *off?*'

What was the matter with him? Why was he so worried? Had this goddamn Bureau gotten to him this much already?

The backstairs of the Gaylord was an old, narrow passageway that wound its way from the third floor to the basement, with intervening landings on the second and first floors. Harvey accomplished the trip quickly, remaining close to the wall to prevent the steps from creaking. Within a few seconds he was standing in an alcove near the rear room.

It was very dark, and with the exception of a ray of light that appeared from beneath the door, Harvey could see very little. As he approached the room a conversation of light voices came muffled and intermittent from behind the door.

The alcove was hot and perspiration was beginning to form tiny rivulets on his temples and cheeks. It occurred to him what Ed Timmons had said about how annoyed the Director could become at perspiration rings under an agent's armpits. He wished he had removed his suit jacket. He would have no time for another cleaning before meeting the Director.

He could hear Alberta's clipped, accented voice now, but it was not so authoritarian as usual. Jay had said once that Alberta's accent was German, and that most Germans expressed themselves in an authoritative way. But Alberta's voice was different now. Harvey sensed immediately that it was solicitous, as though concerned that she would offend the person to whom she was speaking. It seemed odd to hear her talking so submissively. Cautiously he moved forward and placed his ear against the door. It was still difficult to hear anything. The conversation was subdued. Beyond a word surfacing now and then, he could make out very little. But then he heard it, '—raville.' Had the voice said 'Nayraville'? He was almost certain it had.

He knelt down and placed his eye against the keyhole. He could see nothing as a key was occupying most of the space. He wondered if there was a window in the alley. No, that would be insane. If he were ever caught out there, it would be the end for sure. 'Out in the alley? Trying to contact your landlady? With no shoes?' No, it would never go.

'If we waited for a decision from Nayraville, nothing would ever get done.' It was the voice of the other person now, much louder as though somewhat distraught. It was a feminine voice. But more than that, there was something strange about it—curiously familiar.

Harvey noticed the light coming from under the door.

55

Maybe . . . just maybe. . .

Stretching himself out lengthwise in the hall, he pressed his eye against the new vantage point. The position rendered him completely oblivious to the two hundred pounds of lumbering Aunt Frieda who turned the corner carrying her nightly glass of port. Having performed the routine from kitchen to bedroom without incident through the years, the senior lady was unprepared for the form stretched out in the blackness. The port and Aunt Frieda landed about the same time with crushing force.

'AW-W-W-W-K!' It was a voice straight out of hell which inspired the voyeur to untangle himself and make the stairs. It is doubtful if liquid oxygen could have provided a quicker ascent to the second floor.

Ed Timmons stood rigidly at the lectern, a look of paternal concern on his face, scrutinising each member of the class like a headmaster prior to a lower school graduation exercise. Dark suits, conservative ties, white handkerchiefs adorning breast pockets, carefully combed hair—oh, oh—'Ernie, can't you do something with that hair?'

Ernie Collier had come to Washington eight months previously with the same crew cut he had worn most of his life. His hair had the stiff, wiry texture of fibreglass brush, and one might just as well have tried to comb a cactus plant.

But the mould did not provide for such individual problems. Crew cuts were taboo. Therefore, hopefully, Ernie had permitted his hair to grow. It had not been long before it became obvious to everyone what Ernie had known from the start. Namely, that his hair was not going to deviate from its original direction. So after eight months, instead of a crew cut one-half inch high, Ernie now sported a crew cut standing a full three inches above his brow and giving every indication of continuing to new heights.

'I just combed it, Ed,' said Ernie plaintively.

'You did?' said Ed incredulously. 'Jesus, it looks as though you got hold of a hot wire. Why don't you go put some more water on it to hold it down?' With little optimism, Ernie headed for the men's room.

56

'Now, try to look intelligent when you go by the Man,' said Ed, apparently satisfied with the rest of the class. 'A lot depends on the impression you make in there. Ahhh ... if your hands have a tendency to perspire' (Ed looked at his palms), 'and that means most of us, it might be a good idea if just before you shook the Man's hand, you rub your palm on your trousers like this. We don't want him to feel as though he's squeezed 19 wet sponges.'

Ed continued with a summary of last minute instructions. 'Now, does anyone have any questions about *anything*? Remember, when I said go through *fast*, I don't mean *too* fast. . .' Ed paused as Ernie Collier returned to the room. 'But not too slow, either. I can't imagine anyone forgetting what he's supposed to say. You've only got one line. Still, if it happens and you forget your name, make one up. Maynard, in your case that might not be a bad idea.'

After a final check of his watch, which he had been winding continuously for the past quarter hour, the counsellor inhaled deeply. 'Let's go.'

It was a curious line of silent men who trooped down Pennsylvania Avenue toward the Justice Building. Harvey, deep in thought, walked quietly beside Jay. The episode the previous evening had left him shaken and pensive. However, he had been very fortunate. The wails from Aunt Frieda had diverted attention, and he had been able to grab his shoes and make a hasty exit from the Gaylord. By the time he had returned, Jay was there and filled him in on the details. There had been surprisingly little aftermath.

Alberta had told Jay that Aunt Frieda had tripped in the hall again, but that similar accidents had happened before, and that although she had received a bad bump on her hip, she was going to be all right. Although Aunt Frieda had complained vaguely about the possibility of an intruder, Alberta had been more inclined to blame the genie in the bottle of port, since it seems Aunt Frieda had been picking up the number of trips to the pantry of late.

With the exception of a slight discolouration on the back of his new grey suit coat and a faint aroma of lingering port, Harvey considered himself fortunate indeed. Still, the

57

meeting with the Director was an unnerving prospect, and there was always the possibility that the Man had organs of smell every bit as extraordinary as apparently were his other faculties. The spectre of the Director stopping the line and sniffing carefully at Harvey Tucker was interrupted by Jay.

'You seem a bit downcast, Harvey.'

'So what's there to be cheerful about? Look at Ed Timmons. You'd think he was going to the guillotine.'

'Maybe it's just an act,' said Jay. 'Part of the psychology to impress us with meeting the Director.'

'You might be right. There does seem to be quite a bit of acting going on,' said Harvey pointedly. There was a slight pause and he sensed his roommate was pondering the remark. For a second he considered going all the way, just flatly asking Jay what it was all about. Instead he said, 'No, I don't believe all this stuff about the Director having a button. He probably indicates the class as a whole looks good to him or they don't. You can't believe half of the stuff you hear around this place.'

Jay said nothing and they continued to walk in silence. When they entered the Justice Building, a uniformed guard took them to a bank of elevators. Two cars that had been reserved for the class opened magically as they approached. Harvey was continually amazed at the precision of everything. It seemed nothing in the organisation was ever out of kilter. Nothing was late. Equipment never failed. No one made mistakes. It was as though the Bureau were an elaborate, finely tuned motor comprised of many intricate mechanisms requiring a precise performance from each, lest the failure of the slightest part cause the entire instrument to go awry.

They were carried smoothly to the eighth floor, a slight humming noise being the only thing that suggested they were moving at all. Following the counsellor, they moved silently down an immaculate corridor, finally stopping before a door on which was printed in black letters 'DIRECTOR, FEDERAL BUREAU OF INVESTIGATION.'

Ed Timmons paused and looked back at the column of agents. Taking his handkerchief from his breast pocket, he dabbed at his brow. Then carefully folding it, he replaced it in

58

the pocket, fussing momentarily with the corners, which seemed to be drooping in the face of what was waiting beyond the door.

Ed no longer tried to conceal his concern from the class. His whole future rested with the next few minutes. Turning again toward his charges, he made a fingers-crossed motion while rolling his eyes toward the ceiling. Then, stretching his neck and fingering his tie once again, he grasped the doorknob and pushed.

The Director's antechamber was a large, delicately furnished room with fawn-coloured carpeting, soft under foot like spring turf. Although there were but two small windows, the room had a bright, cheerful air about it which seemed to reflect the disposition of its occupant, who sat smiling amiably behind a vase of russet and yellow mums perched on the corner of her desk.

This, then, was Miss Handy, the Director's secretary for over 30 years and described by him as the *one* indispensable person in the FBI—a rare tribute and one that the tenure of service in the other positions seemed to bear out rather well.

As the agents entered, Miss Handy nodded pleasantly and pushed a button on her intercom. 'The agents are here, sir.' She said it rather breezily. She was a handsome woman in her mid-fifties with white hair, large blue eyes and an aristocratic bearing. With or without her secretarial talent she would have been a complement to any staff. 'The Director will be with you shortly, gentlemen.' Her smile conveyed the idea that such prospects were pleasant, indeed.

Several minutes passed as the class stood around the room in a long spiral, handkerchiefs dabbing at brows, palms rubbing against trousers, each agent adhering tenaciously to his designated position lest any deviation rob him of his anonymity in the sentitive surroundings.

Harvey's eyes shifted to Miss Handy and he was surprised to find the woman regarding him thoughtfully. The exchange was interrupted as a door opened slowly behind the woman and an elderly Chinese appeared. Later Harvey was to learn that this was Ho Ping, the Director's personal orderly and answer to any and all charges that the Bureau engaged in discriminatory hiring practices. When a charge of discrimination was levelled at the Bureau a few years previously, Ho Ping had been attributed a partial Negro ancestry—an assertion that had been regarded with a considerable scepticism by most critics. But there seemed little likelihood of proof or disproof of the claim what with Ho Ping's age and his power of total unrecall.

With a slight bow, the orderly bade the harried-looking group to follow him, and the line unravelled into a long, narrow passageway. There was a solemnity to the manœuvre that was unnerving to the already tense assemblage. The narrow, grim-looking hallway reminded Harvey of the gauntlet through which livestock passed on their way to the slaughterhouse. It was the last avenue to the Director's chamber—as one erstwhile Bureau official had described it, 'sort of a "Bridge of Sighs".'

As they approached the entranceway, Harvey could see a group of older men just beyond the door. They appeared stiff, silent and formal, as though very serious business were at hand. At the door the orderly stepped aside, bowed slightly, and motioned Ed Timmons inside.

Harvey quickly followed the counsellor. Inside, he found himself in a large, Edwardian-type room. Although there were a half dozen Bureau officials standing about, Harvey's eyes riveted immediately on a figure in a grey sharkskin suit standing near a furled flag on the far wall. It was a heavy, block-like figure of medium height, firmly planted as though it had grown in that spot and had roots extending clear down through eight floors of the Justice Building into the soil beneath Pennsylvania Avenue. Those who had expected a formidable figure were not disappointed.

He was an intense-looking man with wiry black hair and a square, belligerent jaw that jutted forth from a deeply tanned face. The dark eyes which peered from beneath the heavy brows showed little cordiality, and his face, although flat and expressionless, indicated the man expected trouble and rather relished the prospect. It was a face it seemed which never laughed, never cried, and whose chief emotional

60

manifestation was anger.

It was toward this formidable countenance that Ed Timmons briskly stepped. 'Hello, sir. Special Agent Timmons, *counsellor* for New Agents Class number five.'

'Hello, Mr Timmons.' The words came out clipped and inexpressive, imparting no more warmth than the face. As he spoke, the Director kept one hand resting on the edge of his desk. Ed Timmons accomplished his presentation and was past the Director in three seconds flat. Then, turning to Harvey, he motioned him to move, and the agent did so with surprising alacrity, leaving Jay a step or so behind.

'Harvey Tucker. How do you do, sir?' The eyes of the Director met his only fleetingly and conveyed no more expressiveness than one might expect from a casual passerby.

'Pleased to meet you,' came the terse reply.

Ed Timmons motioned him toward a door leading from the office. He moved toward the exit and heard the names rattled off behind him as the line shuffled past the Director with speed characteristic of old-time flicks.

'James Von Vlack. How do you do, sir?'

'Pleased to meet you.'

'George Davis. How do you do, sir?'

'Pleased to meet you.'

'Steven Martin. How do you do, sir?'

'Pleased to meet you.'

'M M Em-Emmons,' inordinately loud followed by, 'How you, sir . . . *do*!'

A slight pause and then, 'Pleased to meet you.'

Out in the hall Harvey and Jay became convulsed. Partly from nervous relief, but mostly because of Maynard's incredible blunder. 'Holy Christ,' whispered Harvey, 'did you hear that? "How you, sir . . .*do*!"'

Both tried to compose themselves as Maynard emerged pale and shaken. 'I really goofed,' he murmured.

'Like a bunch of floorwalkers from a department store!'

No one was sure how such a group looked, but presumably it was bad. The interviews had started shortly after they had returned from the Justice Building and had continued

61

through most of the day. The door at the rear of the classroom had squeaked open five times and five agents, including Maynard Emmons, had been summoned. One had returned. It was not Maynard.

During a break late in the afternoon, Jay, deep in thought, was resting his elbows on the brass railing outside the classroom looking down at the skylight when Harvey appeared at his side. 'Rough day.'

Jay looked up at him briefly and then returned his interest to the skylight without answering.

'So what's the matter with looking like a floorwalker?' continued Harvey. 'They're pretty neat-looking guys, aren't they?'

'Yes, I guess so,' answered Jay, clearly not interested.

There was a prolonged silence.

'Hear about the affair in the LA office?' said Harvey finally.

Jay gave a short sigh. No, he hadn't heard.

'Seems three agents were renting an apartment together, and after they moved out, the landlord called the office about some mail or something. Anyway, he mentions that one of the agents had been peeing in bed.'

'So?' Jay looked up at him quizzically.

'So, now there's a big investigation to see who peed in bed. Can you imagine that? You can't even pee in bed without advising the Bureau.'

Jay looked back down at the skylight without answering.

'I wonder if they'll have any more interviews. Every time that door squeaks open I wonder if my time has come. I'll never forget that day I went for the interview with Hawkins. Remember that? The guy who couldn't talk? He was a creepy character. Do you remember him?'

'Vaguely,' replied Jay.

'I still think I saw him down at the Academy that day. Have you ever seen him anywhere?'

Jay glanced up and looked at him closely. Immediately Harvey was sorry he had asked the question.

'Where would I see him?' said Jay. He continued to look at him.

'I don't know. I just thought you might have seen him in the hall or someplace.'

'No, I've never seen him.'

The grey eyes continued to focus on Harvey as the break came to an end.

Neither one said anything as they walked toward their seats, and more to break the awkward silence than anything else, Harvey said to Gabriels, 'Hear the deal in the LA office?'

'No, what happened?'

'An agent peed in bed and embarrassed the Bureau.'

'What?' said Gabriels, looking askance.

'Tell you later,' whispered Harvey, as Ed Timmons assumed his place at the lectern and the class fell silent.

'Gentlemen,' began Ed, looking exceedingly sober, 'tomorrow all notebooks will be picked up to be reviewed and graded. I suggest any of you who have any doubts about the condition of your notebooks spend plenty of time tonight putting them in shape. Now, men, it's been a long day. Those of you who are left have only two days to go and you can leave here with a clean bill of health. Let's stay on our toes, OK?'

After class Harvey excused himself from Jay and walked over to the shopping district to pick up a few presents for his family. It was approaching midnight when he returned to the Gaylord. He had changed into his pyjamas and was brushing his teeth in the bathroom when he was startled to look up and see his roommate staring at him through the reflection in the mirror. Harvey had not heard him come up the stairs.

Jay was the first to break the silence. 'Did you get your presents?' he asked pleasantly.

'Uh huh,' grunted Harvey, finishing brushing his teeth and hanging his toothbrush in the holder above the washbasin. 'I got some perfume for my mom and that record album for my sister.'

'Why didn't you get the perfume from the agent over in the lab?' said Jay, walking into the other room. 'He can make anything you want.'

'Oh, I don't know. It looks better in a fancy bottle with the

63

name on it and all.' Harvey hung up the towel he had been using and opened the medicine chest, preparing to put away his toilet articles, when a curious thing happened. In the other room Jay had struck a match to light a cigarette, and the flame had reflected ever so briefly in the mirror of the medicine cabinet, catching Harvey's eye. He noted that while Jay was out of normal vision, by moving the door of the medicine cabinet he was able to follow his movements through the reflection from a large mirror over Harvey's dresser. In effect the two mirrors afforded him a near perfect view of Jay without moving from the washstand.

Jay sat down on the edge of his bed with his back to the mirror and prepared to remove his shoes.

Harvey pursed his lips, considering for one last second, and then with measured casualness said, 'Jay, do you think the Bureau has any submarines in our class?' Jay paused slightly, and then bent over, continuing to untie his shoes.

'Who knows? Probably,' came the answer in a disinterested tone. And then the inevitable, 'Why do you ask?'

'Because I think I know who's a plant.'

Jay straightened up slowly and stared at the bureau in front of him. He sat motionless and Harvey could tell he was tense. 'So, who *is* the plant?'

'Emmons.'

'Maynard? Why?'

'Sure, can't you figure it? He blows the interview with the Director on purpose and we never see him again. That way he's out of the picture completely, right? That frees him up for another class when he comes back as Hubert Humstone or some other character.' He saw Jay drop his head slightly, and then bend over to remove his shoes. Harvey could sense his relief.

'That seems remote. How long are you going to be in there?'

'Be out in a few minutes,' answered Harvey. He was just about to close the medicine cabinet when he saw Jay stand quickly as though on impulse and softly withdraw a smaller drawer near the top of his bureau. With his free hand he reached far back into the interior of the chest and quickly withdrew some object. Although he could not tell for certain, it seemed to Harvey as though he ripped up a piece of paper. As Jay turned in the direction of the mirror above the bureau Harvey quickly closed the medicine cabinet. Turning off the water he walked into the bedroom. 'We should go over these notebooks once more.'

Jay ignored the comment and entered the bathroom, closing the door behind him. Harvey glanced toward the bureau on the other side of the room. He recalled the first day when Jay had indicated a preference for it. He was determined that sometime before he left the Gaylord he would have a look behind that special drawer. Taking his notebook from the briefcase he crawled into bed. He propped the pillow up behind him, turned on the reading lamp and tried to concentrate. It was difficult.

Within a few minutes Jay returned. 'Unless you can read that in the dark you'd better put it away. Your roommate is going to bed and he wants peace, quiet, and darkness.'

'The roommate can go screw himself,' retorted Harvey. Jay seemed in a jocular mood and Harvey was ready to respond. It was rare that he exhibited any levity. 'You heard Timmons. They're collecting these things tomorrow to grade them.'

'I think it's just as important to be alert on the last day, and alertness to me means eight hours' sleep. Now, turn out that light.'

'My God, what an old lady. If I had to do it over again, I think I'd rather room downstairs with Aunt Frieda,' said Harvey.

'Yes, and if I know you, you've probably tried.'

Soon Jay was snoring with all the intensity of a heavy truck on a steep hill.

'Damn it,' murmured Harvey, slamming shut his notebook.

He got out of bed, adjusted the pillows and then made a last trip to the bath. As he lifted the lid on the commode he was surprised to see a few pieces of white paper floating in the water. It must have been the remnants of what Jay had ripped up and had intended to flush away in the faulty commode. He could feel the blood pounding in his temples as he leaned over and carefully removed the bits of paper.

The following day passed quickly. Instructions regarding reporting procedures while en route to the office of assignment, collection of the notebooks, more papers to sign (no one ever knew what he was signing; the type who would hold things up to read the fine print, after being instructed to sign, long since had been weeded out) and the second to last day of training was concluded peacefully.

It was Jay who excused himself that evening. More personal errands to attend to.

Harvey had placed the pieces of paper between two blotters and inserted them in his textbook on federal criminal procedure. He was anxious to assemble them. Also Jay's absence would enable him to have a look at the bureau drawer. It was risky. There could be hidden security devices. No matter. Before he left he was determined to look.

He purchased a roll of Scotch tape with which to piece together the bits of paper and headed for the Vespers, a restaurant rarely frequented by the agents in view of the high prices.

The maître d' was an obliging little man who changed Harvey's table from a secluded corner after the agent had found it would be too dark to see. The second choice was far better and, after ordering a Manhattan, he carefully spilled the small bits of paper onto the table.

Working with the Scotch tape, he began assembling the pieces. He progressed much more rapidly than he had expected. As each piece fitted into place, it looked as if one word were emerging. A good deal of the paper had been flushed away, but it appeared that the part containing the word was all there. Within a few minutes he had completed the puzzle. One word printed in black ink appeared on the slip of paper—'EXPIATE'. It made little sense. Disappointed, he placed the paper in his wallet.

Following dinner, he went directly to the Gaylord. With the exception of a night lamp in the hall, the house was dark. He went straight to Jay's bureau. After checking the edges for any seals or other security devices, he gently pulled out the drawer. Just as he had suspected, it was slightly shorter in depth than the others. He placed it on the bed and bending

66

over looked into the interior. An open shelf-like structure had been built into the rear of the bureau. He experienced an uncomfortable feeling in his stomach when there on the shelf he saw a small box of aspirin. Next to the aspirin was a snub-nosed revolver. It was too dark to be certain, but Harvey believed it to be a Colt cobra—a small, easily concealed weapon which packed all of the punch of a regular service revolver. The rest of the shelf was bare.

After replacing the drawer, Harvey picked up the dictionary from his desk and lay down on the bed, snapping on the reading light as he did so.

'Experience'. . . 'expert'. . . 'expiate—to atone for; make amends or reparation for.' It meant little to him.

It was only 9:30 when he crawled into bed and turned out the light. It was a luxury he had not enjoyed for the past eight months.

Although laden with several pistols and sets of credentials, Ed Timmons almost floated into the room. Indeed, he was walking on air. 'Good morning, good morning.' It was actually much more than that. It was truly a magnificent morning—the best one in eight months, and Ed was having difficulty containing his ebulience. 'Just drop them on the desk there, son,' said the counsellor breezily.

A young, rather fragile-looking clerk who had followed Ed into the room bearing the remainder of the equipment, deposited his cargo on the desk. After rewarding the young man with an approbative wink and a warm smile, he gazed out at the class, automatically counting heads like a camp counsellor following a swim. Fifteen, just right. Ah, yes, sir, three more hours and they would all be a memory. In eight hours with a little luck he would be aboard the train heading for the oblivion of the Waterville RA.

'Well, gents, this is it,' said Ed, looking out over the hollow-eyed remnants of New Agents Class number five. 'Commencement day. The day we pay homage to the Bureau for the splendid training we've all experienced.'

Smiling, the counsellor raised his hand protestingly, but the class, sensing they were now bulletproof, were considerably more lively than usual.

'Listen, if I were you fellows, I think I'd like to know where my first office was going to be.' Immediate silence. 'Like many other Bureau procedures,' continued Ed, 'the method for determining offices of assignment for new agents might seem a bit arbitrary to some of you at first, but I can assure you that it's proven to be an effective one in all respects. Tom, can you give me a hand?'

An agent in the front row stood up as Ed opened up a large map of the North American continent. With the agent's help, the counsellor pinned the map to the bulletin board behind the desk. The awesome silence that always accompanied the presentation of some ingenious Bureau process prevailed now as the agents watched anxiously.

'Now, let's see,' said the counsellor, consulting a list on the desk. 'Ernie Ahern is first.'

Ernie, a young man from Georgia, swallowed instinctively as Ed opened one of the desk drawers. The counsellor withdrew a large dart and casually threw it in the direction of the map. Then slowly he walked over to inspect the target.

'Well, I don't know, Ernie,' said Ed, moving the feathered end of the dart up slightly so he could pinpoint the spot. 'It landed in Canada and we don't have any jurisdiction there. I guess you'll have to go to the closest spot and that looks like . . . let's see . . . Alaska. Yep, it's Anchorage, Alaska.'

Ernie's expression was that of a person having a tooth pulled. After one look at him Ed broke into laughter. It was the first time anyone had seen him genuinely laugh in eight months.

The raillery directed at the counsellor could be heard clear down the hall and Ed hurriedly held up what purportedly was a genuine list of the assignments. 'Really, fellows, this is it. Come on, now. Christ, they'll hear us all the way over in the Justice Building. Here we go, Ernie Ahern.' The noise subsided. 'Your first office is Detroit, Ernie.'

Ernie moaned slightly. 'I'd just as soon it were Alaska.'

Amid much groaning and joking the list was read off. Invariably the agents from the East were sent to the West, while those from the North received assignments in the South

68

and vice versa. Harvey drew Phoenix, Arizona, while his roommate was assigned to Albuquerque, New Mexico. Few in the class were pleased with their lot.

Ed then presented each agent with credentials, a Smith and Wesson revolver with six shiny silver bullets, and a firm handshake.

Following the informal ceremony, the counsellor looked at his watch, and the tense expression with which the class had become so familiar replaced the serene look. 'Mr Karp is due here in just about five minutes to give his farewell message, so if you—what? He's outside? How long's he been there?' Ed glanced anxiously toward the rear door, where a pair of eyes framed in black horn-rimmed glasses peered through the window. As though propelled by an electric cattle prod, Ed was off the podium and out in the hallway.

Mr Karp's commencement address was every bit as interesting as his inaugural, and as long. Indeed, many of the class believed it was the same talk. But no matter, to Mr Karp it made little difference. Beginning or finishing, they were all new agents, and after all, the main things were, 'The knights of old ... Caesar's wife,' and more importantly. 'Don't embarrass the Bureau, 'cause if you do you'll be dismissed ... with prejudice!' After an hour and a half he was gone in a flurry of adjectives, leaving the class anaesthetised.

Ed Timmons, as fuzzy-eyed as the rest of the class, resumed his place at the lectern. 'It's always good to hear Mr Karp's stimulating talk—he's a *very* busy man,' was the best he could muster.

Ed concluded the training with a few gracious remarks about the associations he had enjoyed (some of which was true) and his hopes that he would be working with them someday in the field (none of which was true). Then picking up his papers from the lectern, preparing to leave, he offered what was probably his most sincere message since he had first come to the training school. 'The best advice I can give you fellows is this. Remember, you're a second-class citizen and have damn few rights, if any. You rarely get a second chance in this outfit. If you screw up, then you're all through. You've got to understand that as long as you're an agent the Bureau owns you body and soul. As far as the agents themselves are concerned, you'll never meet a nicer group of men anywhere. The work itself isn't that dangerous, but when it comes to Bureau personnel policy, then, gents, you've got the most dangerous job in the whole world. So good luck, and remember, don't embarrass the Bureau. The job you save may be your counsellor's.'

By the time Harvey had made his farewells to the others, arranged for his airline ticket, and completed some last minute shopping, it was almost 4:00 P.M. He arrived at the Gaylord just as Jay was finishing packing.

'You had me worried,' said his roommate. 'I thought I might have to leave without saying goodbye.'

'I had to pick up a few things. How do you like the new bag?' Harvey held up the new two-suiter he had just purchased.

'Fine. Very nice. That other one over there has more character, though.' Jay gestured with his head toward the old Gladstone bag in the corner. 'It looks as though it might have been an abortionist's kit or something.'

Harvey ignored the comment. 'What time's your plane leave?'

'Five-thirty. I expect to be in New York by six-thirty.'

'How are you getting to Albuquerque?' asked Harvey. He wondered where Jay was really going.

'I'm not sure yet. How about you?'

'I'm flying. I made a reservation on a flight a week from Sunday.'

'Great. That gives you over a week home. Well, I'm on my way.' Jay placed his bags in the doorway and then, turning, stretched out his hand. 'It's been splendid, Harvey. Good luck to you.'

'And to you, Jay,' said Harvey, shaking the hand vigorously.

The tall figure stooped to pick up his luggage, and as he did so a lock of the yellow hair fell down on his forehead. A toss of his head and the hair was back in place, and then with a knowing wink and a parting smile the man was gone. It was the last he ever saw of Jay Von Vlack.

Harvey turned his attention to his new piece of luggage. It was a handsome bag, a bright beige, made of cowhide. Grasping the handle, he placed it on the bed. There was an identification tag attached, and disengaging it from the handle, he carefully inscribed in large letters:

Harvey Tucker
Justice Department
Federal Building
Phoenix, Arizona

He packed the bag leisurely. With over three hours until flight time there was no hurry. His wardrobe had been expanded during the preceding months, and he enjoyed arranging and rearranging the clothes in the various compartments. It was a tight squeeze, but with the exception of the record album, which he thought it best to carry anyway, he was able to fit everything inside.

He then looked at the old Gladstone. It had been his intention to junk the bag. But he finally decided it had sentimental value and elected to take it home. He placed the government briefcase inside the battered satchel for convenience and set the two bags on the floor.

It was almost six o'clock when he descended the stairs to the living room. Alberta had just returned from shopping and had dropped several parcels into a large chair. She was as attractive as ever in a tan suit with a mink collar. Her blonde hair, instead of being done up as usual, hung to her shoulders, giving her a much younger appearance.

'So, another very special agent on his way.' She peeled a glove from her hand and let it drop carelessly onto the packages. Although she smiled pleasantly, there was a trace of sarcasm in her manner. 'I expect we shall hear crime and espionage drops off sharply now that Special Agent Tucker is making his debut.'

Harvey dismissed the comment with a smile. 'Alberta, the only thing I'm going to miss in Washington is my landlady.'

'Oh, I see. Now that you are leaving, you become very gallant. Why is it I have never received this expression of

71

affection for your landlady before?' She returned his look with an unfaltering gaze. She removed her other glove and then started on the jacket, unbuttoning it slowly with one hand in a way which indicated that it might just be the beginning.

Although he always had been at ease with the opposite sex, Harvey found Alberta just a little too much for him. The charm which he ordinarily used on women somehow eluded him when confronted with the steady green eyes.

'Oh, say, I almost forgot.' He set down his bags and reached into his breast pocket for his wallet. 'I used the phone last night to call home. I wrote down the charges here somewhere. I think it was three dollars and something.'

'I see. I returned home just in time it seems. I suppose the handsome Mr Von Vlack has left me with a few mementoes of his visit also.'

'No, I don't think so, Alberta. Let's see where I wrote that thing.' He removed several cards and papers from his wallet and began sorting through them.

'It will be all right. Just give me whatever you think—it was.' It was little more than a slight hitch in her voice, but it was sufficient. She had seen it. In searching the contents of his wallet, he had forgotten momentarily the bits of paper he had pieced together. They had shown for only a fraction of a second, but she had seen them. It had been a ridiculous blunder on his part. He continued shuffling the papers briefly and then quickly returned them to his wallet. 'I can't seem to find it, Alberta, but I'm sure four dollars will cover it.'

Any doubts he might have had that she had seen the paper were dispelled when he looked up to hand her the money. Her face was ashen. The paper had a far more profound message for the landlady than it had for him. 'Anything wrong, Alberta?'

She raised her eyes to meet his. The coquetry was gone. Her face, although very pale, was impassive. 'Nothing is wrong.'

Harvey glanced at his watch uneasily. 'I'd better be going. I've got to get out to the airport.' He averted his eyes self-consciously and, placing the album under one arm,

72

stooped to pick up the bags. 'Thanks for everything.'

'What time does your plane leave?' Her voice was flat and husky, and her eyes had acquired a hypnotic look as though her thoughts were far off.

'Oh, somewhere around 8:30,' answered Harvey uncomfortably. 'Goodbye, Alberta.'

'Goodbye.' She was standing in the same position, the green eyes looking straight ahead, as he closed the door.

'Hi there.'

'Good evening, sir,' responded the girl briskly. 'May I help you?' She was a tiny thing, standing little more than two feet above the ticket counter, pretty with short brown hair, high cheek bones, and eyes which turned up slightly like a Siamese cat. She was dressed in a navy blue uniform, the skirt of which—although no one could see—had been turned over twice at the waist in order to hitch the hemline the proper length above the knee. She was wearing a brilliant customer's smile and there was a sauciness about her which indicated that she was new on the job but capable and anxious to deliver.

'Indeed you may,' said Harvey, returning the smile. He placed the two-suiter on the scales next to the ticket counter and was about to place the Gladstone bag beside it when he hesitated. 'Are they careful with the luggage?'

The girl regarded the Gladstone for a second and, perceiving her customer was joking, replied, 'We try to be particularly careful with something like that, sir.' She busied herself with Harvey's passenger ticket as the agent placed the Gladstone on the scales.

'Flight 274 will board at exit 7B at 8:30,' she said, handing him the ticket with a pretty smile.

'Why does it always happen this way?' said Harvey.

'I beg your pardon?'

'Every time I'm just about to leave some place I meet a beautiful girl. Why is it that way? Why don't I ever meet them when I arrive?'

It was a difficult question not found in the airline training manual. The young lady struggled with the answer and then blurted, 'I was probably right here and you didn't see me.'

73

She reached down, grabbed the Gladstone bag and two-suiter, struggled slightly with their surprising heft, and dropped them near an opening in the rear wall.

''Bye,' said Harvey, smiling pleasantly, picking up the bag containing the album.

'Goodbye.'

As he turned and walked away toward the terminal restaurant the girl stole a final, slightly wistful look after him.

Harvey enjoyed dinner. He was in good spirits. His initial concern at Alberta's reaction to the paper had given way to apathy. Like Jay, she was involved in some kind of training school activity. But he had made it through all the nonsense. He was a bona fide agent now. No one could take that away from him. He could always leave without a cloud over his head. If things weren't any better in a field office, he'd quit. After all, he'd been looking for a job when he got this one.

With such thoughts Harvey had carefully laid to rest all of the unpleasant feelings he had experienced during the past eight months. Now it was home for a week of comfort and relaxation.

It was almost 7:45 when he made his way through the terminal crowd to a phone booth. Although he had submitted an itinerary of his travel plans, he had to make a final call to the office for any messages before leaving Washington. Also, his mother and sister had promised to meet him at the station in Eagle's Notch and he had to tell them his time of arrival.

'Operator, I'd like to make a collect call to Eagle's Notch, New York, telephone 764-8274.' He supplied the personal data that goes with making a collect telephone call. After several seconds he heard the ringing and then, 'Hello.'

'I have a collect call for anyone from Mr Harvey Tucker. Will you accept the charges?'

'From the poorest man in the whole world?' said a youthful feminine voice. 'Yes, Operator, we'll accept the charges.'

'Hi, Filthy,' said Harvey.

'Don't call me that anymore, Harvey.'

'But, sweetie, I've always called you Filthy,' teased the brother.

'Call me Phyllis, Phyl, Phyllie, anything you want, but don't call me Filthy.'

'OK. Listen, tell Mom I'm flying to LaGuardia and catching the 10:27 train from Grand Central.'

'Just a second. Did you get my album?'

'Yes, I've got it.'

'Oh, thanks, Dolly. You're awfully sweet.'

'Be seeing you in a few hours.'

'All right. 'Bye.'

Harvey held the receiver down briefly to break the connection. He had a dime in his fingers ready to deposit in order to call the office when the operator came back on the line. 'Are you through with your call, sir?'

The possibilities of saving a dime occurred to him immediately. 'Ah, yes, Operator. Now I'd like EX7-4000, please.'

'You can dial that number direct, sir. Hang up for thirty seconds, deposit ten cents and—'

No use. He held the receiver down for several seconds, deposited the dime and started to dial. He had dialled E-X-7-4 when he paused, knitting his brow thoughtfully. The word 'expiate,' which had been deeply rooted in his subconscious, suddenly came to the surface. Of course! Expiate was a phone number—EX 7-4283. Similar to the office number. A feeling of exhilaration swept over him. Carefully he dialled the remaining three letters, A-T-E. He would not have been surprised to hear a mechanical voice come on the line to say, 'I'm sorry, the number you have dialled is not a working number.' Instead, the phone began to ring and he felt his heart start to pound. Once, twice, and then, 'Hello'.

A look of astonishment spread across his face. There was only one voice like that. And then suddenly he knew. That voice. Alberta's friend. 'Hello,' came the voice again, this time impatiently. Ever so carefully, in the manner of one handling a highly explosive device, he returned the phone gently to its cradle.

It had been almost a half hour after the phone call when Harvey was intercepted on the way to the plane by the two

75

agents. A half hour to ponder the meaning of it all. Now, as he sat in the Bureau car between the two men, some of his questions were beginning to find answers in his weary mind. The Gaylord, the dresser, the aspirin tablets, Jay's strange personality, the tattooed numbers in his armpit, the phone number—they were not figments of his imagination. They were real. He had seen them. Jay, Alberta, her extraordinary companion—all confederates in some mysterious scheme. But what? And why Harvey Tucker? Why had Jay asked him to come to the Gaylord with him? Had it been planned this way? Well, he should know something soon. If they were going to question him back at the office then he would ask some questions himself.

His thoughts were interrupted as the car approached the main thoroughfare and slowed down. The driver looked back over his left shoulder, checking the traffic. Harvey was surprised to see it was the man who had taken him to the Justice Building—the man who couldn't talk. The presence of the man sent a slight shiver through his body.

Instead of proceeding toward Washington, the vehicle turned the other way and began gathering speed in the opposite direction.

'Say, what's the idea?' said Harvey. 'I thought you were taking me back to the office.'

'Take it easy, kid,' said the older man. 'It's a different office. Let's see what you got in the bag there.' He took the bag gently from the new agent's hands.

'Just a record album I bought for my sister,' said Harvey. The man inspected it quickly and handed it back.

'Let's take a look in your wallet, OK, fella?' Without waiting for the answer, he reached inside Harvey's coat and withdrew his billfold. 'Let's have some light, Gotty.' The driver obediently turned on the interior light and the man went through the wallet, carefully inspecting the contents. 'Here it is,' he said finally, holding up the paper which had been pieced together. 'How did you come up with this?'

'I thought they wanted to talk to me back at the office,' said Harvey.

'Listen, kid,' said the older man, putting the wallet in his coat pocket, 'you're in serious trouble. A lot more so than you think. Now, we have to know just how you came up with this paper, and why you made that phone call.' Although the man's voice was quiet and persuasive, it had an unmistakable quality of earnestness about it. Harvey sensed he was indeed in serious trouble.

'I saw my roommate, Jay Von Vlack, rip it up a few nights ago, so I pieced it together. He'd been acting very suspiciously and I got curious. Tonight while I was dialling the office number I was looking at the letters on the dial when it occurred to me that "expiate" might be a phone number.'

'Do you know who you got on that call tonight?' asked the older man.

'Yes, I know,' answered Harvey. 'Anyone would recognise that voice. I know quite a bit about the person's activities. At the Gaylord with Alberta . . . Nayraville. . .'

The younger man emitted a soft whistle, but the other agent immediately gave him a sharp, reproachful glance. Then, turning to Harvey, he said, 'Well, why don't you tell us about it? What about Nayraville?'

Almost as soon as he had mentioned Alberta and Nayraville, Harvey knew it had been a mistake. 'I think I've said enough for now. I'll wait till I get to the office.'

'Have you ever discussed any of these things with anyone else?'

'No, I haven't. And I don't intend to start now. When you tell me what this is all about, then I'll tell you what I know.'

The other two agents exchanged glances, and a silence fell over the car. They had driven several minutes when the older man said, 'Gotty, there's a restaurant over there. See if you can get over some way so I can make my call.' Within a few seconds they were pulling into the parking lot of a small tavern. The older agent alighted and disappeared inside.

Harvey made a few efforts at conversation, but found the younger man, although pleasant enough, hardly more communicative than the driver. The best he could elicit was that the young man was Bob, the older man Everett, and that new agents sure knew how to get themselves in a load of trouble.

Almost 20 minutes had elapsed when Everett reappeared with a heavy frown which was incongruous on the agreeable features. 'Magic Lake, Gotty,' said the man, entering the car. There was the course sound of wheels skidding against gravel as the driver propelled the vehicle onto the main highway.

Harvey felt the younger man shift uneasily in his seat. 'That's a little rough, isn't it, Everett?'

Everett emitted a weary breath. 'Maybe so,' he said. 'Maybe so.'

'Where are we heading now?' asked Harvey indifferently.

There was no answer, only silence and the humming noise of speeding tyres on the pavement.

It was wondrously bright that evening. Elongated, silver-tinged clouds sailed swiftly past a large, floating moon, which beaconed at irregular intervals like a welder's torch, casting its bluish light on the countryside.

The Bureau car had been travelling at a great speed for what seemed to Harvey almost an hour. He had watched through the windows as the terrain became progressively mountainous and desolate. Scarcely a dozen words had been uttered since they left the tavern. It was as though the two men on either side of him remained quiet in deference to the driver, who could not participate. Bob had offered him a cigarette, which Harvey had declined, and the younger agent had commented in a somewhat resigned voice, 'It looks like a long night.' Beyond this there had been no conversation.

Harvey knew it was senseless to talk. The men in the car were miles away in their own thoughts. It was obvious that they were not at liberty to discuss anything with him. As far as they were concerned, he was just another new agent who had managed to screw up. Of course, there was always the other possibility. It might be that it was all just another link in the endless chain of training school subterfuge, kind of a grand finale as the last test to check the mettle of a new agent. The slip of paper, Alberta, Jay, maybe all had been meticulously laid out in accordance with the training school prog-ramme—more Bureau schematism designed to evaluate an agent's ability to follow through on leads to a logical conclusion. The more he thought of it, the more it seemed possible. Could be there were 15 other Bureau cars racing through the night with perplexed new agents in the back seats.

At any rate, he was tired. If ever he did get that week at home, he was going to bed and not getting up. Screw the Bureau. Screw the Director. Screw 'em all. He nestled back into the seat between the two agents and started to whistle very softly.

'Screw 'em all. Screw 'em all. The long, the short, and the tall. . .' Soon he was dozing.

'It's just over this rise, Gotty.'

The voice startled Harvey, and he blinked out the window as the car turned off onto a dirt road.

'How much farther is this place?' asked Bob.

'Another mile or so. Not far,' said Everett. 'The road's pretty bad. You'll have to take it easy, Gotty.' The driver nodded his head in acknowledgement.

The road was little more than tyre tracks which bumped and wound their way through heavy foliage. It seemed more than a 'mile or so' when Everett leaned toward the driver with more directions. 'Now right up here, Gotty . . . OK, here. Turn right.' They pulled into a clearing which overlooked a large lake. 'OK, cut the motor and lights.' Everett opened the door and slid out. 'OK, Tucker, here it is. Shangri-la!'

Harvey felt his heart begin to beat faster. He half expected to see Gabriels, Jay, Ed Timmons and the others out in the bushes somewhere. The whole thing suddenly took on a juvenile aspect. Here they were, grown men prowling around in the woods on some banal training mission. Still holding the album, Harvey yawned and alighted from the vehicle.

Once out of the car, however, his thoughts were interrupted. Before him lay a remarkable view.

A black body of water, sequestered by tall peaks and jagged rocks, stretched into a distant gorge from which cascaded a high falls pouring long and ribbonlike in the moonlight. It was a breathtaking scene, but the most incredible aspect of it all was the total silence which prevailed. Although the falls seemed no more than a mile away, nothing could be heard from the falling water. It was like watching a silent movie.

Magic Lake itself was a still, black, sinister-looking pool in which it seemed nothing swam—nothing lived. Indeed, the only sign of life in the quiet darkness was the intermittent croaking of a bullfrog, but even this had a dull, dead sound.

It seemed to Harvey that the loudest shriek in that strange quietness would be reduced to a muffled bleat. It was an unnatural silence, total, weird—terrifying in a way.

'Some view, eh?' observed Everett to no one in particular.

'Fantastic,' said Harvey, his voice filled with awe.

'You mean the quiet?' said Everett. 'Yes, it's impressive. Something about the rock formation which affects the acoustics. Also, that falls is an optical illusion. Actually it's hell of lot farther away than you think. Even in the daylight it looks closer than it is, though. It looks from here like it drops in this lake, but it really goes into a gorge beyond. Quite a sight when—'

'Let's get it over with and get the hell out of here,' interrupted Bob. 'This place gives me the heebie-jeebies.'

'What are you so nervous about?' said the older man. 'You'd think you were being worked on instead of this guy.'

Harvey took the remarks in stride. It was obvious the men were starting their role playing. Well, if their plan was to try to scare him, and apparently it was, then they had brought him to the right place. The driver appeared from the other side of the car carrying a long chain and a small metal box.

'Forget the chain, Gotty,' said Everett. 'Tucker here is a sensible guy. He's not going to go anywhere, are you, Tucker? Now, look. You can save us all a very unpleasant night. We've been down this route before. Eventually we're going to find out every goddamn thing you know. We can start off by Gotty pulling you around that lake by your heels a few times. And if that doesn't work, then we can use the barbiturate in that box there. We can start shooting you with sodium thiopental, only it's going to take a lot longer and be much tougher on you.'

So that was it. The final test. How well could he stand up under threat of physical intimidation? But what if it were all real? Impossible. Yet Julius Rosenberg had gone to the electric chair thinking they were bluffing. That's what the instructors said. That he had been in a fog entering the execution chamber, apparently still thinking it was part of the deal put to him by the warden at Sing Sing. 'Talk. That's all they want. Your espionage contacts. You and your wife don't have to be executed.' And it had been the same way with Rudolph Elba, according to Ed. They had threatened Elba with the chair, too, but he had been resolute. It was the most difficult situation that confronted an espionage agent—talk or die.

Yes, it was only natural they should test him. Agents would always fall into enemy hands as Francis Gary Powers of the CIA. How would they react? Would they cop a plea? It was only natural they would want to know this before an agent left training school. But it was too much. A poor charade at best. The two agents couldn't have carried off the part of heavies in a high-school play. Gotty was the only one with any character. There was something about him that would scare anybody.

'So why don't you start filling us in,' said Everett. 'Tell us what you know about Nayraville and some of those other things you mentioned.'

Harvey said nothing. A great silence prevailed over the area, broken only by the sounds of the voiceless man rummaging in the trunk of the car.

'OK, kid,' said the older agent finally. 'Move over there.' He motioned toward a spot where Gotty was busy unfolding an inflatable rubber raft. With a wry grin Harvey moved to the designated spot.

'You got one last chance, Tucker,' said the man in the same patient tone. 'And then it's a trip with Gotty around the lake. Anything you want to say?'

'Yes,' said Harvey, noting the heavy chain which Gotty picked up and carried toward him. 'I'd like to leave my body to medical science.'

'Well, you got big balls, Tucker,' said Bob, who seemed to be getting progressively nervous.

'Oh, come off it,' exploded Harvey. He had played the game as long as he could. He was probably flunking the test, but he was beyond caring any more. 'I've had enough of this crap. You guys are as phoney as free dancing lessons. I've had

81

you pegged since I got in the car. All this silent crap. This mute here probably talks like an old lady with—'

He never finished. The driver hit him flush in the mouth with the two-inch chain, shattering his front teeth. The blow sent him sprawling to the ground.

'Oh, my God!' spluttered Harvey, in a voice somewhere between rage and dismay. He struggled to his feet still clasping the album with one hand and holding his mouth with the other. 'You stupid son of a bitch!' There was a bewildered look on his blood-spattered face, and tears were streaming down his cheeks.

The driver was raising the chain again when Everett shouted at him. 'Cut it out, Gotty! What's the matter with you! The idea was not to mark him up.'

Harvey felt his lips hanging heavy and rubbery as they swelled but there was no pain. He shook his head slowly from side to side in disbelief. It couldn't be true. It must be a nightmare. He was on the train and he'd fallen asleep. That was it. He was on his way home and he'd fallen asleep. He clutched the album to his chest. It felt good. But then it was coming back. The horrible awareness that it was all real. It wasn't fair. He knew nothing. He had been just bluffing. Now his teeth. . . He began to shake.

'Listen, Everett,' said the younger man. 'This guy is no gook, you know. It's one thing pushing around a—'

'Shut up! Go ahead, Gotty, put him in the raft.'

The silent man with the strange, impassive features drew a foreign-looking pistol from his belt and motioned with it toward the rubber raft. Harvey shuddered and started to close his eyes.

Suddenly the moon slipped behind a cloud. A last-second gift from God. Harvey dashed for the black pool. Two shots rang out in rapid succession, but he was still on his feet. A third followed quickly and a bullet ricocheted off a large boulder and struck him in the leg, pitching him into the soggy marsh with the force of a cannon ball.

As the older agent stooped down casually to pick up three spent Luger cartridges, the quiet man walked slowly toward the prone figure.

'For God's sake, Everett, you can't let him—'

'We got no choice now,' said Everett, turning away.

Harvey watched the figure approach. Again the Luger was pointing flush in his face. 'No—please, God!' Another explosion and the impact slammed the head into the morass. Dying gasps came at intervals.

'Better hit him again, Gotty,' said Everett, walking up to the scene. 'He doesn't give up easy.'

The man shook his head negatively as he stared down at the twitching figure. The form gave a last, compulsive shudder and was still.

'Here, grab his legs, Gotty.'

A swollen lumpy cloud rode past, unveiling the yellow moon and silhouetting the two figures as they dragged the body to the rubber raft. 'Wrap that chain around the legs and hitch it to the weight. Make sure it's tied good.'

Noiselessly one of the figures paddled out through the bright path of the moonlight. Soon there was a splash, and then all was still but the muffled croaking of a frog.

PART TWO

Jay Von Vlack

'Albuquerque! You're out of your mind. Hell, if it weren't downhill most of the way I'd give odds you wouldn't make it to the Cross County Parkway in that wreck.'

Whitey Barrett, proprietor of the Nayraville Garage, blew his nose forcefully into the blue bandanna which was arranged ascot-like about his neck. 'The transmission's going, the valves are shot—look at the tyres! Christ, there's more rubber in a pack of safes. I'm telling you, Jay, you'll never make it.'

The subject of the discussion was a black English MG, its lowslung undercarriage resting on a hydraulic lift some six feet in the air. The mechanic moved Jay to one side and depressed a lever. The MG descended slowly to the floor, creaking painfully as the full weight of the vehicle settled onto the springs.

'Thanks, Whitey.' Jay crawled into the cockpit and pushed the starter button. A tired, groaning sound emanated from under the hood followed by a succession of pops and sputters. The engine caught, threatened to expire, and then exploded into a roar. Jay turned and grinned at Whitey, who shook his head sadly, like a veterinarian watching an abused old horse. 'Goodbye, Whitey. I'll drop you a card from Albuquerque.' He tooled the MG skilfully among several sleek limousines out of the garage into the bright morning sun.

Jay glanced at his watch as he turned left onto the main street and started through the small downtown section of the community. At the end of the town he made a left turn onto Northgate and began gathering speed for the steep climb up

87

the hill to where he lived.

Northgate was a lovely road winding its way up the Nayraville hillside through one of the most exclusive residential sections in all the world—Rumstick Hill. It was a neighbourhood to which many aspired but few arrived. A resident of Rumstick Hill was assured of many things, not the least of which was the lineage of his neighbours, and when property changed hands, although it seldom did, it was as much a community undertaking as a service at the Nayraville Episcopal Church.

It was a warm, cheerful day and spring was evident in the patches of sunlight that drifted through the leafage of the elms which bent tunnel-like over Northgate, and in the carefully landscaped terraces that lined the road. Pachysandra, myrtle, and English ivy covered the grounds and dwellings like a heavy green snowfall, creating a soft, hushed tone, and the harsh, straining roar of the MG motor seemed incongruous in the silence.

Halfway up the hill Jay slowed for an elbow-shaped bend in the road that afforded a magnificent view of the town below—a vantage point from which the perspicacious planning of the Nayravillian forefathers was evident. It was a neat pictorial setting no more than nine miles square, carefully delineated from surrounding New York City suburbs.

The business section in the centre of the town consisted of a trim row of immaculate shops set in Tudor buildings offering for sale those convenient items necessary for an affluent community. Surrounding this were several imposing civic structures all designed with a traditionalist's eye, while stretching out farther were meticulously zoned acres of land on which stood some of the older residential mansions.

Interspersing this staid panorama was a surprising number of churches—places of worship such as St John's Episcopal, The Lutheran, St Matthew's Presbyterian, The Dutch Reformed, The First Methodist, all snuggling contentedly beneath a configuration of spires that ringed the community like poised missiles ready to defend Nayraville from any un-Christian elements.

The scene brought a touch of nostalgia to Jay. The early days growing up in Nayraville had been happy ones. But the memories lingered briefly. The events of childhood themselves seemed in retrospect as transitory as the breeze that rustled through the elms above Northgate.

Soon the MG reached the top of the hill. This, then, was Rumstick Road itself, the apex of the community and the epitome of all for which Nayraville stood. He gathered speed on the level ground and shifted into fourth. Another cough and the engine purred as contentedly as ever.

The MG hugged the road, which wound its way through a green sea of luxuriant lawns, trees, and shrubbery. Native stone pillars and imposing wrought iron gates opened into white marble chip roads that threaded back through splendid grounds finally disappearing into profusions of foliage that represented the finest in landscape architecture.

From the main road could be seen tops of stately mansions etched against the sky, while an occasional staid battlement in the form of a Norman tower peeked from the leafage as though to warn any transgressors of the inviolacy of the grounds. It was an opulent setting—an assemblage of estates, servants, and Bentleys—designed to enrapture the most discriminating heart.

The MG slowed finally as it approached a large ivy-covered stone portal that extended from a gatehouse at the end of the road. A small brass plate affixed to one of the wrought iron gates bore the name, 'Lindenwald'.

A woman dressed in servant garb walking toward the gatehouse waved cheerfully at the MG as it drove through the entrance and started up a paved road lined with laurel and rhododendron. Rounding a curve, the vehicle passed before an immense stone edifice, a collage of turrets, arches and towers of Norman design which comprised the main premises of Lindenwald.

At the extreme end of the building Jay eased the MG past a black limousine parked at an angle in the road leading to the entrance of an elaborate garage. A chauffeur, carrying several packages toward the limousine, nodded and smiled. 'Make it all right, Jay?'

'Fine, thanks, Karlo. Lots of room. See Dad around?'

'I just saw him down at the tennis court. Ted was looking for you.'

'I know. I'm going to stop at his office before I leave.'

Jay left the MG in a corner of the parking lot and walked around behind the garage. He descended the stone steps to a white gravel path lined with red and white tulips and yellow trumpet daffodils. Following the path, he wended his way behind an immense cluster of rhododendron, past an entourage of varied coloured hyacinths and crocuses, to the swimming pool—past a greenhouse, finally arriving on a small knoll overlooking a grass tennis court.

His father, his back to Jay, was kneeling next to a bed of Christmas roses near the entrance to the court. The sight of the grey hair and the broad shoulders working tirelessly beneath the forest-green gardener's uniform saddened him. He was not certain of his father's precise age, but he knew he was well over seventy.

Mr Wallingford, the Lord of Lindenwald, had tried on numerous occasions to lighten the day, but his superintendent was implacable in his approach to his duties. For over 30 years the man had set a firm example for his three-man staff in caring for the grounds and creating some of the most exquisite formal gardens in the world. There never would be a slowdown in Johan Von Vlack's approach to his work. It was as though each shrub and plant depended on his personal supervision for its survival.

Quietly Jay descended the embankment and tiptoed toward the figure. As he approached, he heard his father humming as he always did while working among the flowers. It was a soft, almost inaudible sound of contentment—the quiet murmur of one at peace with creation. Gently, in the same way he had done when he was a child, Jay reached his arms around his father and covered both eyes with his hands.

His father gave a short, surprised laugh, and then proceeded with an abbreviated form of the game they had played so many years before. 'Is it Mr Wallingford? Stella? Karlo?' he asked in his heavy German accent.

In years past the man had run the gamut, from the lord of

90

the estate down to the last chambermaid, to the great joy of the little fellow, who had responded to each guess with a delighted, 'No!'

Taking Jay's hands in his own leathery palms, the elderly man held them as though he were holding his most delicate flower, and then squeezed them gently in the same manner he had squeezed the soiled little hands which had helped him in the flower beds 25 years before.

In a turret at the rear of the main house overlooking the grounds a witness to the scene stood at a window of his private study. Although he was approaching seventy-four years, David Wallingford had retained the faculties of a much younger man. Once-bright-yellow hair had long since turned white, but the hairline was still tight and full above a smooth brow. Tan skin stretched tightly over high cheek bones, and the prominent jaw was as strong and firm as a young man's. Possibly the only noticeable ageing process were the heavy lines that extended from the corners of the deep-set grey eyes. He was an alert and handsome man with the bearing of a brigadier.

The gentleman had observed many such moments of affection between the gardener and the boy, and the incident produced on his features the same resolute expression that similar occurrences had evoked during the years. The jaw stiffened, his lips were compressed into a thin line, and the wide grey eyes watched wistfully as the two figures walked over the knoll toward the garage out of sight.

He then gazed out over the rolling meadows of his estate, averting his eyes as always from the purple leaves which each year brushed closer to the window. He rarely looked down at the thundercloud cherry tree from which they grew. The tree had been planted there years before at his direction to cover a precise piece of ground so that he would know always the spot would remain undisturbed. But almost from the moment of its planting it had haunted him. The tree had grown from a stripling, faster and stronger than any plant at Lindenwald, its gloomy lavender leaves magnificent in their saturninity, as though its roots were nurtured by the secret that lay buried underneath.

91

Jay left his father at the garage and started up a worn path that connected the servants' quarters with the rear of the main house. He had made the trip thousands of times during his life and usually it was made in pleasant anticipation of what waited at the other end. This particular morning was no exception. He had an appointment with Mr Wallingford, and such visits were agreeable occasions.

Halfway up the knoll the aroma of freshly baked bread reached him. The odour stimulated memories of earlier times, when stubby legs had carried him puffing up the unmanicured path to the warm greetings and delicious handouts in the kitchen. Life had been good at Lindenwald. Mr Wallingford had been like another father. Because of an extraordinary interest the man had taken in his rearing, Jay had enjoyed many of the benefits accorded a rich man's son.

His education was illustrative. Nayraville, Phillips Exeter, Princeton, Yale Law School—prestigious institutions where heavy Wallingford endowments had paved the way.

Nor had the interest stopped there. Following military service, there had been the appointment to one of New York's most reputable law firms, where the Wallingford name had launched him. All had been meticulously planned as though the benefactor had considered it his duty to provide the best for the gardener's boy.

In spite of this great interest, there had been little personal association between the two. Beyond an occasional visit, most of the transactions affecting Jay had been conducted from afar. Therefore, any meeting with Mr Wallingford was an important event.

The end of the path terminated at a screen door and here Jay looked into a large kitchen. 'Hello, Vera. Where's Mr Wallingford?'

A heavy woman in a white uniform standing near a large black cooking stove looked up and smiled. 'Good morning, Jay. I think he's in the downstairs study. Just a second. I'll call him. He's been expecting you. . .' Then in a softer tone, 'He's not mad at you, is he?'

'Why, no. Not that I know of,' said Jay uneasily. 'Why?'

'Oh nothing. I probably imagined it.'

The woman walked to the other side of the kitchen and spoke into a small intercom attached to the wall. Within a few seconds she returned and said, 'He'll see you in the downstairs study, Jay.'

'Thanks, Vera.' Jay walked through the kitchen into the hall which led to the front of the house. The woman's remark made him uncomfortable. His father had commented on many occasions about the man's extraordinary temper. A number of similar stories were told by the domestic staff. Though rare, these incidents had had sufficient residual effect to command great respect for what lay beneath the man's cordial manner. When David Wallingford became angry, Lindenwald was no place to be.

In the front foyer Jay stopped under a large glittering chandelier and knocked on the door of the study.

'Come in.' It was a deep, authoritative voice.

Whenever he passed through the door into the downstairs study, Jay was struck by the great dignity of the room and its occupant. It seemed much of the power and wealth of Lindenwald was concentrated in the room. It was underfoot in the soft, deep nap of the elegant Oriental rugs, and in the freshly cut flowers on the rich mahogany tables. It was on the walls in the renderings of the Masters, and in the graceful lines of the furniture. Even the vast silence which prevailed was remarkable, as though the most dissonant sounds introduced would be muffled.

But more than anything, it was in the tall, handsome figure who rose from a chair at the far end of the room. David Wallingford was a gentleman in the finest tradition, and in him Jay saw all of the traits that were lacking in his own father.

In spite of his formal training, there had developed within Jay over the years an excessive awareness of what he considered a social deficiency—his father's status as a servant. Regardless of the occasion, whether an informal dinner party or a cotillion, it would come out. Tall, handsome, charming, possessed of the social graces, but beneath it all was the son of a poor immigrant—a man whose father, after more than 30 years in this country, had never found it necessary to learn more than broken English. Through the adolescent years into early manhood it had been a persistent refrain which had followed him through the doors opened by the Wallingford name—'the gardener's boy'.

There had been humiliating experiences—incidents resulting from a lack of honesty regarding his background. There was the autumn afternoon following the game at Palmer Stadium, when he sat in the Princeton Inn drinking Martinis with the beautiful girl from Vassar. The daughter of an industrialist, she was pursued by some of New York's most eligible bachelors.

It was in dealing with his own credentials that Jay had created his problem. The girl had invited him to a dinner party that evening at her parents' apartment in New York City. Karlo, who was performing an errand in Philadelphia, had agreed to stop by on his way back to transport Jay and his date to New York in the limousine. It had been Jay's intention to present the chauffeur in a perfunctory manner, and then to afford himself the privacy of the glass-enclosed rear seat. It was a fitting way to launch the evening, or so he had thought. The limousine had arrived, but instead of Karlo, sitting behind the wheel wearing a chauffeur's cap was Jay's father. The subsequent embrace and broken introduction had caused him inestimable embarrassment. They had sat three abreast in the front seat all the way to New York, with Jay's main contribution that of an interpreter.

It had been times like those when he wished the handsome, urbane Mr Wallingford had been more than his benefactor. Of course he loved his own father deeply, but he loved him back among the trees and flowers of Lindenwald. Beyond the front gate Johan Von Vlack was a liability.

Jay walked quickly through the room, and David Wallingford greeted him with the same paternal cordiality that had characterised their relationship through the years. But almost immediately Jay knew the man was disturbed.

'You look well, Jay. Please sit down. I'm sorry I missed you last night. I had a meeting down in the city.'

'Thank you, sir.' Jay sat down in one of the two easy chairs that rested in front of the fireplace.

'It feels good to be home even if for only a day.'

94

'We've had some unfortunate developments in Washington,' said Mr Wallingford, lowering his frame into the chair. The frown that had been evident when Jay entered became more pronounced. 'It appears your roommate, this Tucker, found out quite a few things. What happened down there?' He levelled a cool appraising glance at the young man.

Jay was dismayed. So Tucker had been aware. 'I'm not sure, sir. I have no idea how he would have found out anything. He did begin to act a bit odd the past few weeks.'

'He had every reason to,' said Mr Wallingford, a stern look in the grey eyes. 'Apparently he learned a good bit from you. He had your phone contact. That was supposed to be used only in a dire emergency. He claimed he found it on a piece of paper which you had ripped up.'

'I don't see how that could have happened, sir,' said Jay anxiously. 'I did write the number on a piece of paper, but I destroyed it when he began acting suspiciously.'

'He found it all right. What about the aspirin? I understand you let him get one of those too.'

Jay took a firm grip on the arms of the chair. 'Yes, sir. He swallowed it. He had a headache and—'

'It's not hard for me to understand why the controller down there wants you out of the organisation.' The man's face was flushed, and it was obvious he was having difficulty restraining himself. 'He was instrumental in bringing Tucker into the FBI, thinking maybe he could develop into a double agent. That's why you were instructed to room with him. Unfortunately we never approached him. My man did start to talk to him on one occasion, but the Director called unexpectedly. It's regrettable. Had the meeting not been interrupted Tucker might be alive today.'

'Harvey Tucker is dead?' said Jay dumbfounded.

'He is. They were interviewing him, trying to determine what he knew and there was an accident.'

'Oh Mr Wallingford, no. . .' Jay slumped back in his chair. 'But he was just an innocent . . . I'm sure Tucker didn't really know that much. He couldn't have. He was just a young country boy, unsophisticated. . .'

Jay's voice trailed off and he shifted his eyes to the large

95

painting above the fireplace—a portrait of a woman. It was an unusual painting by an obscure artist, with obvious imperfections, incongruous really among the Rembrandts, Renoirs and Corots. The shoulders and body of the subject seemed a trifle out of proportion with the head, and the background apparently had been restored to repair some damage. Yet there was a stunning quality about the subject—a blonde-haired woman with soft green eyes and delicate features. The head was held high, almost monarchical, but there was a sympathetic quality to the eyes and mouth suggesting a rare combination of imperiousness and sensitivity.

The delicacy and intimate charm of the portrait held particular significance for Jay. Once he heard Mr Wallingford's assistant, Ted Summers, say that the expression on the face was astonishingly similar to that of Jay's mother, Werta Von Vlack, who had disappeared when Jay was very young—a comment that had prompted him as a child to stand before the fireplace hoping that the face would move, that the deep eyes which focused on him would blink, that the lips which always seemed about to speak would suddenly part.

David Wallingford regarded his guest intently for several seconds, and his manner softened. 'I know how you feel, Jay. You've never been enthusiastic about the project. And I understand this. I've been involved in international espionage since before you were born, and frankly, there have been more times I should have liked to quit than to have continued.'

The man rose from his chair and walked toward the fireplace, where he rested an elbow on the mantel. He stood quietly for several seconds studying the floor.

'Let me put it this way. I'm aware of the extraordinary adjustment which you've had to make. I realise you've had no real preparation for this work. We took you out of the law firm, gave you a few months regrooming in that camp down in Virginia, put an identification number under your arm, and then expected you to perform. Add to that the loneliness of a double agent's life, not even knowing who's working with you, and as I say, you have quite a psychological adjustment

96

to make.

'But that's the way of our business, taking men who are in sensitive security positions—or someone such as yourself who has the proper credentials—and developing them. If you had my perspective on it all—if you could see how it all ties together—then it would make far more sense to you. However, in the interests of security no one may be told anything more than is required to handle his assignment. Everything must be done on a need-to-know basis.

'A perfect example is that aspirin which you picked up from the dead drop in the men's room each day. You would be surprised to know the number of agents required to photograph the records, get it to the laboratory, implant the microdots in the aspirin, and transmit it all to the coordinating point. Yet, for the most part, the agents involved handle only one segment of the operation. It's like an assembly line, and in some aspects just as boring for those doing the work. What you must keep in mind is the overall objective. You're participating in one of the most sophisticated intelligence operations we've attempted in the western hemisphere.'

Mr Wallingford walked back to his chair, and to Jay he seemed tired and perceptibly older—almost as though he had aged during the course of their discussion. The thought of the man's death and the disposition of the vast Wallingford fortune flashed across his mind. In all likelihood, judging from past events, he would be in the will. Maybe significantly. While he made a conscious effort to avoid thinking of death as a vehicle to his wealth, the thought hovered persistently in the wings. It was times like this that he pondered the enigma of David Wallingford and wondered why a man who had inherited one of the country's great fortunes would dedicate his life to the brutal world of international espionage. How could he be a part of something that could result in the death of a person such as Harvey Tucker?

Wallingford lowered his frame into the chair, and then, as though he had sensed what the young man was thinking and wanted to lay the matter to rest, he turned to Jay and said, 'I understand how you feel about Tucker, but you must remember this. Tucker was one person, and when you

consider the thousands of lives lost each year in these
brush-fire wars, then one life—as grave as it may be—must
assume its proper relationship to all of the others. It would be
well for you to remember that. . .'

He paused and looked long and hard into Jay's eyes. It was
a peculiar look which, coupled with the statement, produced a
strange feeling in the younger man.

Jay dug the tips of his fingers into the padded fabric on the
arms of the chair. It felt good—like everything at Lindenwald,
soft and comfortable.

'What about my assignment in Albuquerque, sir? Will
someone contact me?'

'For the next few months you'll be a sleeper agent. We have
some important assignments for you, but the first thing we
must do is get you set up out there. New Mexico is one of the
top defence-research areas in the country. It has a number of
key facilities such as White Sands Proving Grounds,
Holloman Air Force Base, Sandia Base, Los Alamos—all
top-security installations. Much of the intelligence activity in
the country is centred in this area, and we need as many
agents as possible there. Once you're groomed, you can be of
great help, not only with your assignments within the Bureau,
but related work as well. As an FBI agent, you will have
access to all of these installations which I've mentioned, and
this, of course, will aid our general intelligence activities. But
as I said, the main objective for you right now is to get
established out there. I shall send you a letter advising you
when you're to be reactivated.'

'A letter, sir? Isn't that a bit risky?'

'No, not necessarily. Even in this day of highly
sophisticated technology sometimes the most effective way of
communicating is the simplest. A letter will be all right. And,
Jay, you must do your very best on this assignment. This
project is of enormous significance and its importance
transcends any feelings which you or I might have. We cannot
tolerate carelessness. An agent who is unable to perform is a
serious liability in this business, and his position becomes . . .'
David Wallingford hesitated slightly and averted his eyes.
'Well . . .tenuous.'

'Well, now. Hel-lo there, Jay. Come right in.' It was a deep, melodious voice, a string of notes that bounced happily about at the lower range of the scale, a voice from the past that delighted the heart of a child, inviting him to step in and climb aboard Ted Summers' magic carpet for an exciting trip almost anywhere.

He was a robust-looking man with stormy grey hair that tossed about over a deeply lined brow. His six-foot frame appeared a full nine feet tall to the young lad who stared at his belt buckle. A pair of shaggy dark brows might have appeared sinister to the youngster were it not for the left one, which was in constant motion, rising and falling it seemed almost with the voice. But the eyes were the most fascinating feature. They were dark and mysterious, darting everywhere, perceiving exciting events on the horizon of a young boy's mind.

From the early days a strong relationship had grown between Jay and Ted Summers. The office, located at the extreme end of the south wing of the main house, where the man performed his secretarial and administrative functions for David Wallingford, had been the setting for pleasant interludes. Whether in a game of chess or a lively conversation, the two had enjoyed each other's company, and despite the difference in their ages, a close friendship had evolved over the years.

Usually Jay experienced a good feeling when entering the office. Ted's greetings were always gracious, imparting a feeling that the day was complete now that Jay Von Vlack had dropped by.

Few entered the office who were not similarly affected, including to some degree Ted's superior. It was this same sincerity and graciousness which had attracted David Wallingford's attention many years before, when as a boy Ted had assisted Johan Von Vlack working on the grounds of the estate, and during the ensuing years Mr Wallingford had developed him as a reliable assistant.

For Ted it had been the most fortuitous of circumstances. While still occasionally baffled by the intrigue of espionage and horrified by its sometimes brutal ramifications, he still

99

took great pride in his position. Despite his lack of formal training, his native intelligence and great—indeed, almost desperate—desire to please his boss had carried him far beyond that which would have been normal for a man with such beginnings.

David Wallingford, a man who liked to see his judgements sustained, had been particularly gratified, and his confidence in the man had grown to the point where few transactions now took place at Lindenwald of which Ted was unaware. And for his diligence Ted was accorded all benefits and privileges of a valued aide-de-camp. If the Lord of Lindenwald was a demanding boss, he was a generous one as well.

It had been pursuant to a small task that morning in the upstairs study Mr Wallingford used for his office that Ted had overheard some things that motivated him to look for his young friend.

Jay entered the office carrying a package under his arm. 'I understand you've been trying to reach me.'

'It's good to see you,' said Ted, shaking the hand vigorously. 'I was afraid you might get away without seeing me. Here, sit down over here where it's more comfortable. Put your feet up,' he said, pushing a large ottoman toward a chair.

'You know very well I wouldn't leave without stopping in.' Jay dropped into the large puffy-looking chair offered by his host, and stretched his long legs out. 'I do believe you're the first person who has shown any concern for my comfort in some time,' he said smiling. 'Now I'm glad I got you this.' He tossed the man a light package he was carrying. 'Before you say something about the colour or anything, let me just tell you that it cost me the better part of a day's wages, and it can't be returned.'

Ted untied the package gently and withdrew a dark green smoking jacket that bore the initials TLS on the breast pocket. It was apparent that he was moved by the gift. He kept his head down as he held the garment to his body measuring its size. 'It's too big,' he said gruffly.

'Why, it's perfect,' said Jay. 'You're reacting predictably. I knew you'd either say the size was wrong or there was

100

something the matter with the colour.'

Ted carefully folded the jacket and replaced it in the box. 'Thanks.' It was the same gruff tone. He coughed a few times, cleared his throat, and walked to another chair a few feet away.

'How's business?' asked Jay.

'My business is all right. From what I hear, though, yours is going none too well.' Ted rose from the chair, walked over and gently closed the door, then returned to his seat. 'I overheard Wallingford talking on the phone this morning.' Ted paused to light up a cigarette, and Jay saw that his hands were shaking slightly. Turning his head, Ted exhaled a thin trail of smoke through pursed lips and settled back in his chair. He seemed more relaxed with the cigarette in hand. 'Apparently you goofed up.'

'That's right. What did you hear?' Jay moved slightly forward in his chair.

'Mr Wallingford was talking to his head man in Washington. The man down there is pretty unhappy with your performance.'

'Yes, that's what Mr. Wallingford told me.' A frown settled over Jay's features. 'He wants me out of the organisation. You know how I feel about it. I would just as soon be out. I've never—'

'But do you know who this person is? The controller, that is?' asked Ted.

'No, I don't.'

'Well, it's Avery Hawkins.'

'The Assistant Director?'

'That's right.'

'They call him the Barracuda in the Bureau,' said Jay.

'And for damn good reason. That's what I wanted to tell you. If Hawkins wants you out of the organisation then maybe you should be careful.'

'Careful? I don't believe I understand,' said Jay curiously.

'Well, a few years ago when he wanted an agent under his jurisdiction out of the organisation he ended up dismissing him with extreme prejudice.'

'You mean he had him killed?' said Jay, surprised.

101

Ted nodded and the dark eyes blinked rapidly several times. 'It happened in one of the satellite countries. He ordered it done without even checking with Mr Wallingford. Later on, he claimed that the agent was a security threat, and that the exigencies of the situation required immediate executive action.'

'Are you suggesting that he might have me killed?' Jay's eyes were wide with astonishment.

The older man shifted his eyes and again inhaled from his cigarette. 'I have no idea. This is a wild business. All I know is what I've heard Mr Wallingford say. Hawkins is supposedly a brilliant person, but he is very young for the responsibility he has, and apparently he's somewhat impetuous. Since you're under his supervision I thought I should let you know. After all, your roommate got killed, right? I understand it was an accident, but who ever really knows about these things?'

Jay shook his head slowly in disbelief. 'I've made a big mistake, Ted. I should never have become involved. The whole thing is just awful. Absolutely awful.' He shifted his eyes and focused on a painting at the other side of the room. It was a portrait of an elderly man sitting at a desk, his chin resting in the palms of his hands. Often he had studied the painting and marvelled at its unusual detail. The hands, twisted and skeletal, supported a worn, tired face heavily lined as though fastened together by deep seams. From beneath a furrowed brow peered two sensitive brown eyes.

At this particular moment the painting inspired in him a strange feeling of impermanence. Time was illusive. It was like a breeze floating quietly and invisibly from across the meadow touching all things gently and imperceptibly. And then it was gone, irretrievable. There was so little time. And here he was engaged in a clandestine business in which he had not the slightest interest. A business that he was now finding might well cause a short life to become even shorter.

Anger displaced the anxiety which he had felt initially. It was all bizarre. When Wallingford had approached him the previous year the prospects of becoming involved had been distressing. He had been progressing nicely in the law firm, and he had acceded to the request reluctantly, only after some subtle but convincing pressure had been exercised, and then with the stipulation that it would be for only a two-year period. Although he had been cognisant of some of the perils, never had he considered that he might be killed. The death of Harvey Tucker was now dramatic evidence of this possibility.

'I'm not sure, but I may have seen this Hawkins one night down in Washington,' said Jay. 'Have you ever met him?'

'Yes, He's been to Lindenwald several times. Mr Wallingford is very fond of him. He's a remarkable-looking chap.'

'I'm not sure if I saw him or not. I received a phone call instructing me to go to a certain street corner where a man was waiting for me. Incidentally, it was the same man who came to the class for my roommate when he went to see Hawkins. Apparently he can't talk. Anyway, he brought me to a car a few blocks away. Two people were in the back seat. I'd lost one of the aspirin, they wanted to know what happened to it.'

'Well, you'd know Hawkins. Was he effeminate?'

'I don't know. The other man did all the talking. The one who might have been Hawkins was sitting on the other side. I never really saw him, but somehow I got the idea he was the boss. How did he ever get to be an Assistant Director? From what you all say he's so young and—'

'I don't really know. I never had any contact with him until a few years ago. I believe he grew up in Europe. I guess he's some kind of genius. He started with us right out of law school. Mr Wallingford had him handling some kind of liaison work with the FBI, and apparently the Director took a shine to him and brought him into the Bureau. I did hear Mr Wallingford say once that it was a miracle Hawkins ever got into the Bureau.'

'Why was that?'

'I have no idea. I don't ask questions. If Mr Wallingford talks I listen, but I don't ask questions. But as long as we're on the subject I'll give you my opinion about this Hawkins for what it's worth.' Ted ruffled his brow and shifted in his chair as he pondered his next statement. 'You may not agree with me, and I could be wrong, but it wouldn't surprise me at all if

103

Hawkins might not be a trifle envious.'

'Envious? Of what? . . . Me? Well, what possible reason could there be for him to be envious of me? I don't even know him.'

'Maybe not so much you as your position,' said Ted, speaking softly and, by implication, hoping Jay would do likewise. 'As I said, I could be completely wrong, but he's Mr Wallingford's fair-haired boy, and he knows it. Now, enter Jay Von Vlack, practising attorney in Wallingford's firm, a protégé who's never had anything to do with the intelligence operation and—if you really want me to lay it on the line—*a strong candidate for a share of the Wallingford fortune on top of it*. Well then, who knows what Hawkins has in mind? I'm merely saying that you have all the elements present for competition. And the thing I think you should keep in mind above everything else is that Hawkins probably doesn't think the way you do. Remember, he's been in this business his entire adult life. A life to him is not the same thing it is to you. He's seen too many of them lost. Again, I may be all wrong, but it's still worth considering.'

Jay sat with one arm folded on his chest and the other hand holding his chin, looking glumly at the floor. 'How did I ever get involved in all this, Ted?'

'You had no choice—really. I saw it coming years ago. With your law degree and other qualifications, you were a natural for the Bureau assignment.'

Getting to his feet, Jay started pacing slowly about the room. He stopped briefly before another painting, a rendering of two clowns, and gazed at it abjectly. 'This is absolutely awful, Ted. Why don't you get rid of it?'

Ted Summers started to answer, but then, as though in deference to the younger man's mood, said nothing.

Finally Jay turned and said, 'Mr Wallingford told me that they have some assignments for me in Albuquerque. I'm supposed to be a sleeper agent until they see fit to reactivate me. Honestly, Ted, I have no interest in all this. I'm just going to put in my time and the sooner it's over, the better. I'll finish out the two years as I promised. But this may be one sleeper agent they have trouble awakening.'

Ted nodded and put out his cigarette. 'I understand, Jay. I don't blame you. But I'd be a bit careful for a while. This is nasty business. I'm sure Mr Wallingford would never let anything happen. But as I say, this Hawkins fellow is an unpredictable chap. Also—' Ted paused, considering his next remark, 'I wouldn't discount Mr Wallingford's temper. He's not the same man when he gets mad, you know.'

Jay nodded. 'Don't worry.' There was a pause and he glanced at his watch. 'Well, I'd better be going if I want to cover any ground today. Thanks for everything, Ted. I'll be in touch.' Turning, he left the office, quietly closing the door behind him.

Ted Summers sat for several seconds staring at the door. Finally he shifted slightly and looked at his watch. Almost three o'clock. Another hour. Then he would go down to the Tudor House in town. There, resting in one of the swivel bar stools with the comfortable backs, Ted could sip his nightly Martinis, communicate with Harold, the bartender, and forget Lindenwald, at least for a while.

But there were still 60 minutes to go. They would be 60 disturbing minutes. He could already feel the thoughts lining up on the periphery of his mind. Thoughts from long ago, puzzling vignettes from the corners of his memory, vivid in themselves, but lacking the congruity that would have made them completely meaningful.

The cold, rainy afternoon when the beautiful Werta Von Vlack first arrived from Munich to join her husband at Lindenwald. Glimpses of Werta with Mr Wallingford near the greenhouse. The occasional meetings as she hurried from the private study, the beautiful eyes always averted. The birth of Jay, and the second pregnancy abroad, of which few were aware. Johan Von Vlack's life among the flowers and his imperviousness. The tense whispering behind closed doors. The violent arguments. Werta's disappearance—

Ted rose and walked to the window that looked out toward the rear. Off to his right the building jutted out at an angle. It was there that David Wallingford's personal quarters were located. And it was there, just beyond the corner of the building, that the branches from the thundercloud cherry tree

105

protruded. Each year they had grown farther, almost, it seemed, as though some day they would reach clear down the side of the building to Ted Summers' office.

Often he had thought of the tree, mostly when he was sitting in the Tudor House having his evening cocktails. He suspected that here was David Wallingford's Achilles' heel. Someday he would find out for sure. But adventurous thoughts such as these were no less ephemeral than the glow of the Martinis and were usually confined to the hazy world of the Tudor House.

Now, as he looked out at the dusky leaves fluttering in the afternoon sun, he felt something akin to a pang of conscience. After a deep breath, he exhaled slowly and ran the palm of his hand across his head, smoothing the ruffled white hair. It was an ineffectual movement and the stiff strands sprang back quickly—angry whitecaps on the waters of a troubled mind.

Elston Doolittle of number 12 Esplanada Drive, Albuquerque, New Mexico, was a kind, dignified gentleman at peace with his neighbours and the world. Handsome, with iron-grey hair and light-blue eyes, he was quite able to charm the older girls in the neighbourhood with his soft, suave, easygoing manner. Most of his free time he spent pottering among the flowers in the garden next to the small grey-shingled ranch house in which he lived, and from there the gracious gentleman was not at all averse to taking a few minutes from his gardening to make small talk with passers by. So charming was he, in fact, that it was questionable if all the trips made past number 12 were necessary ones.

His business hours were almost Babbitt-like. Each morning at exactly 8:00 an observer might see him backing his grey two-door Chevrolet down his driveway. At 6:05 each evening one would see the blunt nose of the vehicle reappear and ease its way quietly past the privet lining the driveway, back into the garage.

This, then, was Elston Doolittle of number 12 Esplanada, a true homebody, the personification of ease, comfort, and regularity.

But Elston Doolittle, special agent in charge of the

Albuquerque FBI, was a horse of a different colour. The metamorphosis took place at exactly 8:21 each morning when the S-A-C leaned over the sign-in register at the office and wrote, 'E Doolittle—8:11.' This slight misrepresentation in time gave Elston exactly 19 minutes of voluntary overtime since the regular starting time was 8:30. Had he signed the register 8:21, he would have received no overtime credit whatsoever, due to a peculiar Bureau rule that required the employee to sign in at 8:15, or earlier, to qualify for morning voluntary overtime.

The excitement of it all, however, would start the gastric juices flowing (this, in spite of an airtight excuse he had prepared some five years earlier in the unlikely event someone should challenge the extra ten minutes) and by 9:30 A.M he was making a fast draw of the Tums tablets to appease his Bureau belly. His ulcer was reputed to be the size of a new agent's .38 calibre shot group at 60 feet, and by the time he had read his Bureau mail, received a few teletypes from the Director, and handled one or two conferences involving major cases, his stomach was badly in need of the poached egg and glass of milk that awaited him at the lunch counter around the corner.

He was an immense man towering some six feet four inches above his size 14 double E's, with a frame that gave every indication of serious problems when it came to the Director's new weight chart. He had been special agent in charge of the Albuquerque office for the astonishing period of five years—an accomplishment based on a policy not altogether unsuggestive of his last name, and his success at eluding serious Bureau criticism in recent years had been uncanny. So much so, in fact, that in recent months his confidence had developed to the point where he was seriously considering converting from a 30-day to a yearly lease. But probably the most singular manifestation of his confidence was reflected in his garden. He had started to plant perennials.

But if Elston Doolittle's phlegmatic temperament changed radically once in the office, it was not reflected in any rash undertakings. He had long since relegated any raids or the like to his assistant, 'Jumping Joe' Holloway. As for Elston, he confined his excitement whenever possible to a few TV shows and an occasional shot of Rock 'n' Rye in the pantry.

Nor did his conservative approach vary when it came to new agents. Elston likened his position at S-A-C to a man rowing a round-bottomed boat with less than an inch of clearance. A trait he appreciated above all else in any passengers was the ability to sit quietly—a quality notably lacking in rookies. Since first having received word that a first office agent was on his way, Elston had resolved to see to it that the new man did little more than check office indices—a tedious process involving coordinating references in various files—and then only on innocuous cases.

And so it was by reflex one morning that after his secretary had announced the arrival of Jay Von Vlack, the S-A-C reached into the middle drawer of his desk for the Tums.

'Well, now, it's good to see you,' lied Doolittle, resuming his chair after shaking hands. 'How was the trip out?'

'Very good, sir,' came the reply. 'Beautiful country out this way.'

'Yes, it certainly is. Drive out, did you?'

'Yes, sir. As far as Oklahoma City, that is. I'm afraid I had some mechanical problems there. I had to take a plane the rest of the way.'

There was a lull in the conversation as Doolittle paused to ponder this bit of information and latest passenger. What he saw was something of which he did not necessarily approve. The young man impressed him as a trifle cool for a new agent. It had been Doolittle's experience that most young men confronted with their first S-A-C were a good deal more eager in their manner, while this one seemed, well—almost a trifle uninterested in it all. And that name. The last time he had heard a name like that was in a movie about World War I aviators.

It all added up to trouble as far as Doolittle could see. A young single agent had to be bad news, and when he was as handsome as this one, all sorts of things could happen. Somebody's wife would fall in love with him, or he'd end up getting some steno in trouble. He never saw it fail. And the way he talked—that accent. Invariably anyone he met who

108

talked like that turned out to be a phoney.

It was times like this when he took comfort from his controversial policy of hiring only the homeliest girls available. It was a tried and proven procedure. 'Show me a homely girl and I'll show you a good girl,' he was fond of saying, 'a good, honest, hardworking girl who isn't going to get involved with some agent and screw us all up and get us all transferred. Besides, they don't run off and get married as soon as you get them trained.'

It was a philosophy with which it was hard to argue. The Albuquerque steno pool and clerical staff had the lowest turnover rate in the city, and in view of Doolittle's policy, it seemed that nothing was going to alter this accomplishment.

'Well, you'll be assigned a Bureau car while you're here. That's just for official business, you understand. You've read all the rules governing the use of Bureau vehicles, I imagine.'

Doolittle leaned back in his swivel chair, which creaked ominously under the weight. 'I just made an examination of the fleet last week and noted some exceptions.' As the S-A-C reflected on his examination, worry lines wrinkled into place transforming his face into an aged plum. 'Seems the agents are damned untidy lately. I find all kinds of things in the cars—soda crackers more than anything else. Agents eat them between meals for their ulcers, you know. Goddamn crumbs everywhere! Have any trouble with your stomach yet? Good. You're lucky. Actually there's no reason an agent should get ulcers. If he obeys the rules and does things the way he's supposed to, he's got nothing to worry about.'

Jay nodded solemnly as Doolittle paused momentarily to prop his huge feet on the desk in front of him. Leaning far back in the chair, he clasped his hands behind his head and regarded the fledgling agent thoughtfully between the V-shaped sights formed by his crossed feet. In this position, as though lounging in a chaise on his patio, he delivered the Doolittle interpretation of the *Manual of Rules and Regulations*.

Following this, he escorted Jay downstairs to the main office, where the agents' room was located. The only one in at the time was Jumping Joe Holloway, who was in the

109

photographer's developing room. A red light signified no entrance was permitted.

'Joe, come on out,' said Doolittle. 'There's a new agent here I'd like you to meet.'

'Right, Chief. Just about through. Got a few mug shots on an impersonation case here.'

Within a few seconds the red light went off and from the room emerged a sandy-haired man of average if somewhat harried appearance. He was wearing a large leather belt from which dangled an arsenal of weapons. Aside from some 50-odd rounds of ammunition, there were a blackjack, a pair of handcuffs, several sets of keys, a small dark packet that looked as though it might contain anti-snake venom, and a large pearl-handled .357 magnum.

'I think I've got a good one here, Chief,' said Joe, displaying a wet photograph. 'I've had this lad under surveillance for two days and it—'

'Joe,' interrupted the Chief, frowning, 'why do you spend all this time on a simple impersonation case when we don't have a single, solitary lead on the Leopard Boulevard job? You know the heat that's on that thing.'

Turning to Jay, the Chief related a brief description concerning the robbery of the Leopard Boulevard National Bank apparently perpetrated by four Indians from one of the nearby reservations. 'We've been getting nowhere on the case and the Director's all upset. It seems we should have developed something by now. Hell, by the time you weed out all the children and squaws there aren't that many left that could have pulled the job. You hear that, Holloway?' said Doolittle, turning back to his assistant with a stern look. 'There aren't that many left who could have pulled this thing off, understand?'

Joe understood. Avoiding Doolittle's gaze, he looked down nervously at the mug shots in his hands. Softening his voice, the S-A-C then introduced Jay.

'Von Flack just arrived from new agents' class. I thought you could introduce him to the other agents.'

'Von *Vlack*,' corrected the new agent gently. No one appeared to notice.

110

'Well, there's no one here right now, Chief,' said Joe. He shook hands uninterestedly with Jay while looking at the S-A-C.

'I realise that,' snapped Doolittle impatiently. 'Just show him around, and when the others come in, make sure he gets acquainted.'

'Yeah, sure, Chief,' said Joe unenthusiastically.

Feeling his duties to the new agent completed, Doolittle dropped a final, pointed reference to the Leopard Boulevard job and started from the room. Suddenly he stopped and, walking back to the assistant, said softly, 'Have you heard anything about anyone from the Bureau coming out here?'

'Gee, no, I haven't, Chief,' said Joe. 'There's a rumour about a possible inspection in Phoenix, but nothing here. Why do you ask, Chief?'

'Oh, nothing,' said Doolittle, a look of concern on his face. 'I was just talking to a friend down at the Bureau. He mentioned he'd heard that a couple of Hawkins' men were out this way. Better get the word around for these guys to stay on their toes.'

It was quite apparent she was confident with men. She had every reason to be. Honey-blonde hair, light blue eyes, approximately 140 pounds delightfully assembled on a five-foot-nine-inch frame—few men would not have been struck by her extraordinary appearance.

'*Secret* agent? Really now, you must be kidding.'

It was a lovely voice, light and friendly, but with a trace of huskiness which Jay found stimulating. Thoroughly charmed but uncertain how to reply to the comment, he took an inordinate amount of time returning his credentials to his pocket. After flicking a piece of fuzz from his dark suit, he adjusted his tie and returned his eyes to the lovely face smiling at him through the barred window of the registrar's office. 'It's *special* agent, not secret agent.'

'How can you say that with a straight face?'

'I beg your pardon.'

'It sounds ridiculous,' said the girl, her eyes brightening in a way that indicated she was enjoying the agent's uneasiness.

111

'Honestly, don't you think that's silly? Calling someone "special"? It sounds positively unctuous.'

The combination of the girl's appearance and teasing remarks had left Jay tongue-tied. At Elston Doolittle's direction, he had spent his first few weeks in Albuquerque checking records at nearby installations. He had become accustomed to impressing people with the authority of his credentials and was totally unprepared for the kidding—even though apparently it was intended good-naturedly. It was obvious the face framed in the window could indulge in liberties that might have proved exceedingly risky for a less attractive young lady, but as he struggled for an appropriate answer and could think of nothing, he decided on a cool approach.

'Miss, I came here to get information in which the government is a party in interest, not to discuss the merits of my title.'

The smile in the window faded slightly, and he had begun to experience some remorse at having crushed the lovely, fragile thing when, 'Are you a rookie?' Again the genial smile.

'I beg your pardon, young lady' (somewhere in her late twenties, she could not have been much younger than he), 'but by any chance were these bars installed to protect you?' He was referring to the vertical shafts that covered the opening like those in old bank tellers' windows. That did it. A slight shrug, and the smile was supplanted by two arched brows.

'What can we do for you?'

'Denton, Robert Denton.' He spoke cryptically. Attended the University of New Mexico from 1947 to 1951. I'd like to review his transcript, please. It's a confidential matter having to do with the internal security of the country.'

The girl walked to the files on the far side of the room. Jay watched her go, wishing there were some way to start the interview all over. He was admiring the girl's figure when he caught the grumpy eye of an elderly woman seated at a desk in a far corner. It was the briefest of exchanges, but the message was evident. It was an unflinching gaze that bespoke 60 years of uncompromised virtue.' Jay turned away uncomfortably, but within a few seconds, with studied casualness, the grey eyes were back on the girl. She was fairly large, sturdy but well proportioned, with long shapely legs. It was a strong figure, the type he found sexually stimulating. He tried to think of someway to improve the situation. He would have to act quickly. 'I beg your pardon, Miss. The middle initial is P as in . . . peace.'

The girl turned briefly toward the window, where a hopeful smile now supplanted the grim expression of a few minutes before.

'No hurry. Please take your time,' he soothed, with a slight wave of his fingers. It was awkward and he felt like a fool. Apparently the girl shared his feeling because she gave him a cool look and returned her attention to a rotary file.

No, he had ruined it. Absolutely the most beautiful woman he had seen in New Mexico, and he had destroyed it all in the first two minutes. He straightened up as the girl came back carrying a file.

'Here you are, special agent. Robert Denton.'

'Thank you.' Jay sent his most cordial smile through the window. The girl hesitated and then responded brightly. Ah yes, back in the saddle. God, she was great. He scanned the records, making a few brief notes, and then said, 'May I have your name, please . . . as the person who furnished the records?'

'Kent,' replied the girl pleasantly. 'Gertrude Kent.'

'Middle initial, Miss Kent?'

'R.'

'Position.'

'Oh, most people just put down Registrar's Office, University of New Mexico.'

'Righto, Miss Kent.' He jotted down the name on his folder. 'I appreciate your help very much. Oh—say, do you know of any place on the campus where they serve lunch?'

It was awkward, and the elderly woman in the corner looked up suddenly.

'There's a cafeteria at South Hall,' said Miss Kent, resting her elbows on the ledge under the window, apparently disposed to continue the conversation.

113

'I see. Is that far from here?'

'No, just across the quadrangle, turn right, and it's the third building. It's almost twelve o'clock. You'll probably see people heading in that direction.'

He toyed with the idea of asking if he would see *her* there, but noting the older woman's state of progressive agitation, he decided against it. 'Thank you, Miss Kent. I'll see you one day.'

'Bye. Stop in again.'

He certainly would. It might mean inventing a few Robert Dentons, but he would be back. As he turned to leave, he shot a quick peace feeler in the form of a smile toward the eyes peering from the other end of the room. He was rewarded with a chilling stare that would have frozen the ears on a brass monkey. No hany-panky there.

Jay sat in the bleachers overlooking the practical pistol range, watching the agents firing their pistols from the prone position. In accordance with Bureau rules, once each month all agents had to qualify with Bureau weapons, and it was pursuant to this requirement that agents of the Albuquerque office were spending the day at a nearby firearms range.

Wrinkles of fat smiled up from the backs of bald heads as the men, arms stretched full length in front of them, strove to overcome inhibiting midriffs to get a sight picture. One by one they staggered to their feet and shuffled down the asphalt path to the next firing position, their hands corset-like at their sides trying to contain the flabby muscles.

This was a sitting position and the old-timers eased themselves onto the hot asphalt with all the delicacy of a spinster depositing herself on a public utility. (An unusual conciliatory gesture by the Director had permitted those veterans suffering from haemorrhoids to stand at the ready at this point on cold or damp days.) Then amid grunts prompted by abused sciatica, they pushed forward to the standing position, firing from behind a post. Finally, a puffing double-time brought them to the last station, which was close enough to the target for a gimlet-eyed evaluation to show that it would take some liberal scoring to qualify.

114

It was at this point that the associate agent, who followed each shooter closely during the course to offer helpful suggestions, discreetly bent down to recover spent shells as the man who had been shooting went forward alone to score his target.

'Scores!' boomed the voice from the control tower.

Starting from the left, the agents shouted out their achievements while quickly ripping their targets from the holders and meticulously shredding them as though they contained highly secret data. 'Ninety-nine. Ninety-six. Ninety-eight. Ninety-nine. Ninety-eight.'

Jay watched with some suspicion as each agent strode purposely toward the incinerator with the remnants of his target.

This, then, was the practical pistol course, or PPC as the agents referred to it, impractical as the name itself. Like many Bureau procedures, it was a holdover from yesteryears, clung to with a grim tenacity lest any change in an established practice suggest something within the organisation had been less than flawless.

But the PPC was only of momentary import to Jay. What was of much more significance was the older, dark-complexioned agent who sat behind him in the bleachers. The man was a a recent arrival in the office, and it was rumoured among the other agents that he was there only temporarily on some type of special assignment. His presence had caused a good deal of uneasiness throughout the Albuquerque office, and it was apparent that even Elston Doolittle was feeling the pressure. For three days in a row the S-A-C had arrived at the office before eight o'clock.

Yet if the man's presence was causing concern among the older agents, it was nothing compared to what it had been doing to Jay. The reason was that a full two days before the man showed up at the office, Jay noticed him sitting behind a newspaper in a restaurant. When he arrived at the office, Jay had suspected immediately that the man had had him under surveillance. This, coupled with Doolittle's remark about Hawkins' men being in the area, had made for an unpleasant state of mind.

115

'All right, next group,' came a voice from the tower. 'Secure 50 rounds and come to the firing line.'

Noting a vacant alley on the range, Jay decided to shoot the PPC and get it over with. As he climbed from the bleachers, he saw the dark-complexioned man rise and start following him from the stands. It made him uncomfortable. He hoped the man was not going to shoot with him. The PPC was laid. out in a way that required some agents to move to forward positions while others were still firing from the rear. It would be very easy for a stray bullet to kill a man—accidentally.

Jay's state of mind approached anxiety when he saw the man take the alley directly next to him. At the sound of a whistle from the tower the agents commenced firing. Jay emptied his pistol at the target and reloaded the cylinder very slowly. He noticed the man next to him was equally slow. They were the last to rise and move forward.

At the sitting position he took an inordinately long time squeezing off the six rounds, but the other man, although finally rising and moving forward ahead of him, was still very slow. It was at this time that one of the older agents who was acting as Jay's coach spoke up.

'Hell, Von Vlack, you're never gonna finish the course on time. What's the matter? The way you're screwing around, you'd think you wanted to be the last one finished.'

Jay didn't answer. He noticed the other man had caught up with the other agents. He holstered his weapon and moved forward.

'Hello, Miss Kent! Care to join me?'

It was several weeks after Jay's first visit to the Registrar's office, and he was sitting at a table near the serving line in the campus cafeteria. He had sat at the same table on a number of other occasions and had visited the office hoping to see Gertrude Kent, but to no avail. Now, as the young lady approached the cashier at the end of the line, he was determined not to let the opportunity pass him by.

The girl turned toward him with a surprised expression and paused, as did 50 other persons waiting to see if she would accept the invitation. Then, with a look that indicated some

116

mixed emotions, the girl nodded, smiled, and finished her transaction with the cashier. The hush that had settled over the room during the movement of decision was replaced by the heavy drone of campus conversation.

'This is a very pleasant surprise,' said Jay. He stood and pulled out the other chair as the girl approached carrying a tray.

'The FBI seems to be spending a good deal of time on campus,' she said smiling. 'Are you investigating something today?'

'Indeed I am, Miss Kent. In fact, you may be able to furnish some information about the subject of my case. It's a beautiful blonde lady who's disrupting the orderly function of the FBI.'

The girl laughed gently. 'I see. Well, maybe if the FBI concentrated on its function, this lady would be less disruptive.'

She followed the comment with a dazzling smile that paralysed Jay. He would have liked to respond with some pithy comment, but somehow the girl overwhelmed him, and the right words seemed elusive. The same thing had happened at the Registrar's office. When he first saw her in the cafeteria, he had sat for almost five minutes waiting for her to go through the service line, thinking of the things he would say, and now, in less than two seconds, she had rendered him speechless. It was an unusual experience for one who had always demonstrated reasonable confidence with the opposite sex.

'It's a bit awkward calling you Miss Kent. May I call you Gertrude?' said Jay.

She paused as she was about to take a bite from her sandwich. 'Please, not Gertrude. My friends call me Cricket.'

'I'm Jay Von Vlack, Cricket.'

'Yes, I know,' she said, breaking into the confident smile. 'It's *Special Agent* Von Vlack.'

'Shall we forget the "special agent"? We had a regrettable beginning because of that.' Jay knitted his brow slightly. 'I'm just plain Jay.'

'Oh, I see,' she said, fluttering her long lashes in mock

117

surprise. 'Now it's just plain Jay. You seemed rather proud of your title that morning a few weeks ago.'

'I'm sorry about that, Cricket.'

'All right. I'm just teasing. All is forgiven, OK—Jay?'

She was fascinating. Those eyes, a faraway blue, light and hazy like the distant ocean sky where it joins the water, yet having some strange limpid quality that somehow made them as delusive as that imaginary point.

'You don't sound like you're from the Southwest, Cricket.'

'Originally I'm from San Francisco,' she said. 'And you?'

'I live in a suburb just north of New York City.'

'I thought so. You have a . . . well . . . sort of a special accent, shall we say?'

They continued to exchange conversation as they ate lunch, but as they talked it soon became apparent to Jay that she was not furnishing an abundance of information. Rather, it seemed, whenever they got on the subject of Cricket's background she artfully directed the conversation away. Beyond the fact that she had just recently come to Albuquerque and was working part-time in the Registrar's office, he learned very little. What emerged for Jay was the picture of a woman with a sophisticated personality which he found difficult to reconcile with the provincial setting in which she was working. But it was a wonderful experience for a man who was lonely and who had gone for many months without any feminine companionship. He sat throughout the lunch marvelling at the faultlessness of the girl's features—the clear skin, the blonde hair, the small nose and soft, natural lips; all an exquisite, delicate painting too beautiful for real life it seemed.

'Do you have lunch here often?' he asked when he saw she was nearing the end of her lunch. 'Maybe I'll see you tomorrow. Same time, same table—what do you say?'

Cricket laughed easily, a soft, tingling cantillation that fluttered about Jay like a thousand glittering snowflakes. When she laughed everything else was forgotten. Espionage, the Bureau, the Director—all were heavy clouds dipping beyond the horizon, and there was only this girl. It was a powerful feeling he had never before experienced.

118

But then she was standing, about to leave. 'I'm glad to have met you, Jay.'

'I'm not going to have to wait for another lead at the Registrar's office, am I?' he said, getting quickly to his feet. 'That other woman in there doesn't seem too receptive to my record checks.'

'Mrs Fryhoffer?' said Cricket. 'Oh, she's very nice. Sometimes she just doesn't feel well.'

'Would you care to have dinner some evening?'

A detached look came into the strange eyes, a certain preoccupation that hinted of more interesting times with other faces.

'Would you be free Saturday?' said Jay, as she hesitated. 'I understand the Latin Club out on the Mesa is very nice.'

'I'm afraid not, Jay. Thank you, but I won't be able to. I'm going to be busy. Maybe you'll be back to the Registrar's office sooner than you think.' She started moving away.

He knew he was losing her. There might not be another opportunity. The telephone was difficult. Maybe she was going with someone, or worse, she might be engaged. An outstanding girl like that, there would have to be a great deal of competition. 'Say—Cricket, before you go, mind if I give you a call? Maybe we could arrange something for another time—that is, unless there's some reason. . .' His voice trailed off, hoping for some encouragement.

From Cricket came a betwitching laugh of reassurance, and Jay Von Vlack was enchanted as he had never been before. 'Of course. I'd love to hear from you. Call me sometime. Please.' Again the amused expression and the eyes twinkled mischievously, suggesting a reverie of delightful secrets in which somehow he knew he would never share.

Of the many traits that formed the personality of Jumping Joe Holloway probably the most conspicuous in its absence was any sense of inadequacy on his part. A lesser spirit long since would have yielded to the vice-like pressures of the job and relinquished his position as Assistant Agent in Charge for a more sedentary role as Resident or the like.

But not so Joe. He was an unsinkable vessel, withstanding a

withering barrage from his boss one day and the Bureau the next, but sailing on with an air of imperturbability that was puzzling to both superiors and subordinates. Nor had all the salvos come from the Bureau and Doolittle. The Director himself had seen fit on 11 separate occasions to comment in scorching prose on the ability of the A-S-A-C from Albuquerque.

Yet, in spite of it all, Joe's spirit was undiminished, and he continued to think of himself in superlatives. As an investigator he was the best. 'Hell, you have to get letters of censure. Show me an agent who hasn't received a letter of censure, and I'll show you an agent who doesn't do anything.' When it came to firearms there wasn't a faster draw in the Southwest. (His trigger finger was even faster—he had blown the toe off his boot in a fast-draw exhibition a few years back.) His overtime was the highest, his weight the lowest, his fugitive apprehensions the greatest, and in his youth he had been a two-time Golden Gloves champion.

One morning a few months after Jay had arrived in Albuquerque, Joe was sitting with his feet propped on his desk, Doolittle-style meditating on these credentials, when Doolittle's voice came cracking over the intercom.

'Holloway! Holloway, come up here!'

As though 500 volts had just been sent coursing through his chair, Joe was on his feet and out of the door. Braking suddenly, he shot back into his office to grab a sheaf of teletypes. It was always a good idea to have something in his hand when summoned by the boss. Thirty seconds later he stood breathing heavily in front of the S-A-C.

'What took you so long?' snapped Doolittle, rising and walking toward the window behind his desk.

This was bad. Joe knew all the symptoms. Doolittle was strictly an armchair investigator. Anything that would get him on his feet had to be bad news.

'Read that letter, Holloway!'

Although Doolittle was looking out the window, there was no question in his subordinate's mind to which letter he was alluding. Joe had spotted it the second he had entered the room. Anything whatsoever on the boss's desk other than his feet was bound to catch one's attention, for Doolittle was a clean-desk man. Nor did Joe have to get much past the doorway to see that the letterhead on the paper signified it was from the Director. But the most alarming factor was the colour of the letterhead. For all personal correspondence the Director used a light blue letterhead—that is, with the exception of letters of censure. The missive lying in the centre of Elston Doolittle's desk was a funeral black!

'Read it!' exploded Doolittle.

Joe, shocked out of his momentary stupor, reached quickly for the letter. It was short. That was good. The severity of a letter of censure and its ramification, like a heart attack, could be measured somewhat by its duration. While the Director's style of writing at best was terse, he could, as evidenced by a 'home run' (a term applied to the black ink when it completely encircled the memo) go on at some length depending on the motivating factors. In this particular instance it appeared he had been only mildly stimulated.

Dear Mr Doolittle,

I am amazed and astounded to learn that your office has not yet developed any logical information pertaining to the Leopard Boulevard bank robbery. This failure most certainly can be ascribed in large part to the totally inadequate confidential informant coverage in your territory. I want you to understand that I am holding you personally responsible to see this matter is brought to a rapid logical conclusion. Continued derelictions will not be tolerated, and will result in immediate and severe administrative action.

Very truly yours,

Director
Federal Bureau of Investigation

A few beads of perspiration appeared on Jumping Joe's brow. Unwilling to face the tirade which he knew was imminent, Joe started to reread the letter—slowly.

'I didn't say to memorise the goddamn thing!' A huge hand

121

snapped the letter from Joe's fingers, and Doolittle's massive frame began a heavy pacing behind the desk. 'My first letter! My first letter, mind you! My first letter *in over six months*, and why?'

Joe had a good idea 'why' but chose to remain a listener.

'I'll tell you *why*. Because I have an incompetent, unreliable, stupid assistant, that's *why*!'

Joe took small consolation from the fact that he had had the right answer.

'An assistant who doesn't know enough to get off his ass and develop an informant programme, that's *why*. What have you been doing around here all this time, anyway? Why aren't you out on the bricks instead of sitting around the office on that dead ass of yours? How many informants do we have now? Never mind! I know. One! One stinking lousy, Bureau-approved informant. And it's a goddamn security informant at that. Never mind, I know. That old bug-eyed bitch down on Dresser Street who reports on her neighbours.'

'But Chief, that's a hotbed of—'

'Hotbed, my ass! You know there's no communists, Black Panthers or any other security problems out here. What good's a security informant? There's not a goddamn thing to report on. You know that. But if I know you, you're probably trying to develop a communist cell down there so that nut will have something to report on. I tell you, Holloway, you're on your last legs. I've stood for as much as I'm going to around here. If you don't come up with something on this case within the week, you can haul out that winter underwear.'

Joe shifted uneasily, trying to avoid the burning eyes in the hovering figure. Doolittle didn't have to spell it out. The winter underwear meant Anchorage. His boss alternated between Anchorage and Butte as possible areas of banishment. As Doolittle paused, Joe sensed it was time to say something. 'Well, Chief—'

'Well, Chief, bullshit! What in hell has happened to our informant programme, anyway? I know what's happened to it. I just reviewed the file. We never had any programme. That's what happened to it. We've got seven potential security informants and no real security subjects. They're all

122

reporting on each other. Don't you know how stupid that is, Holloway?'

'Well, Chief, we've got 27 potential criminal informants and—'

'PCIs be damned! Every goddamn bellhop and hustler in town is a PCI. We got more people on our payroll than the Unemployment Bureau, and all we ever learn is that somebody's opening up a new cathouse. You can be replaced, Holloway. You know that, don't you?'

Joe knew. He nodded pleasantly, and not knowing what else to do, he smiled.

'No, you never could be replaced.' The boss was off again. 'You're too goddamn stupid to be replaced. I wish the hell they had a smaller office to send you to.' Doolittle had just about shot his wad. Joe noted the orchid hue had gradually lifted from his boss's face, supplanted by his normal ashen look.

Doolittle slumped into his chair and plopped both feet on his giant-sized ottoman. After measuring his assistant carefully through the V-shaped sights, he delivered one final volley and lapsed into silence.

Finally Joe broke the silence. 'Is that about it, Chief?'

'Yes, yes,' murmured Doolittle, waving his assistant toward the door with a hopeless gesture. 'Oh, wait a minute. How's that new agent doing, Von—whatever his name is? I saw him wearing his gun yesterday while he was checking indices. Why the hell does he wear his gun when he's checking the indices? Isn't there some way we can take that thing away from him? All we need to have happen now is have a new agent accidentally blow some clerk's head off.'

'You know, I'm glad you mentioned that, Chief. This new agent appears very unusual to me. You know how most new fellows are. They want to get involved in everything and screw us all up. But not this guy. He says he likes it in the indices. Ever hear anything like that? Somebody who likes to check those damn files. And that teletype from the Bureau requiring a weekly summary of his assignments. Doesn't that strike you as unusual, Chief? We never had to do that on a new agent before. And another thing. I understand his

123

roommate in training school never showed up at his first office—just took off somewhere and nobody knows where he went. This guy keeps to himself, too. Doesn't associate with anybody. And you know how he talks, Chief. Everyone in the office is mimicking that accent of his. To tell you the truth, he strikes me as if he's scared of something. I've never seen him without his gun. The other agents have the feeling he doesn't trust them.'

'That's a switch,' mumbled Doolittle. 'A new agent not trusting the older agents.'

'It's the truth, Boss. Last month at firearms he was shooting the PPC and wouldn't go to a forward position until the other agents went first. I think he's kind of a paranoiac, Chief.'

'Well, he probably is. We all are. Anybody who could last in this outfit a year and not be paranoiac would have to be nuts. Well, keep your eye on him. Give him leads to check records around town. Nothing heavy, understand? I'm holding you personally responsible if he screws up, you know that.'

Joe knew. 'Anything else, Chief? I've got an informant contact at 10:30 and. . .' His voice trailed off.

'What informant?' asked Doolittle, a note of hope creeping into his voice.

'Ah—T-2,' answered Joe, his eyes moving uneasily toward the door.

'T-2? Who the hell is T-2?'

'Well, ah—you know, Chief. The ah—Dresser Street dame.' Joe noted the familiar bluish colour creeping back. With a quick, nervous wave he slipped out the door.

For the first few months things went according to Elston Doolittle's plan for first-office agents, and other than an occasional lead to check records at some nearby installation, Jay's activities were confined to the office indices. It was all right with Jay. He developed an affinity for the vault in which the records were kept that was puzzling to his associates. To most men the mere thought of spending so much time in the basement of the building was tantamount to a stretch in the stocks.

Jay had returned to the university on several occasions, but

124

there had been no sign of Cricket Kent. Such visits had been curtailed as the result of a deteriorating relationship with Mrs Fryhoffer, but he had not abandoned the project. He had become acquainted with the other agents. There were nine in all assigned to the headquarters city—all old-timers who had finally made it to their office of preference. To a man, they demonstrated qualities conducive to the operation of Doolittle's shaky boat, and Jay was accorded all the welcome of a late arrival in a crowded life raft. 'Like a bunch of old grannies pickling preserves for a church bazaar,' he confided to one of the young clerks, who promptly reported the observation to one of the grannies.

It was not until early one morning near the end of his fourteenth week in Albuquerque that Jay received any significant assignment. He was sitting on a stool in the indices, his back against the wall, feet propped on an open file cabinet, when Joe Holloway popped into the vault.

'How would you like to get out of town for a while?'

'Out of town?' said Jay. It was a disconcerting thought. Since the event the previous month at the PPC range he had come to appreciate his assignment in the indices. Although the mysterious, dark-complexioned agent had disappeared shortly thereafter, the incident had produced residual anxieties, and Jay was most comfortable in the security of the vault. It seemed remote that anything could happen to him in there regardless of what Hawkins' intentions were. Also, an extended trip would rule out any contact with Cricket. 'Well, I'm right in the middle of this file project, Joe. I'd just as soon—'

'Hell, man, you can't spend the rest of your Bureau career down in the basement. You've got to get some experience. I'm sending you down to help out O'Rourke—he's the Carlsbad Resident Agent. He's getting way behind. Over half his cases are delinquent. Grab a plane out of here this afternoon. O'Rourke will meet you at the airport. Incidentally, tell him that Doolittle's been reviewing the informant programme, and he'd better rustle up some PCIs pretty quick, or he'll be getting some personal mail from the Director.'

125

Standing precisely 74 inches to the brim of his broad Stetson, his hand outstretched, and a wide welcoming smile creasing his ruggedly handsome face was Bob O'Rourke, a third-generation New York Irishman who had found the Southwest much to his liking. The initial amenities and enthusiastic handshake reflected a genuine cordiality, and Jay's impression was that, unlike the old-timers in Albuquerque, Agent O'Rourke was truly glad to see him.

'The car's over this way,' he said, taking the bag from Jay's hand and starting toward the parking lot. 'Did Joe fill you in on the white-slave case?'

'No, he didn't.'

'Well, I've got a surveillance going over at the Regency Hotel. It's a white-slave case on a subject named Pinky Miller. He's running all these high-priced pros all over the Southwest. They know me at the hotel, so you'll have to conduct the surveillance. I've developed the bell captain as an informant. He's got you planted in the room next to the subject's girl friend—a hustler named Cyndy Powers. Very special. Terrific-looking babe. Fifty bills a crack, and nobody comes away with any complaints. Not bad for one trick, huh?'

'No, I guess not. I'm supposed to surveil her?'

'That's right. The informant's fixed it so you can cover her room. Both rooms have medicine cabinets, and they're back to back, only the mirror on her side is two-way. When you open the cabinet on your side, you'll see a small screw hole. You can look through there and catch all the action.'

'Sounds interesting.'

'It beats the *Late Show*. I've got a radio for you in the car. After each trick you radio the description of the John to me. I'll be a block or so away with a state cop. We'll pick up the Johns and get statements from them. This way we prove the immoral-activity part of the statute. You'll have to keep a log in case you have to testify. We want to try to develop any evidence we can, showing Pinky is transporting her across state lines for purposes of prostitution. It shouldn't be too tough.'

'I see. How many statements will you need to make your case on Pinky?'

'Well, we should try to get a quite a few. Johns have a hesitancy about testifying. Especially the ones we'll be dealing with here. Anyone who can afford 50 clams for a piece of tail has got to be unusual. When trial time rolls around a lot of them will start changing their story.'

'Not that I'm complaining,' said Jay, 'but why do we have to watch her room? The informant could furnish descriptions of the Johns, couldn't he? I mean, he sees who—'

'Yeah, but we'd never get a statement. Unless we catch them in the act, no one's going to admit they've been involved in any illicit activity. They'd all deny they went the route. Some will admit they were in the room, but they invent all kinds of reasons why they were there. Listen, there's nothing more virtuous than a guy who's just got his rocks off. You'd think you were talking to a monk. No, the only way we'll get any statement is by pressing these guys. You know, telling them a few of the details, like the size of the mole on their ass—stuff like that. Remember, most of them are probably married, and nothing heats things up at home like climbing on a witness stand to tell how you blew 50 bills in a cathouse.' The agent grimaced slightly as though such a consequence held a particular distressing significance for him. 'But we'll try to line up enough single guys,' he added, brightening. 'It's easier on them. They're more apt to co-operate.'

Jay was pondering this bit of married-man's philosophy when they arrived at the car. He had almost walked by the vehicle when the older agent said, 'This is it.'

'This is the Bureau car?' asked Jay incredulously.

'This is it,' repeated O'Rourke, opening the rear door and swinging the bag into the back seat. 'It's a little dirty. I've been so damn busy I haven't had a chance to wash it recently.'

The condition of the car had nonplussed Jay. The exterior was encrusted with several layers of mud to a degree that it was impossible to tell the colour. Inside, articles of every description, including a few Bureau letters, were strewn about. Jars of baby food were intermingled with toys, and beach regalia hanging from hooks and draped over the seats served to create a cabana effect. A grocery list was dangling from a switch on the Bureau radio. Jay thought of Doolittle's concern at the cracker crumbs he had discovered in Albuquerque.

Moving a towel and child's driver's seat, Jay climbed into the front seat. 'You have a few children, I see.'

'I got children,' said O'Rourke with a note of wryness, 'but not a few. A platoon's more like it.'

'Must be very nice,' observed Jay, for want of something better to say. The comment drew no answer. 'Joe mentioned that you had some delinquent cases.'

'Yeah, it's impossible to keep the goddamn things current. I just get them under control, and then a lead comes in on some top-level matter like the Who Case or something, I have to drop everything. Then I'm right back where I started.'

'The Who Case?' said Jay. 'What's the Who Case?'

'Oh, that's a top-secret case. That's the code name. Not supposed to talk about it even with the agents—'course everyone does. Don't let Doolittle ever hear you, though. He heard one of the teletype clerks just mention the words Who Case, and he suspended him. Mr Who is the code name for a top-level subject who directs certain phases of the Soviet espionage apparatus operating in the western hemisphere—supposedly one of the key men in the KGB. The Bureau's been trying to establish his identity for years. The way I get it, they think he's been able to infiltrate some sections of the Bureau.'

There was a pause as Bob O'Rourke reached for the grocery list dangling from the radio. Steadying the wheel with one knee, he took a pen from his shirt pocket and made a note on the paper. 'Gee, I'm glad I thought of that. She would've been all over me if I forgot the Enfamil.'

Bob O'Rourke's comments were a shock to Jay. Could he be referring to Mr Wallingford? He probably was. The infiltration of the Bureau was their prime objective. But he had never been told that the Bureau was aware of anything. His entire role took on a different character. It was obvious that Hawkins and the others were controlling the leads, but just the fact that the Bureau was aware that they were being infiltrated increased the risks greatly.

He realised he was on the verge of more information, but

128

he resisted the impulse to ask questions. It would be natural for any new agent to ask questions, but still he had to be careful. He had to remain calm. More would come in natural fashion if he could just keep O'Rourke talking. He sat quietly, feeling the nervousness in the pit of his stomach, hoping the man would return to the subject after handling the domestic matter.

'Yes, as I was saying, don't ever mention that I discussed the Who Case with you. It's a very sensitive thing. It's driving the Bureau crazy—toughest thing they've ever had to cope with. You'll hear about it. Don't worry.'

'No, I won't say anything,' said Jay. 'It does sound sensitive. I should think it would make the Bureau very vulnerable to any Soviet activities.'

'It certainly does. The problem is, it can't be controlled. Once they have a toehold in the outfit, they can bring other spooks in. If it's unchecked, eventually they can control the whole organisation. That's what's been driving them crazy in Washington. From what I hear, they've got a blue-ribbon squad working the thing.'

Jay waited, but it seemed that the man was not going to elaborate further. It was risky asking questions, but he decided it was worth it. 'I wonder if this blue-ribbon squad has been able to develop anything.' The minute he said it he was sorry. It sounded awkward to him. But the comment drew no reply.

After a long pause that suggested to Jay that O'Rourke might be far off mentally solving some unrelated problem, the older man cleared his throat and said, 'I just talked to the informant before you landed. He's waiting for you at the hotel. Just register under the name Harder. He'll see you get to the right room.'

After giving him a tan suitcase that contained the radio, O'Rourke dropped Jay near the hotel. 'This is about as close as I'd better get. Give me a call on the radio about 10:00, OK? If there's any activity before then, just write it down in your log. Good luck.'

The Regency was one of the foremost luxury hotels in New Mexico, but the wing to which Jay was led by the informant was of an earlier period and had not been renovated.

'We got to be quiet now,' said the informant, a short, bulky man with heavy ebony features.

He stopped before one of the doors and set down the bags. Quietly he unlocked the door and motioned Jay inside.

Jay hesitated, looking back down the hallway. 'After you,' he said, gesturing toward the dark interior.

Inside was a small foyer that opened into a small two-room apartment. The informant placed the two suitcases on a double bed. He then snapped on an overhead light and, placing his finger to his lips in a silencing gesture, walked to the windows and drew the draperies. Sounds of a feminine voice came from the next apartment.

'Is that Cyndy?' whispered Jay, motioning with this thumb.

'Yeah, that's her.'

The informant pointed to the medicine cabinet on the wall above the washbasin. 'Mr O'Rourke tell you about that?' he whispered.

Jay nodded.

'Remember, you got to keep it dark in here when you open the cabinet door.'

'I understand,' replied Jay. The place was eerie.

With a final comment concerning his availability, the informant was gone. Jay immediately locked the door. He noticed that a chain latch had once been on the door, but that the chain was missing.

He removed his suit coat and draped it over the back of a chair. After loosening his tie, he sat down dejectedly on the edge of the bed. Bob O'Rourke's comments had made him apprehensive. He had said a blue-ribbon squad was working the case. Were they aware of his activities? Was Jay Von Vlack now a subject of the Who Case?

The sound of a voice laughing in the next room cut his attention, and rising, he walked to the medicine cabinet. Remembering the light, he walked to the door and turned the switch. Then cautiously he opened the door of the cabinet. A small stream of light came through the screw hole in the right side of the interior. Jay pushed his head into the cabinet and put his eye to the hole.

*　　*　　*

130

At home she had been Muriel, in Las Vegas it was Sue. New York, Chicago and other metro markets knew her as Cynthia, while in El Paso and points south it was Cyndy. But to the ageing New Mexico judge she was just plain Cyn—delightful, beautiful, sensuous Cyn.

The few gratifying moments left in the man's withering existence occurred in room 707 of the Regency, where, discarding the mantle of his office and everything else, the magistrate abandoned himself to his Cyn.

It was just such a moment, and the Judge, clad in turquoise shorts and long, juristic-looking stockings, was sitting on the edge of a chair absorbed in the matter at hand. The fact that the matter was standing sideways between his legs seemingly more intent upon fixing her hair in the mirror than reciprocating his interest appeared not to bother the man an iota. Rather, the senior jurist had become so absorbed in exploring the contours and crevices of the young woman's nude form that what the head was doing at the moment seemed of little importance. Holding the girl as though she were a bass viola, he had one hand clasped tightly on her buttocks while the other, with a deftness that belied the gnarled fingers, was fondling all ventral objects avidly.

Suddenly, as though acting on impulse, the man reached up and, taking a nipple between his thumb and forefinger, gave a slight tug as though plucking a ripe olive from a branch. Gentle as it was, the manœuvre brought a short gasp from the instrument of his affection. 'OK, Judge, enough of this crap.'

The girl disengaged herself from the hands and, turning, placed the comb she had been using on a table. 'What do you say, ready for the saddle?' She was not heartened by the prospects of the aged patron grinding away on top of her, but the hands were simply too much. And with the judge's circulation being what it was, the fingers would become progressively colder as he became more excited.

The girl moved across the room and unceremoniously deposited herself on the large double bed, assuming the position that occupied a good amount of her evening hours.

'C'mon, Judge. You'll be my first fuck today.'

The judge emitted a tumbling, grating laugh that

131

terminated in a hacking cough. Shaking convulsively, he made it to his feet and moved toward the bed.

'Oh, boy,' muttered the girl, rolling her eyes. It was times like this when she wondered if she had chosen the right profession. For want of something better to do, she started counting the number of undulations as the Judge began. She had reached 115 when the telephone rang.

'Goddamn!' from the Judge.

'It's all right, honey, hang in there,' assured Cyndy, reaching one arm languidly toward the phone above her head on the bed stand. 'Hello... Oh, hi, Sweetie... Working, what do you think?... No, that's all right... What?.. No, that's too late... No, tell him tomorrow... I know, but—Listen, honey, I don't care. Even a pussy needs a rest, you know... OK... OK... See you tomorrow, honey... OK, 'bye.'

She had no sooner replaced the phone on its cradle when it rang again.

'Goddamn,' said the Judge. 'What you doing, running an answering service on the side?'

'Easy, honey. Hello... Oh, it's you... Yes, he is... About ten minutes ago... Don't worry, I'll let you know... Yes, I got it right here. 572–4631... Say, before I forget. I been thinking. How you gonna get the money to me? I don't even know you. How do I know this isn't some kind of gag?... Why not give it all to me this week?... OK... OK... Only thing is, if you shove it under the door when I'm out, and I don't get it, then the deal's off... OK... Don't worry. I'll keep you filled in.'

She replaced the phone carefully so as not to interfere with the Judge. 'Not bad,' she thought. 'Not bad at all.' Five hundred bucks just to keep the caller informed when the creep who was peering through the hole in the next room came in and went out. Not bad at all. She wondered how he was enjoying the show through the hole—the 'unused screw hole' she called it. Amazing how some guys got their rocks off!

Reaching up, she picked up a package of gum. Holding both hands above her head so as not to interfere with her patron, she unwrapped a stick, bent it double, and put it into her mouth. After chewing a few times, she blew a large bubble, which she cracked in the Judge's ear. 'How we doing, honey?'

In the next room Jay softly closed the cabinet. Crossing the room, he dropped into a chair and sat quietly in the darkness. As the cracking sounds of Cyndy's gum came from the other room, he took out his handkerchief and carefully mopped his brow.

Almost two weeks had passed before Elston Doolittle became aware of Jay's assignment. It was one of those infrequent cold, stormy days in the Southwest when the rain came down hard in long silver threads and the baked, crusty earth was unable to absorb the water. Inadequate drains quickly filled up, and the gutters were soon ankle-deep in muddy, swiftly moving water.

Joe Holloway was on his way to deliver an 'important package' to Mrs Doolittle. Joe couldn't be certain, but from the size and heft of the package, he judged it to be a pot roast. He knew the boss usually had a pot roast on Wednesday. Doolittle himself was using the time to conduct a surprise inspection of his assistant's desk and was finding it, as always, in intolerable condition. It was pursuant to this administrative function that he came across one of O'Rourke's reports, and noted Jay's name.

'God almighty!' he hissed, moving out the door. As he whisked past the receptionist, he shouted, 'Send the idiot up to my office as soon as he gets back!'

'Which idiot is that, sir?' asked the girl politely.

'Holloway!'

'Oh, yes, of course,' answered the girl, as though she should have known.

An hour later, breathing heavily and water dripping from his ears, Joe stood looking at the face framed between the crossed feet. 'But he can't stay in the indices forever, Chief. He has to get some experience. I told you how the Bureau seems to be interested in his activities for some reason. Maybe he has a rabbi down there. And you know how the Bureau feels about that vice case. They want the thing closed out as

133

soon as possible.'

'Nonsense! Can you imagine those two down there closing out a setup like that? Why, they'll nurse that thing along forever. Would you close it out? The hell you would. With all we have to do, here you are fooling around with a ridiculous vice case. You still haven't anything on that Leopard Boulevard job, have you?'

Joe was becoming rattled. The large vein in the boss's forehead had begun to bulge, and within a minute he would be tough. He wasn't certain which of Doolittle's questions was the best to answer, but since the Leopard Boulevard case was going absolutely nowhere, he decided to stay on the subject of Von Vlack.

'But, Chief, this isn't just an ordinary white-slave case. The thing has gotten real big. This guy Miller is an international pimp, and the Mexican authorities claim there's dope traffic involved.'

'If there's dope included, why don't we refer it to the Bureau of Narcotics? We need more closed cases around here. Our statistics have been off for two months now. What about auto recoveries? You sure the police are reporting all the recoveries to us? At any rate, you shouldn't have put that young agent down there.'

'Well, he's not really that young, Chief. Besides, there just isn't anybody else available. The case load averages over 50 per man right now.'

'What about Jefferson? You could have used him, couldn't you? A mature agent. It would have been much better.'

'We've been reducing his cases like you said, Boss. He retires in six weeks, you know. Besides, you know Harold, Chief. He'd fall asleep at the peephole.'

'Well, I don't like this whole thing one damn bit. Remember, don't let them use any technical surveillance equipment down there. Does the Bureau know they've got a two-way mirror? Good Christ, here we are tying up all our manpower peering through mirrors at people screwing, and we're getting absolutely nowhere on the Leopard Boulevard case. We aren't getting anywhere, are we?' He fixed his assistant with an eye that meant business. 'Are we?'

134

'Ah—well—Chief, I'm glad you mentioned that case. I've been wanting to talk to you about that one.' Joe looked down at the pool of water that had collected at his feet, and cleared his throat nervously. 'You know, sir, that one's a lot tougher than the Director thinks. These Indians are pretty tough to communicate with, you know what I mean? Now, we just may have something going. We've been trying to develop a few informants out there and...'

Doolittle became lost in the maze of leads that Joe hastily conceived. Von Vlack and the Las Cruces vice case were all but forgotten until Joe was leaving.

'Remember, Holloway, I'm holding you personally responsible for the new agent. If he embarrasses the Bureau, I'll see to it that you're busted to a grade-nine clerk.'

'Don't worry, Chief, I'll give that matter my preferred and continuous attention.'

'OK, OK,' replied Doolittle, motioning him from the room. Holloway's use of the stereotype Bureau language was a constant source of annoyance to his boss.

Joe had just about made it through the door when Doolittle's secretary appeared. 'There's a teletype coming in on the Leopard Boulevard case, Mr Doolittle.'

Joe tried to squeeze past the woman out the door.

'Hold it. Stop right there, Holloway! Let's get over to the teletype room.'

They arrived in the teletype room and watched over the operator's shoulder as the bold, black letters formed on the page.

TO: S-A-C, ALBUQUERQUE

FROM: DIRECTOR, FBI

RE:UNKNOWN SUBJECTS, BANK ROBBERY
   LEOPARD BOULEVARD NATIONAL BANK
   ALBUQUERQUE, NEW MEXICO

KANSAS CITY INFORMANT OF UNKNOWN RELIABILITY
WHO HAS FURNISHED BOTH RELIABLE AND UNRELI-
ABLE INFORMATION IN THE PAST ADVISES LEOPARD

BLVD JOB EXECUTED BY FOUR KNOWN KANSAS CITY HOODLUMS MASQUERADING AS INDIANS. INFORMANT STATES SUBJECTS EXUBERANT AT SUCCESS OF JOB AND PLANNING ADDITIONAL BANK ROBBERY IN NEW MEXICO WITHIN MONTH. INFORMANT STATES SUBJECTS FEEL BANKS IN NEW MEXICO (PLEASE HOLD DELAY ON LINE)

....
....SOFT TOUCH....

                                             DIRECTOR

After the last clackety clack from the teletype had reverberated about the room, a deathly silence filled the air. A large globule of moisture rolled down Joe Holloway's nose, poised at the tip momentarily, and then splattered onto the teletype just below the word 'DIRECTOR.' If Joe hadn't just come in from the rain, the teletype operator could have sworn it was a tear.

                                        November 19, 1970

Dear Jay,
  Business has been exceedingly brisk of late, and I trust you will understand that, while I have not written sooner, we do think of you often here at Lindenwald.
  Sometime within the next two weeks a friend of mine will be passing through Albuquerque, and I suggested that he stop by to see you. He is unfamiliar with the Southwest, and I should appreciate anything you might do to be of assistance to him.
  Lindenwald is enjoying splendid weather with leaves turning in colourful profusion. We miss you and think of you often, and always with affection.

                                        Fondest regards,

                                        David Wallingford

Sing Street was one of the older streets in Carlsbad, bordering the original part of the Regency on the south side. By day it was a lazy, cheerful spot where sunbeams laced the branches

136

of the tall elms lining the road and fell in brilliant patches
upon the trim white houses assembled tightly like a keyboard
underneath; where birds sang and children played in the tiny
yards, and daily chores were conducted always, it seemed,
with a deferential regard for the nodding heads on front
porches; where sounds floated lightly across the lawn, drifting
up to the windows of the Regency, signifying a pleasant,
salutary atmosphere.

By night, however, Sing Street took on another character.
With darkness came a deathly quiet—quiet, that is, but for the
soft rustle in the branches overhead. It was this sound—a tiny,
low musical tone like a tea kettle far off, occasioned by the
barest breeze—from which the street derived its name.

A few scattered streetlamps did little to cheer the place.
Rather, the slightest motion of air would set them to swinging,
thereby enlivening the shadows from the murmuring limbs
overhead.

But at this moment there was not a breath of air, and Sing
Street was as still and lifeless as a drawing. From a distant
tower a clock struck 11:00, the last bell hanging on the night
air accentuating the forlorness of the hour.

Rounding a corner onto the scene, Jay strode on his way
back to his apartment at the Regency. As though on cue, a
slight breeze infused Sing Street with a soulful moan and a
cast of grey dancing shapes.

Jay added a few inches to his stride. He had travelled the
route many times while going to and from the Regency, and
always it inspired in him the same feeling of dread—as though
someone, somewhere amidst the undulating shadows were
matching, waiting.

It took him only slightly longer than the breeze to move
through Sing Street, and with purposeful strides he turned the
corner onto the main thoroughfare, where the entrance to the
Regency was located.

The informant caught his eye briefly as he entered the
lobby. The bell captain looked quickly away and rubbed his
forehead with his left hand. No one at home in 707. That was
good. He had already taken in three 'matinees' earlier, and
prospects of another turn at the screw hole were dispiriting.

Besides, he had just been presented with an awesome amount of work. Bob O'Rourke had been called to Washington that afternoon. It was unusual. He was not due for inservice for a few months. He left behind a pile of hastily explained memos pertaining to a variety of cases.

Among those termed the 'worst dogs' were leads on five separate bank robberies ranging from Carlsbad to El Paso, two theft-of-government-property cases at Holloman Air Force Base, a complaint from a victim in Hobbs charging police brutality, and a subsequent complaint that his injuries would be all healed before any FBI man had come to see them, a stack of Atomic Energy applicant investigations a quarter of an inch high, and a complaint from the White Sands Proving Grounds concerning missing designs of a drogue parachute under development for use in connection with the government guided-missile program. It was agreed that the white-slave case would be held in abeyance pending O'Rourke's return, when it would be presented to the US Attorney.

Left as an investigative aid, and with the solemn observation that he hoped Jay would not rack it up, was O'Rourke's domesticated Bureau car.

Inside the apartment Jay spread out a map on a coffee table. Soon he was absorbed in planning his itinerary for covering the leads outlined by the Resident Agent.

It was almost one o'clock when he turned out the lights and went to bed. But sleep did not come readily. He lay uneasily on his back interpreting the tired creaks and groans of the antiquated structure.

He lay awake for over an hour before finally dozing off. How long he had been asleep he did not know, but suddenly he was wide awake staring at the outline of the fire escape through the window. He lay rigid, watching, listening intently—almost so that he could hear the very air about him. Suddenly there was a noise from the foyer. A quick, sharp, metallic sound followed by complete and total silence.

Several seconds passed, and then a far-off, scarcely audible moan drifted through the window from Sing Street. It was an eerie sound that died quickly, leaving the room once again as

138

silent as a crypt. Jay pulled the blanket tightly against his chin and closed his eyes. A few minutes passed and he had begun to console himself with the thought that his imagination had been overactive, when before him the bottom of the window curtains fluttered slightly. Someone had opened the door to the apartment.

Jay rose quickly to a sitting position and reached for the pistol next to him on the bed stand. The cold metal felt good in his hand. Withdrawing the gun from its holster, he shook it slightly, listening for the rattle of the cartridges in the cylinder to assure himself it was loaded.

'You won't need that, Von Vlack!' It was a pleasant, almost friendly voice that came from just beyond the bedroom door.

Jay watched as the outline of two figures formed in the doorway.

'Put down the pistol, Von Vlack. I have a message from Nayraville. My name is Everett Reeves.' While he could not be certain, from the man's build and the sound of his voice he guessed it might be the blonde man who had talked to him from the car the night he had been summoned while in training school.

Jay sat motionless for several seconds. Then slowly, almost reluctantly, he returned the pistol to the bed stand. 'Would you mind turning on that light on the wall there?' His voice sounded horse and far-off.

'Leave it dark, Everett.' It was a strange voice that came quickly, almost impulsively, from the other person in the doorway—a feminine voice that appeared to have been intentionally lowered to a more masculine range.

'Sorry, Von Vlack, we'd better keep it dark,' said the man. 'The lights are out in all the other rooms. Besides, we'll be here for only a few minutes. We have an assignment for you. Now listen very carefully. We'll go through this only once. If there is anything you don't understand, then interrupt me. Among those cases left you by O'Rourke are leads involving missing drawings connected with the missile programme at White Sands Proving Grounds. These drawings have been intentionally misplaced in order to give us access to the restricted laboratories in which the missile scientists are

139

working. You will contact Colonel Bloodworth, the commanding officer of the installation, Wednesday morning. He will refer you to Major Littlefield, who is in charge of all security. The Major will presumably escort you to the laboratories where you'll undertake your investigation. Should he for some reason not offer to do this, you'll have to request tactfully that you be permitted to interview those who had access to the plans. Your objective, once in the laboratory, will be to establish contact with Franz Ostermeyer, one of the scientists. There will be only six persons in the entire building. Ostermeyer will be seated in the first office on the right as you enter the building. You'll have no difficulty recognising him. He's quite tall with light hair and glasses. He'll be watching for you sometime around 11:30. When he sees you, he will remove his glasses with his left hand and place them in his breast pocket. Now, are you with me so far?'

'I understand,' said Jay.

'OK. Ostermeyer will have in his possession a slide rule that looks like any other conventional slide rule, only slightly thicker. When the right moment arrives he'll pass this slide rule to you. Now listen carefully. This is very important. The slide rule contains invaluable information. If for any reason you believe you are suspect and the ruler might be taken from you, throw it to the ground. A percussion cap will detonate an explosive, and the ruler will be destroyed. You will, of course, exercise care to see that you don't bump or jar the instrument unnecessarily, for obvious reasons. We'll contact you shortly for the ruler. Now, do you have any questions? It's a relatively simple assignment.'

'I'd hardly call it simple,' said Jay. He was irritated by the man's condescending manner, but even more by the implications of the job he had been asked to perform. 'That is, after all, one of the top-security bases in the country. Passing information out of it would be difficult under any circumstances.'

'Just remember,' said the voice with a touch of impatience, 'you're legal, an FBI agent, cleared for top-secret activity. You should be able to move about fairly freely.'

140

'What happens if I have some problems? How should I get in touch with you?'

'Don't worry,' said the man. 'If you get in trouble, we'll know it as soon as you do. Just remember, this is an extremely important assignment and it would be most unfortunate should you fail. Good luck.' Everett Reeves moved toward the door.

'Just one second,' said Jay. 'What about this slide rule? If I have to detonate the thing—how big an explosion is it, anyway?'

The figures hesitated in the doorway momentarily. 'Adequate,' came the feminine voice with a note of finality.

'Blueprints? Missing? Indeed! Sounds like a matter for Major Littlefield. Although you really don't think they're missing, do you? I mean, you know scientists, Von Vlack. Probably the most absent-minded men on the North American continent are in that laboratory over there. You don't think there's anything else involved, do you? That is, spying, sabotage—any of that rot? I rather think they've just forgotten where they've put the confounded things, don't you?'

Colonel Bloodworth seemed only mildly concerned that top-secret plans had been discovered missing on his base. In fact, to Jay it seemed that the man might actually be pleasantly intrigued by it all.

The commanding officer was a cheerful person with a deep, resonant voice, and when he laughed, which was a great deal, the hearty guffaws that virtually rattled the windowpanes seemed as though they should have rolled from a cavernous, hairy chest rather than the frail little body behind the desk. The Colonel's frame was further dwarfed by the large leather chair in which he sat, and while Jay could not see his feet, he suspected that they might very well be dangling above the floor like those of a small boy. Two shaggy grey brows matched a thick growth of closely cropped hair, and a pair of shiny black eyes twinkling from a tan, weather-wrinkled face suggested a pleasant if somewhat mischievous personality.

Probably the only displeasing thing about the man was his habit of nervously nibbling on the underside of a small grey

141

moustache that graced about three quarters the length of his upper lip—a most distracting mannerism since it gave one talking to him the unsettling feeling that the Colonel was trying to keep from laughing. But all else about the senior officer was quite pleasant, and despite the fact that he was in the twilight of his career, facing a starless future, he was as bright and colourful as the trim rows of campaign ribbons lining his chest.

'When I stop to think of all the money we spend on security around here,' continued the Colonel, 'it seems kind of purposeless if no one ever tries to steal anything. A good spy case would sort of justify the whole thing, if you know what I mean.'

'Well, that's a way of looking at it, Colonel,' answered Jay. 'But I'm inclined to agree with your first theory—that is, that someone probably just dropped the things in the wrong drawer by mistake. Probably a routine interview with the men in the laboratory will clear things up.'

'Yes, I guess you're right,' said the Colonel, a trace of disappointment in his voice. 'Let's take a walk over and see Littlefield. I'd like to follow through on this with you.'

Jay grimaced as they emerged from the building into the sunlight. The morning sun reflected sharply off the pure white gypsum sand, and it took several seconds for his eyes to adjust to the brightness.

'The security office is down there near the entrance to the base where you parked your car,' said the Colonel. 'Only take us a minute to get there.'

'Fine,' said Jay, his mind on the impending meeting. 'What time do you have, Colonel?'

'Eleven-ten,' said the Colonel, taking the occasion to wind his watch. 'It's this building right up here. Incidentally, while I am thinking of it. Von Vlack, don't let Pete Littlefield bother you. He's a little excitable. Doesn't care much for those German scientists who work over there. You'll see. He doesn't mean any harm, though. Pete's bark is worse than his bite.' The Colonel climbed the stoop of a small, rectangular building and held the door for Jay.

In a small room located in a makeshift section of the

142

building was the Security Office. Sitting behind piles of official-looking documents was a wild-eyed individual. Tall, reed thin, balding, a perennial nettled look on his brow, the man seemed ill-prepared for the journey he was undertaking into middle age. He was drinking from a large mug of weak tea when his visitors walked in.

'Parachute plans? Oh yes, naturally. This week it was the parachute plans, last week they couldn't find some kind of manual, next week it will be something else.'

The man began rummaging through the myriad of files stacked not only on his desk, but on the floor surrounding it. 'I'm not sure where I put the memo I had on the blasted thing.'

'Maybe you sent the file over to Personnel, Pete,' said the Colonel helpfully. 'Remember, that's what happened on those security clearances last month.' Then, turning to Jay as though the Major were not in the room, 'He sent half a dozen top-secret security clearances for incoming transfers over to Personnel last month. By the end of the day almost everybody on the post knew about the transfers. Didn't you, Pete?' He looked back at the Major for confirmation of the statement as though the Major's goof had been an accomplishment rather than an incredible blunder. The Major nodded his head curtly as he foraged through the dunes of white paper.

'Guess you're pretty busy around here,' said Jay, sensing an unpleasant situation developing that might hamper his mission. It was already 11:15, which left 15 minutes to make his contact.

'Busy! "Busy" isn't the word for it!' exploded the Major, ready to get a few things off his chest. 'It's crazy! Downright crazy! This whole place could go up like that!' He snapped his fingers sharply. 'They don't know what they're doing out there in those bunkers. They send those telephone poles up, and by the time they realise they're out of control and blow the head off, it's too late—they're hundreds of miles away. A few weeks ago one landed 50 yards from the guardhouse down there.' While the Major did not say so, there was something about the way he glanced at the Colonel that suggested the commanding officer was not without fault in

143

these matters.

'You mean the guided missiles?' asked Jay, in a surprised tone.

'Guided! Haaa! A few months ago another one ended up in a graveyard over in Juarez. You call that "guided"? We've had a helluva time trying to get it back from the Mexican government.'

'Really?' said Jay. 'I thought they had those things pretty well under control by this time.'

'Haaa!' snorted the Major. 'Those lousy Krauts out there—you can't trust the buggers. Goddamn independent, too. You'd think they won the war and we were working for them. If I had my way, I'd pack the buggers up and send 'em back where they came from.'

The Colonel turned toward Jay, beaming. 'See, I told you.'

'Ah, here it is,' said the Major, drawing a file from one of the stacks. 'Now I remember this. Why don't we take a walk next door to the lab? I'd like to straighten them out on a few things.'

'Fine' said Jay, standing up quickly. 'Actually there's no need to take up your time, gentlemen. I'm sure I can find my way OK.'

'Not at all, not at all,' said the Colonel, standing up. 'We'd like to see the FBI in action.'

'Yes, we'd better go,' agreed the Major. 'Those Krauts are pretty tough to talk to. You may need a little help with them.'

It was close to zero hour when they entered one of the buildings that formed the complex where the German scientists conducted their research. At a desk inside the door a young academic-looking lieutenant came to his feet when they entered.

'Good morning, Colonel, Major.'

'Morning, Lieutenant,' said the Colonel, motioning the younger man at ease. 'This is Agent Von Vlack, FBI. He's here to talk to you people about the missing documents.'

'Missing documents, sir?' A perplexed look creased the brow of the Lieutenant. He looked from the Colonel to the Major and back to the Colonel.

'Blueprints of the parachute.'

144

'Oh. Oh, those. Oh, we found them, sir. They were misfiled. In my memo to the security office I indicated they were probably in with something else. We never really thought they had been lost . . . or anything like that. I sent a recovery notice over to the security office yesterday afternoon. I found them myself.'

While the Lieutenant related how he had located the misplaced documents, Jay carefully looked about the room. Almost immediately he caught the eye of a tall, blond-haired man with glasses, standing just beyond the doorway in an office off to the right. The man looked away immediately and removed his glasses with his left hand, placing them in a breast pocket underneath his smock. Jay took a deep breath to steady his nerves.

'Well, I guess that takes care of our missing documents, Von Vlack,' said the Colonel. 'Sorry to get you down here for nothing.'

'Ah—as long as I'm here maybe I should talk to the other people, Colonel. Just for the record, you understand.'

'Why, yes, certainly,' said the Colonel. 'Lieutenant, who had access to those documents?'

'Well, let's see . . . there's really only three of us, sir. Captain Brandt, myself, and Herr Ostermeyer over there.' He motioned with his head toward the other office. 'Captain Brandt isn't here now, but I could probably—'

'That's OK,' said Jay quickly. 'I can get all the facts I need from you and the other man. Well, Colonel, I don't think I shall have to hold you or the Major any longer. I'll just finish up here and—'

'Quite all right, Von Vlack, we'll just wait around till you're through, and show you the way out.'

'Oh, that won't be necessary, sir. My car's right outside at the gate.'

'Not at all, Von Vlack. We'll see it through with you.' The black eyes twinkled agreeably.

'I see,' mused Jay. 'Very well, Lieutenant, would you give me the whole story—from the time you first discovered the plans missing?'

The Lieutenant launched into an earnest explanation of

how the blueprints were misplaced. It was approaching noon by the time they entered the small office in which Franz Ostermeyer was seated. Almost immediately Jay saw the slide rule. It was resting on a corner of the desk within easy reach of anyone sitting nearby.

Quickly but gracefully the German came to his feet. He was an austere fortyish-looking man with sharp features and long, straight blond hair. After a brief introduction, Jay quickly took the chair nearest the ruler and began the interview.

The German seemed completely impassive as they talked, and Jay wondered if beneath the cool-looking smock the man's heart was pounding like his own. He placed his right elbow on the desk so that his forearm rested casually alongside the ruler.

'Does it happen very often that documents are misplaced in this manner?' said Jay.

'Of course,' said the German in a haughty voice. 'We are not perfect, you know. We do make mistakes like everyone else.'

This observation was too much for the Major, who sat fidgeting throughout the interview. 'I'll vouch for that!' he said acidly. 'In fact, from what I've seen around here, you people are trying to corner the market on mistakes.'

'My dear Major,' said the German, his voice fairly dripping with condescension, 'we are scientists involved in a highly complex undertaking which should benefit all mankind. There is a good deal more involved than sitting at a desk all day shuffling bureaucratic rubble.'

It was obvious to Jay that things were going to deteriorate. The Major, apparently interpreting the remark personally, looked as if he had just taken a strong blow to the solar plexus. The Colonel, on the other hand, seemed almost gleeful, the black eyes sparkling in anticipation of the major's rebuttal.

'Now, just one minute, Herr Ostermeyer,' said the Major, his voice quivering with anger as he leaned forward in his chair, 'let's hold it right there. You seem to forget that it was this bureaucratic rubble that saved your ass from a Russian firing squad. It seems to me you and your crew have goddamn short memories!'

146

He picked up the slide rule and gave it a sharp whack on the desk for emphasis.

Jay's jaw fell open as though hinged. Herr Ostermeyer never batted an eye, but his prominent Adam's apple made two trips from his collar to his chin like a fast-moving elevator.

The Major, not above pulling his rank, proceeded to remind the scientist of their relative positions in the scheme of things, wagging the gold slide rule under the German's nose in the process. Jay knew it was only a question of time before the Major was on his way to the Juarez cemetery. The best thing he could do was to leave and let Herr Ostermeyer handle the situation. After all, it was his slide rule.

'Excuse me, Major,' he said, with a touch of panic, 'but I'm late for an appointment.'

'Have to go, do you, Von Vlack?' said the Colonel, interested primarily in the Major's straightening-out process and affording the agent only token attention.

'Yes, sir,' said Jay, standing up while eyeing the flailing slide rule. 'I'll send you a copy of my report.'

'Do that. You can find your way out, can't you? If you don't mind I'll stay here and straighten things out with the Major for a few minutes. Good luck.'

'Good luck to you, Colonel. Goodbye, Major.'

But the Major was not listening. He had pulled all stops in his lecture to the German, who watched Jay leave through aggrieved eyes.

At the entrance to the building Jay heard the cool voice of the scientist. 'Major, may I kindly have my slide rule before you ruin—' Jay winced as he heard another sharp whack of the ruler against the desk.

Walking swiftly, he was soon in the Bureau car and about 50 feet past the guard gate, when a terrific 'PHUMP-BOOM!' announced that the Major had finally straightened out the laboratory.

Jay never looked back. Instead, he took one of the beach towels draped over the seat and carefully mopped his brow. The conical mounds of gypsum sand stretched endlessly before him in the desert, a shimmering white in the torrid noon sun.

147

Back in Albuquerque things were going poorly, indeed, for Elston Doolittle. With the effrontery of only the most daring of the underworld, the Leopard Boulevard mob had struck again. What had made the crime so sensational was the fact that they had not hit one of the more lucrative banks, such as the First National in Santa Fe or the Bank of America in Alamogordo, or even one of the relatively easy touches such as a Wells Fargo truck, but, rather incredibly, had returned to the same lonely outpost on Leopard Boulevard. The job had netted them little more than 7,000 dollars, but the repercussions had been tremendous.

Elston Doolittle, embroiled in the aftermath, was pacing the floor of his office, levelling a tirade at the three agents assembled in front of him.

'Look at those movies. How? How in the name of Christ could you ever have mistaken that motley lot for Indians in the first place?' Doolittle was referring to the movies taken by the concealed camera that had been set up in the various banks after the teletype informing of the contemplated robbery. It had been only an afterthought on the part of Joe Holloway when he had installed one in the Leopard Boulevard bank, feeling that it was inconceivable the gang would return to the scene of their last job. After viewing the film, which was marvellous in its detail, Joe was a bit sorry that he had had the thought, for it clearly showed the subjects had spent relatively little effort on their Indian masquerade. The four of them had poured through the front door carrying Thompson submachine guns, and while their faces were heavily painted with pancake makeup, there the similarity had stopped. One had red hair, another had a cigar butt protruding from his mouth, while still a third had virtually no disguise at all save sunglasses and, in fact, was wearing a sweat shirt that read 'Kansas City Chiefs'.

'But, Chief,' protested Joe, 'all the bank witnesses—'

'All the bank witnesses be damned!' thundered Doolittle. 'And if you call me "Chief" just once more, I'll give you two weeks on the beach! Who ever heard of a red-headed Indian with a tommy gun? I don't know how you ever got out of New Agents' School. You know crime-scene descriptions aren't worth a damn.' He ground out a cigarette in the mound of butts that had built up in his ashtray. 'Now I want each one of you to understand. You've got just a few hours to come up with something. They can't possibly leave the state. The state police have every outlet covered. The big thing is time. Every minute that passes improves their chances. I want every informant contacted and every available man put on this case. Have you notified all the Resident Agents to come in?'

'Yes, sir, Ch—Right, sir!'

'Now I want a two-hour progress report on this matter from here on. OK, let's hit those bricks.'

Jumping Joe snapped to his feet and jingled his way from the office, followed quickly by the other agents.

Elston Doolittle slumped into his chair, holding his forehead with the palm of his hand, once again reading the last part of a teletype that had just come in:

CONCENTRATE ALL RESOURCES ON LEOPARD BOUL-EVARD CASE. IMPERATIVE THIS MATTER BROUGHT TO IMMEDIATE SUCCESSFUL CONCLUSION. S-A-C ALBU-QUERQUE PLACED ON PROBATION EFFECTIVE THIS DATE PENDING DISPOSITION CAPTIONED CASE.
                                            DIRECTOR

A siege of dark thoughts had descended on Doolittle when his secretary, a frail, frightened-looking maiden of middle age, appeared in the doorway. 'Mr. Doolittle, Mr. Von Vlack is calling.'

'Who?'

'Mr. Von Vlack. The new agent.'

'All right, I'll take it,' he said with a heavy scowl. He reached for the phone. 'Hello, Von Flack? . . .That's right, everybody was advised to come into the headquarters city. . . No, I didn't hear of any explosion. . . I see. . . One of the laboratories? . . . I see. . .You think it was the same building you were in huh? I see. . . It happened after you left, you say? . . . I see. . . Well, they're always blowing up something down there. I can't get too excited about it now. We'll wait till we're notified officially. By that time O'Rourke might be back, and he can handle it. Right now you get back up here.

149

We're going to need every available man on the Leopard Boulevard Case.' Doolittle slammed the phone into its cradle. 'Miss Quinby!'

The secretary fluttered back into the doorway, her steno pad at the ready. 'Yes, sir, Mr Doolittle?'

'Tell Holloway when he comes back to keep that new fellow away from the action. Seems to me he's one of those people things happen to. He's at White Sands only a few hours and one of their laboratories blows up.'

'Denton . . . Robert.' Jay cleared his throat nervously. 'P,' he added weakly. He ventured a half smile, and the iron features staring back through the window of the Registrar's office responded with all the warmth and cordiality of a cigar-store Indian. He had called the Registrar's office only a few minutes before and had been elated finally to reach Cricket. It was a real shock to round the corner in the hall fully expecting to see a phantom of delight, only to be confronted with the frosty visage of Mrs Fryhoffer.

'I thought you reviewed his file once before.'

'That's right,' said Jay. And then with a forced smile, 'I believe this illustrates how thorough we try to be in the FBI.' Inside the office the effort at levity was ignored. The face framed in the barred window was a portrait of a prisoner whose stay of execution had been denied.

'Seriously, though,' continued Jay, stretching his neck in the tightening collar, 'there are a few additional notes I'd like to make from the records.'

An exasperated expulsion of breath and the woman walked toward the files on the other side of the room. Jay turned his attention to some trace of Cricket Kent. A pair of white gloves and a handbag resting on one of the desks were encouraging signs. Protruding from the handbag was the corner of an airline ticket. No wonder he had been unable to contact her. Maybe she had gone back to San Francisco. At any rate, she was here now, and that's what was important.

Yes, things were looking up. Not only in the Registrar's office but elsewhere. The Leopard Boulevard mob had eluded the state police road blocks, and things were back to normal in the office. Jay had been assigned little more than leads to check records since then. The White Sands incident had worried him considerably. Bob O'Rourke, investigating the explosion, had questioned him closely, but he had stuck to his story. Everything had been in order in the laboratory when he left. It was the absolute truth. Jay had offered little else. He had tried to contact Ted Summers to see if he had any information, but the man was in Europe. He had expected some word from Everett Reeves, but there had been nothing. Maybe they had written him off. It was all right with Jay. Time was passing and it was on his side. Each day brought him closer to the expiration date of his two-year commitment.

And right now he had a golden opportunity. After several weeks of trying, he had finally contacted Cricket. He was determined not to let the opportunity pass.

'Robert Denton!' The irritable tone of voice and the way the file was slapped on the window shelf served notice that this was the last time Mr Denton was to be produced.

'Thank you, Madam,' said Jay pleasantly, ignoring the woman's irascibility. He fumbled for his pen until the leathery custodian moved away, and then slowly began thumbing through the file, making sketches on a piece of paper as he did, pretending he was making notes. He had sketched a moderately good profile of a man in a cap when he felt a figure peering over his shoulder.

'Hi there.'

He turned quickly toward the greeting and looked into the remarkable eyes of Cricket Kent. The russet-tinged skin, the wide smile, the confident, upturned chin—at that instant Jay was certain that he had never seen anything quite so beautiful.

'Just uh . . . digging up a little more information,' said Jay.

'So you are,' came the prompt reply. 'Mr Denton again, huh? Drawing a picture of him this time, I see.' She leaned forward to inspect Jay's drawing more closely.

'Sorry,' said Jay uncomfortably, pushing the sheaf of paper into his folder. 'Confidential matter. You understand. Say, where have you been, anyway? I've been calling you.' He shot a glance through the window in the direction of Mrs Fryhoffer, who had moved into a farther office but who was

151

still painfully visible.

'Oh, I've been here and there.' Cricket smiled. 'I only work here a few days each month—just while they're closing their books. They get very busy then.'

'No wonder I couldn't get you. What time of the month are you here usually?'

'It varies, depending on the accounting office. Whenever they need girls to help out.'

'Cricket, it's a bit awkward talking under these conditions. I was just hoping that maybe you'd have dinner with me. Saturday night.'

Cricket hesitated briefly and then said, 'I'm very sorry, Jay. I can't Saturday night. I hope you won't think I'm avoiding you, but I'm afraid I'm going to be busy for the next few weeks. Could you call me sometime next month? I'd be delighted to have dinner then. I promise.'

The smile she added did little to cheer Jay. 'But I don't even know where to call you. Would you mind giving me your home phone number?'

'Why don't you just call me here, OK? Sometime next month. I'll look forward to it.'

'Of course,' said Jay dubiously. 'If that's the best we can do. But couldn't we—'

'Miss Kent.' It was the irritated voice of Mrs Fryhoffer. 'There's another long-distance call for you.'

'Here, I think Mrs Fryhoffer would prefer you left Mr Denton with us,' said Cricket. She withdrew the file from under Jay's arm, where inadvertently he had tucked it with his folder, and, with a final smile and wink, disappeared inside.

'The Goon Squad's coming in.'

'The Goon Squad?' said Jay.

'That's right. The inspection team.'

'Is that the purpose of the meeting?' asked Jay.

'That's right.'

Jay sat talking to Elmer Purdy, one of the older agents, in the front of the squad room. Elston Doolittle had called for a meeting that evening, and several of the agents had already assembled. Rumours of an impending inspection had been

152

prevalent for several weeks.

It was precisely 5:30 when 245 pounds of lumbering Doolittle appeared in the doorway of the squad room.

'OK, men,' said Joe Holloway, who had been watching for his boss, 'let's all grab a chair up here in front.'

Within a few seconds the agents had assembled quietly and Elston Doolittle, in a voice heavy with foreboding, was delivering his traditional preinspection talk.

'Most of you have probably heard rumours about the inspection by this time. Well, all indications point to a real tough one. But as I've always said, if you're doing things right, then you haven't a blessed thing in this world to worry about, right?' He paused and looked searchingly about the room for affirmation of his statement. Never was a man's gaze averted more unanimously as some two dozen eyes stayed riveted to the floor.

'Now, I'm particularly concerned about the Bureau cars. I want each man to report to the contract garage Saturday morning with a rag and a can of Simoniz. We must get our fleet in apple-pie order. Each one of you should go over your car with a fine-tooth comb. Get those cracker crumbs out of the glove compartments. Check the air in the tyres. Check the radios, and make sure there's a registration in each car.'

He paused to look down and to shuffle several index cards on which were written his preinspection notes. 'Now, start reviewing all your cases. Remember, a delinquent case is a dangerous case. It's bound to attract attention. Get something in the files to make them current, and save us all a lot of trouble.

'Now, on the subject of voluntary overtime. If your VOT is below the office average, then you know you're in trouble. You all know the Director's feelings on the subject. Every man must pull his oar and handle his fair share of the work load. And remember, if you're over the average, it's almost as bad because then they'll be asking questions about why you can't handle your work in the allotted time. The simple fact of the matter is that you should be *average*.

'Now, time in the office. You all know my feelings on the subject, I'm sure. I don't want to see anyone in the office

153

between 8:30 and 5:00 as long as the inspectors are in town.

'Insofar as informants are concerned, I expect each man to have at least one Potential Criminal Informant and one Potential Security Informant by the end of the month. The time for efficiency reports is rolling around and I can absolutely promise you that any agent who does not have at least one PCI will receive a minus in this classification on his efficiency report.

'The next subject is weight. It goes without saying that I expect to be looking at some pretty lean bodies around here within the next few weeks. Those of you you who are borderline, and that's most everybody, should stop eating right *now!* And don't rely on gimmicks to pull you through. This stuff about taking enemas and the like the night before a weight check just doesn't work!' Doolittle's eyes probed the group, pausing significantly here and there on a drooping jowl or lumpy midriff. 'There's absolutely no reason why we should be criticised for something like excess weight. I've been told a person can lose as much as 20 pounds in one week if need be. One good thing about dropping weight fast is that it leaves you looking haggard, and I think we'll all agree that it won't do any harm to look as though we're pretty tired, right? The main thing is we want to put our best foot forward during this difficult time.'

As the S-A-C continued with his talk the group of agents sat hushed and solemn, listening attentively.

' . . . so, men,' concluded Doolittle, 'remember, those of you who have been doing things the way they're supposed to be done don't have a single solitary thing to worry about. Just stay on your toes, stay out of the office, and let's get these guys out of Albuquerque as soon as possible!' With a slight wave he walked heavily from the room.

A buzz of conversation filled the room as Joe Holloway stood up and moved uneasily toward the spot vacated by his leader. He always was uncomfortable following Doolittle, sensing the letdown which came over the group and the anticlimactic nature of his presence. Also, the chief's talks usually precipitated a multitude of questions which the assistant had to field.

154

'Hey, Joe, what is this crap about Saturday morning with the Simoniz, anyway?'

'Yeah, what's coming off? We never had to buff the goddamn things before.' A chorus of voices filled the air and Jumping Joe held up his hands for quiet.

'Hey, settle down! Take it easy, will you?' Joe looked anxiously over his shoulder toward the door where Doolittle had made his exit. 'You all know what happened during the Detroit inspection last month. The cars got written up pretty bad. You know the Director really feels for the cars.'

As the grumbling subsided, Joe launched his own preinspection talk. 'Now, like the Chief says, if we've all been doing things the way we're supposed to, we got nothing to worry about, which means that we all got a helluva lot to worry about, right? You all know who heads up the administrative division, and he never gave anybody a break in his life. So don't look for any sympathy if they get you.

'First of all, above all else stay out of the office. If you've seen all the movies, then go to the library or someplace. There's a great little museum down near Roswell which just started up. It's a perfect spot to spend a few days for you guys who haven't been there. The main thing is stay the hell out of here. The time-in-the-office figures are the highest they've been since the Mad Bomber used to set off the blasts in the theatres up in New York City. The Director's ready to blow his cork and let's not be the ones who do it. But keep in mind wherever you go that there's been talk about some of Hawkins' men being out here. Don't ask me to elaborate on that because I can't. All I know is that this place seems to be popular with a lot of brass all of a sudden.

'Now, you guys with no PCIs, you better contact a few bellhops pretty quick. And forget about the graveyards. There isn't a tombstone in Albuquerque that isn't already in the informant files. Make sure your work boxes don't have any old files in them. As far as your delinquent cases are concerned, just send me anything. I'll post a routing slip if I have to. Don't use the coffee shop around the corner or the one near the garage. Don't be signing each other in and out to boost your overtime. Make it legit as possible during the

155

inspection. In this connection, make sure your wives know you won't be coming home until later so they won't be flooding the office with phone calls looking for you.

'If you got any old-dog cases, try to get them closed out before the inspection. If an inspector should stop you and ask you if you have any problems, obviously you don't. Make sure you stay in touch with the office. If you're not in contact by your car radio, then be sure you call in at least every two hours. Don't leave your desk unlocked. Make sure you're wearing your gun. Shine your badge...

'And remember, fellas, above all else, if they nail you, then go down like a man. Don't go grabbing at straws and pulling the rest of us down with you.'

> *... I like thee sweet fresh rain een my face,*
> *Diamonds on lace, no got, so what?*
> *For Row-bart Tay-lore I wheestle on stomp.*
> *That ees why thee lady ees a tromp!*

The voice of the Latin-American vocalist died away and the orchestra took over. It was a brisk rendition not without its nostalgic effect on the senior couples who were dancing, inspiring them to the nimble movements reminiscent of the thirties, when the song was first popularised.

Jay had finally made it to the Latin Club with Cricket Kent, and a more enjoyable evening he had never spent. Following dinner, they had sat at a table talking, having an occasional drink and watching the efforts of those dancing.

At that particular moment Jay was fascinated by the activity on the dance floor. The elderly couples had abandoned what restraint was practised earlier, and seemed carried away with the music. A short, squat gentleman, his face buried between two colossal breasts that surrounded his head like a pair of enormous earmuffs, kicked his way uninhibitedly through a Charleston. Another man looked uneasily about for his partner, who had been swallowed up by the whirling mass. A third gentleman, tall and slender, guiding an equally tall, slender lady, endeavoured to retain some dignity by gliding about on the periphery of the action,

156

unaware that they were on collision course with a quarter-ton team yawing badly in a determined Peabody.

'I'm beginning to understand why you're not interested in going out there,' said Jay. 'We might just as well try to dance on the Major Deegan.'

'Major Deegan?' said Cricket.

'That's an expressway back home.'

The evening was drawing to a close, and for Jay it had passed much too quickly. It had been a happy interlude in a strained day. Earlier he had finally been able to contact Ted Summers, who had just returned from Europe. Ted had told him that Mr Wallingford had had a slight heart attack and was at the Nayraville General Hospital, but was recovering nicely. Ted indicated he had not been back long enough to learn much, but already he knew that Mr Wallingford, and apparently Hawkins, had been distraught over the way Jay had handled his White Sands Assignment.

This bit of information, coupled with the knowledge that Hawkins' men were in the area, had resulted in a worrisome day. But in the past few hours with Cricket he had been able to forget his problems.

It was with some misgivings that he glanced at his watch and acknowledged Cricket's observation that it was getting late.

'I've had a marvellous time, Jay.'

'You know, you never did mention where you went the last few weeks, ' said Jay.

'I told you. I was tied up with some personal things.'

'But didn't you go away?' asked Jay curiously. He assumed she must have gone out of town after seeing the airline ticket in her bag.

She paused to draw on her cigarette. 'Why do you ask?' she said, adding a smile.

'Oh, I don't know. When you said you were going to be busy, I assumed you might be leaving town.'

'Yes, as a matter of fact, I did leave town. I went to visit a friend.' She looked away, implying that she was not interested in pursuing the subject further.

It had been an unusual exchange. Jay wondered what sort of friend. Was it a boy friend? The thought gave him an

157

unpleasant feeling in his stomach. With each succeeding minute he had become drawn more closely to the girl. Her laugh, the way she talked, her smile, even the briefest glance triggered an inner response. Yet in spite of the time he had spent with her, and as delightful a conversationalist as she was, he still knew little about her personal life. Most of his questions had been answered after a fashion, but the answers were uninformative. Beyond the fact that she was from San Francisco, that she lived in Dean Sutton Hall, which was the women's dormitory, and worked in the Registrar's office, he had been able to determine little else of significance. It was frustrating. There was a good deal more to the girl. Precisely what, he was not sure, but there seemed a sophistication, a suggestion of worldliness perhaps, which was difficult for him to understand.

'You're beginning to fade away on me again,' said Cricket, interrupting his thoughts.

'Fade?'

'Yes. Every now and then that faraway look comes into your eye, and I'm here all alone. You're really not very good for a girl's vanity, you know. What do you think about?'

'I was thinking about you,' said Jay, forthrightly. 'As a matter of fact, I was thinking about . . . *us*.'

Cricket gazed at him unfalteringly. Although there was a smile at the corner of her lips, she did not smile.

'You are suave, aren't you?' she said finally, smiling and breaking the silence. 'And when you say those things with that aristocratic accent a lady should watch out. I suspect a biography of Jay Von Vlack would reveal some broken hearts. Tell me, doesn't the FBI frown on ladykilling?'

'The FBI frowns on a lot of things,' said Jay. He paused and then added, 'If they frowned less and acted more constructively they'd be much better off.'

'Really? I don't think I understand.'

'It's too complicated a story right now, Cricket. Sometime I'll tell you about it, though. I'd like to tell someone.' He started to say something else, but at that moment the music reached a crescendo. He used the time to light their cigarettes. When the music stopped, he said, 'How would you like to go on a little picnic tomorrow afternoon? The weather is supposed to be nice. We could take a ride someplace.'

The girl leaned back in her chair and a curl of smoke from her cigarette rose slowly, veiling her face. It was moments such as this that he found puzzling—almost fascinating—about the girl. Whenever he asked a significant question, she would pause or, if she was smoking, maybe inhale her cigarette, and watch him closely as she considered her answer. It was a sophisticated mannerism, as though pondering the question were more important than giving the answer. It made him a trifle uneasy.

'Not tomorrow,' she said finally. 'Possibly next weekend.'

'Why, that sounds great,' said Jay. 'How about Sunday? Shall we make it definite?'

'Yes, it might be good to take a drive. Maybe we could go up into the mountains.' She leaned forward through the curtain of smoke and pressed out her cigarette. She ground the remnants into the tray with a thoroughness and finality that struck Jay as peculiar—sort of a determined mannerism that appeared out of character.

A couple brushed by and the candle on the table flickered, almost died, but then sprang back brightly, its light dancing in her blue eyes. The orchestra swung into the final refrains, and perspiring pates glistened candescently like mushroom caps in the rain as round figures bounded about the ballroom chasing the fading years. Suddenly a shriek as a large matron tripped and went reeling across the dance floor with devastating results—a corseted missile ignited by music and wine.

'This is the most logical way for them to come. They'll drive up that road and will have to leave their car down there. Now, Purdy and I will be in this gully, Lawson and Carpenter behind those rocks over there, and Joe, you and Von Vlack will be on that ledge. Now, remember, the main thing is to keep your fire directed toward that bank so that none of us get caught in the cross fire.'

With the determination of one preparing for a last stand, Elston Doolittle, wrapped in a bulletproof vest, was directing

159

preparations for the ambush of the Leopard Boulevard mob. That afternoon Kansas City informant T-1, of unknown reliability but who had furnished reliable information in the past, had advised that the gang planned a rendezvous at a small mountain lodge near Las Manos.

Doolittle, frantic with anticipation, had loaded his assistant, six agents, seven shotguns, two gas guns, a gas mask, a bullhorn, four pairs of leg irons and handcuffs, and several hundred rounds of ammunition into two Bureau cars and had roared away toward Las Manos for a showdown with the desperadoes. So enthusiastic had he been, in fact, that en route Elston's car had been stopped for speeding and he had been obliged to invite the local sheriff, Peeky Salazocka, along on the raid.

A contact with the proprietress of the lodge, a woman who operated the retreat with the help of two daughters, had revealed that she expected four men that evening. The woman had told the agents that the reservation had been taken by one of her daughters, but that both girls were in town and unavailable for any other information.

'Remember, men, these subjects are desperate. They're undoubtedly heavily armed and may be carrying machine guns. I'll make the initial statement over this bullhorn. Remember, Von Vlack, when I shout, "FBI!" you snap on those spotlights. After I identify us, it's up to them.'

In addition to his assignment with the lights, Jay had been designated to watch the sheriff to insure that the officer did not impede the apprehension through some error.

A number of horror stories were told which involved local law-enforcement officers who had exercised rash judgement during critical periods, and the Bureau no longer took any chances in such matters. An agent was assigned the job of diplomatically keeping the officer on the periphery of the action to prevent him from botching things up.

Jay was not happy with the assignment. He had to cover a few leads in Peeky's territory, and the brief association he had had with the officer had been very distasteful. Now as he sat down on the ground next to him, Peeky favoured him by elevating the pointed ends of his black moustache into a broad smile. The result would have given pause to the staunchest critic of fluoride. For what might have been a perfectly acceptable expanse of gum was marred by the remnants of four front teeth, three of which suggested the colouring, if not the alembic qualities, of chlorophyll. The fourth, a gold-capped incisor, glowed anomalously.

Nor did the rest of the officer's appearance show appreciable improvement. Wisps of thinning hair combed in ebony streaks across a leathery scalp served to do little more than exaggerate the oddity of Peeky's cranium, which rose pyramidally between two ham-sized ears. Two hooded black eyes peered from under a protruding brow, while a large lavender-coloured nose sagged down over the moustache in a way that suggested to Jay that both features might have been purchased as one unit from a novelty store. Completing the unfortunate portrait was a three-day stubble of beard bristling from a chin that disappeared Andy Gump-like into the neck.

But if the exterior of Peeky Salazocka was displeasing, it was, nevertheless, a vast improvement over what was inside. The Sheriff was notorious in the Southwest, having been named as the subject of several civil-rights violations, all of which had been carefully closed by the Bureau. The most recent charge had been one that he had placed a bicycle padlock around a prisoner's testicles in an effort to extort a confession.

Peeky's nickname had been derived from his penchant for rigid security matters involving female prisoners. Shower periods, personal searches and seizures (in the literal sense), physical examinations—indeed, he would undertake a vaginal inspection himself should the occasion warrant it—all found the constable in proximity, standing at the ready.

No, it was hardly the picture of a police officer. Rather than the figure in blue at the school crossing, Peeky projected more the image of what lurked around the corner with a bag of candy. But now, as he took his place beside him, Jay was more concerned about the impending showdown than his morals. Another unnerving possibility was that the stakeout might linger on into the weekend and cause him to miss his

161

date with Cricket.

'You fellows might just as well relax,' said Elston Doolittle. 'We've probably got a long wait ahead of us.'

As dusk settled the men took their designated positions and began the long watch. It was approaching 1:00 A.M. and a bright moon rode high over the ridge in the western sky. Peeky had been in a talkative mood, and in spite of Jay's efforts to ignore him, he continued with a nonstop monologue that covered everything from what was wrong with the government to the contributions he had made to the FBI over the years. It was on the latter subject that he was dwelling at that particular moment.

'In all my years I never give an FBI man a ticket for speeding. I bet I stop one a month. You guys are always rushing somewhere. Like today. The minute I seen those two cars with you guys, I said to myself, "There go some FBI men." Just a few days ago I nabbed another one. Fella named Hawkins.'

'Did you say Hawkins?' Jay felt his heart sink.

'That's right. Know him?'

'Was his name Avery Hawkins?'

'I don't know as I remember his first name. He was from Washington, D.C. Didn't look too much like an FBI agent. At least, none of the ones I ever seen. To be honest with you, he looked—'

Just then there was the roar of an approaching car speeding up the mountain road. The two men quickly rolled into prone positions. The metallic clicking of weapons came from around the clearing that formed the perimeter of fire as cartridges were lodged into chambers and the agents made ready for the ambush.

The car came to a stop in the area just beyond the clearing as had been expected, and sounds of people alighting from the vehicle could be heard.

'I only heard two car doors close,' whispered Joe Holloway.

'Maybe it's only a two-door sedan,' offered Jay.

'Either that or they're all getting out on the same side,' observed Doolittle dryly. 'Now keep quiet!'

The sounds of footsteps drew closer and finally figures

162

emerged over the ridge. The agents took careful aim, and Jay, after assuring himself that the Sheriff had his big .44 pointed in the right direction, lay down behind the lights and zeroed in on the spot where the subjects would appear in the clearing. Elston Doolittle carefully raised the bullhorn to his lips and—

'You go on ahead, honey.' The canorous tone of a feminine voice hung on the night air. 'I'm going to the bathroom here so I won't wake up Mom.' The girl, a slender young lady in her mid-twenties, proceeded to unbutton her shorts.

No one in the raiding party knew what to do, least of all Elston Doolittle. Never in his experience had he been confronted with such a situation so fraught with embarrassment to the Bureau, and not knowing what to do, he fell back on the old agent's code of 'First, do nothing'.

Peeky Salazocka was the only one sufficiently collected to react at all, and his voyeurism was not to be denied. 'Hey, Von Vlack,' he whispered, 'lights! Let's have the lights!'

Jay, waiting tensely behind the battery of lamps, uncertain what was happening, flipped the switch.

Following the pandemonium Elston Doolittle assembled his team around the Bureau cars below the stakeout area. Haggard from the tense wait and the loss of 18 pounds in preparation for the inspection, he gave his last order of the night. 'Fuck 'em! Let's go to bed. Holloway, go up there and tell those ladies to call the office if they hear anything.'

'Please, don't ever tell anyone you've been in a Bureau car.'

'Why not?' said Cricket.

'My boss has a great feeling for these cars. They're supposed to be used only on official business. He gets excited when he finds even cracker crumbs. That reminds me. Don't leave any earrings—anything like that.'

'I don't think that will happen.'

'I hope you didn't misunderstand. I just meant something might fall off—naturally.' God, the conversation was going nowhere. He'd be better off if he kept quiet.

In line with plans they had made at the Latin Club the previous week, Jay had picked up Cricket at Dean Sutton Hall, and they had started out for the Sandia Mountains.

163

Thoughts of spending the afternoon with the girl had been on Jay's mind all week. Now that he was actually with her in the car, he sensed a strained atmosphere. He had made several efforts at conversation, but Cricket seemed pensive and unresponsive.

They reached the outskirts of Albuquerque and started the steep climb into the Sandia Mountains. Clumps of cactus and sagebrush covering the desert soon gave way to heavier vegetation as they entered the mountain forest. It was a warm day and the breeze that came through the window, ruffling Jay's hair, felt good.

'Well, tell me more about yourself,' said Cricket, apparently disposed to talk. 'Why did you go to Princeton? Did your father go there?'

Jay considered the question. He was tempted to handle it in one of the ways he had in the past. Instead, he decided on a candid approach. Why not? He really thought he loved the girl. It would be best if she knew him for what he was. 'Yes, my father went to Princeton. One day, to be precise.' He proceeded to tell the girl about the day his father had picked him up in the limousine, sparing none of the details. Cricket was delighted with the story, and encouraged by her reaction, he went on to tell about his life at Lindenwald.

'Whatever motivated you to join the FBI?'

'Oh, many reasons. I'll tell you about it one of these days.'

They had driven for several miles, talking intermittently and enjoying the deep coolness of the forest, when suddenly Cricket put her hand on his arm and squeezed it gently. It was the slightest of gestures intended to draw attention to a side road up ahead, but to Jay it was an exciting contact.

'There's a little spot up here to the right which has a wonderful view,' said Cricket. 'I think it may be down that road.'

Jay slowed and turned off the main highway onto a narrow road that was little more than a path threading back through a dense area of forest. They had travelled about a hundred yards when they emerged into an open plateau that looked out over the plains. It was a breathtaking view. The city of Albuquerque stretched out in the distance—a lush green oasis in the parched, wrinkled landscape.

'Why it's fantastic,' said Jay. 'It's as though we were flying.'

'It is marvellous, isn't it?' said Cricket. 'Shall we get out?'

Jay followed the girl from the car several yards, where she stopped at the edge of a precipice.

'Be careful, that's a real drop down there,' said Jay, looking over the ledge uneasily. 'This is like being on a cloud.'

'I had the same feeling the first time I came here,' she said. She turned toward him and smiled, almost expectantly he thought.

Uncertainly at first, he took her hand. He noticed that it was perspiring, as though she were nervous. It gave him more confidence. When she responded with a gentle squeeze of his hand, it was all the assurance he needed. He put his other arm around her waist and drew her closely to him. At first she seemed tense, but then he felt her relax against him. It was an extraordinary feeling. Her body was strong and firm—almost powerful, he thought. He lifted her chin gently and gazed into the blue eyes. For a few fleeting seconds as they stood on the edge of the precipice, the mood of the lovely day seemed to reflect in the beautiful face, and Jay was thrilled as he had never been before.

'Do you have any idea how I feel about you, Cricket?'

'Please. Don't talk. Just kiss me.'

He placed his lips against hers and felt her mouth open slightly. Her tongue came against his and at the same time he felt her hips come against him provocatively. For one passionate instant he held her tightly, feeling her body go limp, submissively.

Suddenly a car burst through the foliage. Cricket pulled away from him abruptly. Within a few minutes the serenity of the moment had yielded to the ebullience of two teenage couples who bounced from the vehicle. Had Mrs Fryhoffer arrived it would not have been any different.

Jay grimaced as he replaced the phone on its cradle. He had just talked to Mrs Fryhoffer, and as usual it had been an unpleasant exchange. He had called the Registrar's office seven times already that week in an effort to reach Cricket

Kent, but to no avail. Also, Mrs Fryhoffer was becoming suspicious. He had exhausted every disguise possible in his voice short of using a dialect, but he sensed the woman was on to him. She could not be that rude to everyone who called.

Jay had stopped off at his apartment en route to the western part of the state, where he was going to cover a lead for Joe Holloway. He considered making another call to Dean Sutton Hall, but decided against it. He had already made several, but Miss Kent was out and they did not know when she would be back.

He had not seen Cricket since their date the previous Sunday. It had been a wonderful day, that is, until the other car had come. It had all ended there. She had been barely communicative during the trip home.

Jay glanced at his watch. Almost five o'clock. It was a long drive ahead. He picked up his revolver from the table, spun the cylinder to be sure the chambers were loaded, and then shoved it into the holster on his hip. He was pulling on his suit coat when the doorbell rang. It was the landlady.

'This special delivery letter came for you earlier, Mr Von Vlack.'

Jay thanked the woman and closed the door, noting the Nayraville postmark on the envelope. Quickly he opened the letter. It was from Ted Summers.

Dear Jay,

I have bad news. To begin with Mr Wallingford is still in the hospital, and a good deal of his authority has been delegated to Hawkins. Both of them are very unhappy with the way you handled your Albuquerque assignment. Hawkins claims you're responsible for the death of one of their key men and wants you out of the organisation. He's already instituted procedures to see that you're fired from the Bureau, feeling that if you're dismissed with prejudice it will throw the Bureau off inasmuch as they've been running routine checks on you as a result of your roommate's disappearance. If your departure is precipitated by the Bureau it's less likely to

166

prompt questions.

As far as I can determine, they're going to try to get you in some kind of a position where you embarrass the Bureau, probably through some illicit affair with a woman—'swallows' they call them. (You being single, they feel this is the easiest way.)

Supposedly Hawkins is going to have you transferred to Chicago within the next few weeks. They don't want to bring attention to any activities in New Mexico at this time and they feel they can handle your case with a good deal more anonymity in Chicago.

I may be wrong, Jay, and I certainly hope I am, but somehow this all has a familiar ring to it. A similar thing happened a couple of years ago when Hawkins decided that one of our men in a satellite country was a security liability, and he had him dismissed with *extreme* prejudice. I'm just afraid that he may feel that once he has you out of the Bureau he can liquidate you without its attracting too much attention.

My suggestion is that you exercise great caution to see that you don't get into any situation where they can fire you—at least until Mr Wallingford gets out of the hospital and regains control. I don't think Hawkins will try any wet stuff while you're still in the Bureau. Tucker's disappearance has heated things up enough.

At any rate, your case apparently is high priority with Hawkins, and the assignment has been given to one of their top agents, an individual operating under the code name 'Peachy' who supposedly has you under surveillance at this time.

Sorry I don't have better news. Again, I trust you will destroy this after reading.

Kindest regards,
Ted

Jay read the letter several times, and each time it plunged him deeper into despair. Finally he walked to the sink and lit a match to the letter. He watched the edges slowly blacken, curl, and disintegrate. Turning on the water he flushed the

167

remnants down the disposal and then left the apartment. Within a few minutes he was in the Bureau car leaving the outskirts of Albuquerque. Off to the north he saw the Sandia Mountains, a bulky dark blue mass in the fading sky.

As he drove across the desert, his sense of loneliness and despair intensified. Before him through the windshield the golden hues of twilight stretched brilliantly across the western sky, mellowing and finally fading into the cool tones of approaching dusk. The desert was slowly transformed into a grey and hostile place as objects friendly by day took on strange cloaks in the gloom. Cactus plants and clumps of sagebrush became indistinguishable from other crouching forms, and to the lonely figure in the Bureau car, the only familiar features in an otherwise desolate landscape were the telephone poles that came and went rhythmically through the dark.

There is not the marked contrast between seasons in the Southwest that one finds in other regions. Summer fades into fall, fall quietly slips into winter. The changes are almost imperceptible. That is, all but spring. Springtime, no matter the place, has its distinctive qualities, and New Mexico is no exception. It is not so visual there, but when it comes, it does so with most of the exhilarating effect it has in other areas.

It had come this particular night. It had settled over the university campus in the form of a lovely evening, wonderfully balmy and fragrant. It was about 7:30 and shadows had spilled into darkness. Although stars had not yet appeared, a slim edge of the lunar sphere already hung low on the mesa.

Such a nightfall should have proved stimulating, indeed, to a young man in love, but as he stepped from his car in the parking lot and strode across the lawn toward Sutton Hall, Jay could see few encouraging signs in his future.

It had been almost a year since the disappearance of Harvey Tucker. A year—exclusive of the White Sands incident—remarkably free of danger and intrigue in view of its portentous beginning. Before Ted Summers' warning Jay had begun to take cautious comfort from the thought that possibly his role as a double agent might have ceased, that the forces that directed his espionage activities had elected to write him off, and that conceivably he was to be permitted to fade away as an old spy whose position had been rendered obsolete.

But in spite of the solace derived from such thoughts, deep inside he knew that never would he be permitted such a peaceful severance from his contract. With Ted Summers' letter the smouldering anxieties had been rekindled, and he had spent the following week trying to adjust to the realisation that he could well be a target for liquidation.

He had become hypersensitive, suspecting virtually everyone, reading nonexistent signs into all kinds of situations. Every person with whom he came in contact was a potential enemy. Even Cricket was not above scrutiny. Not that he really suspected her in this vein. After all, he had stumbled on her by accident. Still, they knew he was doing record checks and would be at the Registrar's office. She could have been planted there. The lovely, beautiful Cricket? God, it was impossible.

Things had begun to happen. Just that morning he had received word of his transfer to Chicago. An assignment to the volatile city, where the lingering odour of dead flesh on the night air could not always be ascribed with certainty to the Southside stockyards, hardly evoked confidence in one marked for death.

But such gloomy reflections were inconsistent with the beating of a romantic heart, and as he drew close to the dormitory Jay began to experience a slight, tremulous sensation, the same anticipative thrill he always felt when he was about to see Cricket Kent.

As he approached Sutton Hall distant sounds of conversation interspersed with laughter drifted from the rows of lighted windows in the dormitory. It was the time of day when young ladies applied finical touches in preparation for their dates, while less attractive roommates feigned preoccupation with worthier interests. Jay wondered idly if Cricket's voice was among the bantering that floated from the open windows. The possibility that she was still gone or,

169

worse still, was preparing for a date, again crossed his mind as it had several times during the trip over.

He had spent the previous week at Santa Fe helping out the Resident Agent and had returned only a few hours previously. He had called Sutton Hall, but the lines were busy as they usually were on Saturday evenings. After several unsuccessful attempts he had elected to come unannounced.

Inside the door of the main entrance of the dormitory a thin, sallow-faced girl, sitting behind a switchboard, was handling telephone calls and greeting visitors. The churlish look on her plain face and the abruptness with which she pulled and plugged the spaghetti-like cords clearly demonstrated a disaffection for the role. But there was little in her manner or appearance to suggest that the switchboard would have much competition for her attention.

'Good evening,' ventured Jay, when a lull occurred in the activities. 'Is Miss Kent at home, please?'

'*Miss* Kent! Hah!' The girl plugged in one of the cords. 'Hello, Mrs Grant? There's a man here asking for that Kent person.'

Jay had little time to wonder what was transpiring before a grey-haired woman appeared in the door behind the switchboard. 'You were looking for Miss Kent?' she inquired, focusing a cool look at Jay.

'Ah . . . yes m'am,' responded Jay uneasily. 'I uh . . . I had a date with Miss Kent tonight.'

'Date indeed?' retorted the woman. 'I don't know who you are, young man, but I suggest if you want any further information about *Miss* Kent, you contact the local authorities. We've furnished everything we know about that person to the police. *Miss* Kent left here quite abruptly, and understandably so, since one of the girls found out quite by accident that *Miss* Kent was in reality *Mister* Kent!'

Outside the dormitory a soft breeze rustled the bushes nestling against the adobe walls of Sutton Hall. As he walked across the lawn toward the parking lot, sounds of light, young laughter sprinkled from the darkness behind him. Off to his left beyond the spire of the university chapel sailed a banana moon, a thin-edged crescent snipped out of the black sky—a

170

killer's moon.

'I don't think it's good to talk on the phone like this, Jay.' Ted Summers' voice was concerned. 'From what the papers say, the FBI has more taps than Anheuser-Busch. Maybe your line is—'

'I'm talking from a pay phone,' interrupted Jay. 'Besides, I just don't care that much anymore. I've even considered going to the Bureau and telling them what I know. At least I'd have some protection.'

'C'mon now, Jay. Settle down. You know you don't mean that. Our whole future is tied in with Wallingford. Things are a little tough right now, but it will work out. Wallingford has been pretty good to you all these years. And let's face it, you've got every reason to think it might be even better in the future. Besides, that's dangerous talk.'

'No more dangerous than my present situation. Just consider what's happened these last few weeks.'

'But how can you be sure it was Peachy? You could be jumping to conclusions. It could have been any transvestite. From what I hear they're all over the place. Some of these chaps look more like girls than girls do. Maybe one got into the—'

'She was no transvestite,' interrupted Jay irritably. 'Things have been damn confusing lately, but I still know a girl when I see one.'

'Well, you're the one who said that they—'

'I know it. But it must have been some mistake. Maybe she was dressed as a man or something. After all, she's an espionage agent. It could be that she was utilising a disguise and someone saw her.'

There was a long pause, and then Ted said, 'I still don't think it was Peachy. It just doesn't sound like the way they operate. You say she was working at a university?'

'That's right. But it was just a couple of days each month. They knew I would be checking records there and would have to meet her. No, I'm certain it was Peachy. For all I know she may have been planning on killing me. I remember one afternoon standing on a ledge with her. She easily could have

171

pushed me off.'

'I still think you're jumping to conclusions. Hawkins wouldn't permit it. Not while you're still in the Bureau. Besides, after thinking about it I'm beginning to doubt if Hawkins would ever try to liquidate you. I know what I said in the letter, but you are pretty close to Mr Wallingford and I doubt if Hawkins—'

'Yes, but remember, you said that this Hawkins is unpredictable—that he had an agent dismissed with extreme prejudice without even checking with Mr Wallingford. And look what happened to Harvey Tucker.'

There was another long pause as Ted Summers considered the truth in the statements.

'No, sir. I'm disgusted with the whole sordid business,' continued Jay. 'Tell Mr Wallingford I want to get out of this mess as soon as possible—that I want to resign.'

'Jay, I'll tell him whatever you want, but I think you're making a mistake. If Hawkins does plan to get rid of you you'll be playing right into his hands. Don't you see? Besides, in another few weeks Wallingford will be back in control of things. And I am in a pretty good position to hear what's going on. He relies on me quite a bit right now.'

Another long pause followed and Ted said, 'Are you still there, Jay?'

'Yes,' came Jay's voice in a disgruntled tone.

'Where are you staying if I need to call you?'

'I'm at the Hilton in Chicago,' said Jay. 'I just got here. I don't know how long I'll be in this hotel, but I'll keep you advised.'

'All right, I'll be in touch with you in a few days. In the meantime, try to relax,' said Ted. 'Also—and I guess it's unnecessary to say this—but if I were you, I'd avoid anything that even remotely resembles a swallow.'

Fate had dealt unkindly with Henry O'Connor. It had bestowed on him those qualities of piety, effeminacy, and fastidiousness which, together with a rigid abstemiousness, would have enabled him to become an ideal mother superior, but then had provided him with the wrong gender. Instead, he

172

had ended up as Special Agent in Charge of Chicago FBI Office.

Henry had started his Bureau career some 30-odd years before as a stenographer, and in spite of the intervening years, in which he had served in increasingly important positions, there was still about him the aura of the steno pool. Maybe it was the prim way he seemed to sit on the edge of his chair, or possibly the manner in which he crossed his legs, but whatever, it evoked the same concern among the agents—'Henry? Hmmmm. . .'

Jay had heard little about O'Connor before arriving in Chicago. One of the agents who had known him in New York had provided a terse description: 'If you're a Roman, you don't drink or fool around with the women, and you play bridge, then you'll make it with O'Connor.'

But regardless of the agents' opinions, O'Connor had managed to endure in the system, and if there was one individual quality that could be singled out as the reason, it would have to be his unwavering obedience to the Bureau. When the Director said 'Jump,' Henry soared.

Jay arrived in Chicago just one month to the day after Henry had received a letter from the Director advising that he was overweight. It was a regrettable incident since, had the weight check come just three weeks later, it would have been well into the Lenten season, which was the time when Henry had found it most propitious to undertake his annual diet. But as luck would have it, he had been nailed and the results had been predictable. Instead of dropping the five pounds directed in the letter, Henry had gone overboard. Now, sitting across the room from Jay was a cadaverous figure in ill-fitting clothes, whose face sagged in baggy folds like a worn, deflated football.

O'Connor's disposition—testy even on a full stomach— had deteriorated with the fast.

'As you may or may not have heard, Mr Von Vlack, we run a strict organisation here in Chicago, in strict compliance with Bureau rules and regulations. I like to have that thoroughly understood by the new arrivals. Do we understand each other?'

173

Jay nodded and shifted slightly in his chair.

'Now, the Chicago office is a large one,' continued O'Connor, his long, slender fingers delicately toying with a pencil, 'and we specialise here a good deal more than they do in Albuquerque. By that I mean we have squads which handle only certain types of cases. That does not mean that you will not handle a variety of cases as you go along. As you know, our Director insists that each agent remain familiar with *all* phases of the Bureau work.

'Now, we have had a very successful year here thus far. In fact, next week I shall go to Washington to report personally to our Director on our accomplishments. I am happy that I shall be able to report substantial progress in virtually all areas over last year. Fines and recoveries are up 12.6 per cent, convictions show a substantial increase of 17.9 per cent...'

O'Connor proceeded to outline the office statistics for the first half of the fiscal year. It seemed an odd subject of conversation with a new agent until Jay suddenly realised that Henry O'Connor was practising for his presentation in Washington.

Following the recap of the statistics, the S-A-C paused, sniffed several times, squeezed the tip of his nose, and picked up a paper from his desk. 'Now, Mr Von Vlack, to start off you will be assigned to the espionage squad. Mr Carl Horning is the supervisor of this squad and his office is in the squad room right down the hall. We're conducting a goodly number of surveillances these days, and you'll find the cases assigned to you deal pretty much with this type of Bureau work. Now, I touched on the subject of personal conduct before, but I want to reemphasise some of the Bureau rules pertaining to personal conduct. In particular I want to stress that Chicago has numerous temptations for a young man. Women, drinking—you know what I am alluding to, Mr Von Vlack?'

'Yes, yes, of course,' responded Jay, shifting again. Indeed, he knew. In fact, if things went the way he intended, his social life would be no more exciting than that of a Trappist monk.

'The main thing is that you understand my personal feelings on the subject,' continued O'Connor. 'Drinking I have found in particular leads to compromising situations. Frankly, if it

174

were up to me, I should not permit agents to drink at any time. We are, after all, on call 24 hours a day, and one never knows when one might be required to perform one's duty. In fact, it's the so-called off-duty hours when things happen, and an agent's reactions spell the difference between success and failure. It's been proven, you know, that just one drink—one drink, mind you—can slow the reactions of a person immeasurably, and you know what that could mean, Mr Von Vlack.'

Jay pursed his lips and nodded solemnly.

'Generally when an agent becomes involved in some personal misconduct it's because of alcohol—*or a woman*. Do you drink, Mr Von Vlack?'

'No, sir,' said Jay emphatically. 'Not any more.'

'That's good! Ah . . . now . . .' Henry O'Connor sniffed a few times, picked up the pencil, put it down, pinched the end of his long nose between his thumb and forefinger, lifted each side of his buttocks and then said, 'Very good. Well, now, I want to take this occasion to wish you every success here in our office. May your stay with us be a long and rewarding one.'

O'Connor rose and extended a slender hand. 'My door there is always open and you should feel free to visit me anytime. Of course, if you feel there is something concerning our office—or anything, for that matter—that I should be informed of *personally*, then you may rest assured it will be kept *absolutely* confidential. Do you read me, Mr Von Vlack?'

'Yes, sir, I certainly do,' said Jay. As he shook the hand and acknowledged the thin smile, he thought of the plan to discredit him. If Hawkins wanted an assistant axe man for the job, then he had made the perfect selection in the person of Henry O'Connor.

In addition to the special agent in charge and the assistant special agent in charge, the Chicago office was administered by three supervisors who headed up the espionage and criminal squads. The supervisor's position was a thankless one, caught between the fire from the Bureau and the disdain

175

of the agents. The pressure was unrelenting and all three suffered from a variety of blinks, tics, and twitches. Among the agents they were known as Winkin', Blinkin', and Nod.

It was the offices of these supervisors for which Jay was headed as he left O'Connor. The first individual he saw as he entered the squad room was an older agent who sat scowling at his desk, loading a pistol.

'Could you please tell me where I can find Mr Carl Horning?' asked Jay.

'Yeah,' said the agent curtly, without looking up. 'He's up there in Shaker Heights.' The man gave a slight motion of his head toward the offices at the front of the room.

Carl Horning was reviewing a file as Jay entered his office. The supervisor was one of those rare personalities who were able to get along with both the agents and the Bureau. His manner was casual and easygoing, and if it were not for the compulsive winking of his eye, which contorted the right side of his face about every 30 seconds, he would have seemed a relaxed individual.

'Welcome aboard, Jay,' said the supervisor, getting quickly to his feet and shaking hands enthusiastically. 'Glad to have you with us. I'll get Ken Hastings in here. He's single, too. He should be able to help you out with a spot to live.'

Ken Hastings was a tall, angular individual of about Jay's age, with dark hair, rather prominent features, and a frown that looked as though it came naturally with this personality.

He shook Jay's hand disinterestedly, and after a brief exchange with the supervisor, he had Jay follow him. Soon they were seated in a Bureau car heading for the Southside.

'You can hole up with me a few days till you get something,' said Ken, apparently satisfied that the new agent would not make an objectionable temporary roommate. 'Charlie Bryant, the guy who lives with me, is out of town.'

'That's very generous of you, but actually I'd just as soon get a room in some hotel and not bother—'

'It's no bother. A hotel would cost you an arm and a leg in this town. As long as Charlie's gone, somebody might just as well use his pad.'

Ken eased the car out into the traffic on LaSalle Street.

Slouching back in his seat, he turned his body so that his left foot was on the accelerator and his right extended over to Jay's side of the car. His right arm hung over the back of the seat while he piloted the vehicle with one forefinger curled about the spoke in the steering wheel. On his face was an expression of infinite boredom.

'It sounds as though you people are pretty busy,' observed Jay, finding the silence uncomfortable.

'One day busy, the next nothing. This job is strictly a feast or famine. Last week I had a lead on a satellite agent. Important case. The subject was in town for the day and was going to make a contact. I couldn't get even one agent to help me. Had to watch him myself. This week we've been bumping into each other in the theatres looking for something to do. About three months ago we were short and tried to pull a bag job with only one guy on the subject and he ends up losing him. So what happens? We're in the room snapping some pictures and who bounces in but the subject.'

'What did you do?'

'What could we do? We belted him over the head and made it look like a burglary.'

'Did the Bureau hear about it?'

'Nope. They won't know it till one of our guys behind the Curtain gets belted. Everything's an eye for an eye. When we blow one of their cases over here, they blow one of ours over there. It's kind of crazy, you know?'

Ken eased the Bureau car out into the traffic on the South Shore Drive and picked up speed. 'Yeah, the whole thing gets a little monotonous after a while. I hope you like to walk because you'll be doing a lot of it on these surveillances. Man, how these guys love to walk.'

'Does the Bureau get excited when you lose a subject?'

'All depends,' replied Ken, effectively cutting off a sedan that had been vying with the Bureau car for a place in the centre lane. 'If it's an important subject and the Director says not to lose him, then you take your Bureau career in your hands if you do. A few months back three of us got letters of censure for losing a diplomat. They told us not to get made and not to lose the guy. Now, you tell me how the hell you can watch a KGB agent who's tail-conscious, with three guys, and not get made and not lose him. If you try to be discreet and play it loose, then you take your chances on losing him. It's that simple. Not me anymore, though. No, siree. They say don't lose him, then I sit on him—close as me to you.'

Jay was about to speak when Ken said, 'Jesus, I almost went by our stop. You shouldn't get me talking like that.' With the facility of a race driver making a pit stop, he brought the car through two lanes of traffic onto the exit ramp. Within a few minutes they were pulling into a circular drive that serviced the entrance to a modern-looking building. The style of the building seemed incongruous against the background of the older, conventional buildings that surrounded it. Above the main entrance in large, racy letters appeared the name, 'FLAMINGO'.

From the moment he first laid eyes on it Jay could sense that the Flamingo was not a quiet place. Rather, there was a nightclub atmosphere about it that suggested that everything was set to start swinging, but it was still a bit early for the action to begin.

'How do you like it?' asked Ken as they lurched to a stop under a rococo canopy that arched its way out from the front door.

'Very impressive,' murmured Jay.

'Yeah, it's got real class,' allowed Ken. 'She's filled with stews and airline pilots. You can have one helluva ball, but you've got to watch it a little. A few guys have gotten burned in here pretty bad, you know what I mean?'

Jay nodded. He could guess what the agent meant and preferred to take a measure of comfort out of not learning the details.

Ken's quarters were lavish. A gold rug with heavy pile carpeted a large foyer that opened into a spacious sunken living room. A dining room, kitchen, two good-sized bedrooms, and a bath completed the arrangement. The decoration reflected a heavy masculine hand, but was impressive.

'Very nice,' said Jay. He set down his bag inside the door.

'Yeah, it's not bad,' agreed Ken. 'It's a little steep, but

178

Charlie and I would rather go the extra bills and have a classy place.'

'This is Charlie's pad in here. Just hang your gear in the closet there. What time you got?'

'Almost 3:30,' answered Jay, carrying his bag into the bedroom.

'It's a little early,' said Ken, moving toward the telephone in the foyer, 'but I'll call a few stews, and see what I can get started. I don't promise to get you laid the first night, but I sure as hell can get things moving in that direction.'

'Tonight?' exclaimed Jay. On the way down he had decided to spend the night with Ken, but to find something else for himself the first thing the following day. 'Actually, that's not necessary. I appreciate the gesture, but I really should—'

'No trouble,' interrupted Ken. 'Like Carl says, we got to get you off on the right foot. Besides, we haven't had a blast in here since Charlie's going-away party.'

Jay knew it was useless. He heard Ken dialling a number and then, 'Hello, who's this? . . . Oh, hi! This is Ken. Say, get hold of Jane, Gail, and a few others and come on up tonight. . . That's right. . . Fine. . . That's good. . . Great! Bring 'em along. I got a new guy here I want to welcome into town. . . How the hell should I know? She left here four days ago. . . Drunk, what else! . . . OK, see you tonight.'

A few seconds later Ken entered the bedroom, pulling on his suit coat. 'Listen, I've got a couple of personal things to handle. Why don't you stick around and finish unpacking? I'll sign you out when I dump the Bureau car. The booze is in that cabinet over there.' Without waiting for an answer the host breezed from the room.

Bureau Belly was an unpleasant ailment afflicting its victim with a wide range of discomfort. On occasion it was nothing more than a mildly uncomfortable gnawing sensation, like a chipmunk shucking a few hickory nuts in the upper abdomen. On the other hand, it could be a searing paroxysm that raged in the pit of the stomach with the intensity of a Bunsen burner. In its formative stages, often as not, it manifested itself in a hollow, empty feeling and generally was easily appeased.

179

Soda crackers and a glass of milk was the usual remedy prescribed by the agents.

It was just such a snack that Jay was having as he sat in an easy chair before the television set, when he was startled by the telephone. He glanced at his watch. It was almost eleven o'clock. Maybe he had been too optimistic. He had changed into his pyjamas a short time previously, thinking that the party had been cancelled. He picked up the phone.

'Oh - we're - on - our - way,' came a chorus of female voices singing in jumbled unison. 'Yes - we're - on - our - way, Oh - we're - on - our - way. . .' There was a click as the line was cut off at the other end.

'Oh, no.' Jay replaced the phone. He had started toward the bedroom, pulling off his pyjama top, when the doorbell sounded. Grabbing his robe, he headed back toward the foyer. He opened the door a crack and said, 'I'm sorry, but Ken—'

He had no chance to finish as a gust of airline stewardesses swept past him into the room.

'Hi!' 'Hello there.' 'Where's Ken?' 'Yeah, where's lover boy?'

Jay stood holding the door as the group dissolved into mounds of jackets, raincoats, hats, pocketbooks, shoes, and other paraphernalia about the living room. 'Jill, make me a Scotch—just a little water,' said one, walking into the bathroom.

Another disappeared into Jay's bedroom, closing the door with the comment, 'Don't forget to have Andy call me when he gets here. I've got to be back at the field by 2:30.'

Sounds of clinking glasses emanated from the kitchen, and from somewhere in the far corners of the apartment floated music from a hi-fi, as Ken Hastings' guests made themselves at home.

Jay was dismayed and uncertain what to do. He could not order them to leave. He was only a guest himself.

'You must be a new roommate,' observed a contralto voice, not without an accusatory note.

Jay looked toward the sofa, where a pair of iron-black eyes peered from a cloud of freshly exhaled smoke.

180

'Well, just temporarily,' replied Jay. He cleared his throat and averted his eyes. For one frantic instant it occurred to him that maybe Ken was sharing the apartment with others . . . besides Charlie. 'Do, uh, do you live in this building?'

Another expulsion of smoke blossomed above the sofa. 'Sometimes.'

Jay began pondering the vulnerable position in which he had been placed. Here he was in a harem-like situation. Was it a Hawkins trap? A scheme carefully arranged to place him in a position where he would embarrass the Bureau? It seemed unlikely. But he should get out of there. But where? It was eleven o'clock! Stymied, he slumped into a chair near the sofa.

'Why so happy?' asked the husky voice.

Jay regarded the form reclining next to him. She was an attractive, dark-complexioned girl, but the cool, calculating manner and flint like eyes suggested an adventurous spirit he found disquieting. He had to get out of there somehow.

'I'm afraid I had forgotten about the party.' He avoided the eyes. 'I hope you'll forgive my appearance. I—'

'Party? What party?'

'The party here. Didn't Ken talk to you this afternoon about a little get-together?'

'He didn't talk to us. I was in Puerto Rico this afternoon. We just came from the field. Donna, did Ken talk to you about a party tonight?'

'Not to me,' replied a tall, sandy-haired girl who was busy opening cupboards in the liquor cabinet. 'I hope it isn't here. I've got to get some sleep.'

Jay looked from the girl back to the brunette on the sofa and was about to speak when a loud thumping came from the door. 'This must be Ken's friends now,' he said, standing up, an annoyed expression fixed firmly on his face.

'Couldn't be Ken's friends,' snorted the girl. 'They'd have their own key.'

This time there were over half a dozen people in the hall. Several girls, accompanied by a few men in airline uniforms, filed past Jay into the apartment. They accorded him little more attention than a theatre attendant who had just

181

unhitched the velvet rope. One of the girls near the end of the line handed him a partially filled bottle of bourbon with the comment, 'It's all we had.'

He had started to close the door when a chorus of muffled voices seemed to rise out of the floor in the hallway. 'Oh - we're - on - our way. . .' Leaving the door ajar, he moved to a corner of the living room, where he slumped into a large chair.

He watched as a stream of people entered and began to eddy between the living room, dining room, kitchen and bath. The preponderance of the activity seemed confined to the centre of the living room where a heavy veil of smoke began to collect above the mingling forms. The pungent odour of marijuana wafted across the room. Someone turned up the volume of music to its maximum, and Jay felt the floor throbbing beneath his feet.

Despite Jay's half-conscious efforts to ignore it, the droning sound persisted, finally awakening him. The noise was a deep, contented snore emerging from the prone figure of a beefy-looking airline pilot who was sprawled on the floor next to Jay's chair. With his cap turned sideways and the nose and mouth sucking in huge quantities of air, the pilot reminded Jay of a submariner expiring for want of oxygen.

Jay looked at his watch. It was almost 8:30 and bleak rays of light already were streaming through the half-opened venetian blinds that covered the windows overlooking Lake Michigan. Slowly he stretched his cramped muscles and rose unsteadily to his feet. Endeavouring to move his eyes with a minimum movement of his head, he surveyed the apartment. Several partly uniformed bodies of pilots and stewardesses were lying about in various positions. Beer bottles, ashtrays, glasses, dirty dishes, and empty liquor bottles were strewn about the floor. Overturned furniture and lamps in the foyer indicated that a battle of some proportions had taken place near the door. There wasn't a movement in the apartment, save for a pair of ladies panties dangling from the chandelier in the foyer, fluttering slightly in the light breeze that came through the partly open transom above the door.

Carefully Jay picked his way around the prostrate forms

toward the bathroom, looking from one unfamiliar face to the next for some sign of Ken Hastings. Nowhere was the host. The responsibility for the condition of the apartment and its recumbent occupants began to weigh heavily on his mind. There was only one thing to do. He would gather his belongings and push the Down button on the elevator. But first of all, a long, cold drink of water.

He walked toward the bathroom, wondering how he had permitted himself to get so drunk. When he stepped over a broken picture frame into the bathroom, he saw Ken. He was sprawled face down in the bathtub, his body bent bowlike. One arm dangled over the side of the tub as though the man might have made one half-hearted effort to change his position before passing out. He was soaking wet. Apparently someone had pushed him into the tub and turned on the shower. But in spite of his drenched condition and awkward position, he was enjoying the sleep of a babe.

Jay considered trying to wake the man, but decided against it. Better to stay with plan one. He walked over to the washbasin and turned on the cold water. He had started to open the medicine cabinet to look for some aspirin when he saw his reflection in the mirror. Various shades of lipstick had enlarged his mouth three times its natural size, but a good-sized bump under his left eye indicated that all of the sentiments had not been so tender. He had started a delicate examination of the wound when the telephone rang. He hesitated briefly and then made his way toward the foyer.

'Hello.'

'Hello, Ken?'

'I'm afraid Ken can't make it to the phone right now,' said Jay. 'He's a bit, ah . . . indisposed.'

'Well, you better dispose him right away. This is his office calling and it's damned important.'

'I see,' said Jay, hesitating briefly. 'Well, this is Jay Von Vlack . . . ah . . . sort of a *temporary* roommate. I'm an agent. Just got transferred here from Albuquerque. Can I give him a message? Or I could have him call you when—'

'Von Vlack, this is Barney Deneen. I'm the night supervisor. About 20 minutes ago the manager of the

183

Flamingo called in and complained about you guys. He said you been taking the place apart down there raising hell all night. I tried to cover, but O'Connor came in during the call and talked to the guy. O'Connor's on his way down there now.'

'Oh no!'

'Oh yes! You better shape things up down there. You met O'Connor yet?'

'I've met him.'

'Then you know what I mean. Don't forget, you never got this call.'

'Right. How long ago did he leave?'

'About 15 minutes ago. I would've called sooner but a call came in from the Bureau just as he was leaving, and I couldn't shake them till just now. He should be there any second. He probably went down with the siren wide open.'

'OK, thanks,' Jay rang off abruptly.

He raced back to the bathroom. 'Ken! Wake up, Ken! O'Connor's coming to the apartment!' He shook the agent by the shoulder and arm, but the only response was a slight wheezing. 'Ken, for God's sake, wake up!' He slapped the man on the cheeks. Finally he reached up and turned the faucet marked, 'cold'. A stream of water shot down on the prostrate form.

'Son of a bitch!' The screech Ken emitted reverberated through the building and Jay hastily turned off the water.

'What the hell's going on in there?' exclaimed a gruff, sleepy voice from the living room.

Ken Hastings shifted slightly, licked the water from his lips, and looked as though he were becoming comfortable again.

'Ken, don't you understand? O'Connor's on his way here. O'Connor! You know, your boss! The guy who frowns on drinking—and girls!' As he tried to pull the angular body from the tub, Ken opened his eyes. One look at the torpid expression and Jay knew it was hopeless. The man was in a state of drunkenness that probably would last most of the day.

'Are-you-a-vishun-or-a-real-pershun?' slurred Ken, rolling his head and trying to focus on Jay. 'If-you're-real-go-take-a-flying-fuck-at-a-rolling-doughnut.' After this bit of

184

advice, Ken's head dropped onto his chest, and he was back asleep.

Jay was considering the matter when the doorbell sounded—two short businesslike buzzes. He dropped Ken back in the tub. Quickly he ducked out of the bathroom and raced toward his bedroom. At least he had to get out of his pyjamas and into some clothes.

The scene that greeted him as he opened the bedroom door was like something from a canvas at the Metropolitan. The girl who had been awaiting Andy to take her to the airfield was still there, lying face down on the bed. Andy, wherever he was, apparently had come and taken everything to the field but the stewardess, for she was stark naked.

This was it, then, thought Jay. This was the way they were going to frame him. He moved quickly to the window looking for a fire escape. Nothing for 12 floors.

From the foyer came the doorbell again, this time three long impatient buzzes. 'OK, OK!' shouted a feminine voice. There was the sound of someone moving toward the door. Jay shot from the room just in time to see a stewardess wearing a brassiere and skirt heading toward the foyer. It was the dark, hard-looking girl whom he had met the previous night.

'No! No! God, no!' called Jay in a loud whisper. Too late. the girl opened the door. Jay started back into the bedroom, took one look at the nude figure on the bed, and ducked back down the hall into Ken's bedroom. From a crack in the door he saw Henry O'Connor standing rigidly at attention beneath the panties fluttering from the chandelier.

'Young lady, may I ask where Mr Hastings is?' said O'Connor, glancing from the panties to the girl and back to the panties.

'The last time I saw him he was passed out in the bathtub,' said the girl indifferently, walking back into the living room.

O'Connor took one look at the living room and gasped, 'Good Heavens!' He started with swift strides toward the rear of the apartment, where the bedrooms and bath were located.

Jay held his breath as O'Connor paused before the door of the other bedroom, and then grimaced as he pushed open the door.

185

'Jesus, Mary, and Joseph!' exclaimed Henry O'Connor, quickly pulling the door closed. His next stop was the bath. 'My God! And you're supposed to be a special agent of the FBI!'

Jay listened with bated breath as Ken Hastings fashioned his answer. 'Are-you-real-or-are-you-a-vishun? If-you're -real-go-take—'

Jay closed the door in despair.

'Hello, Jay. This will have to be quick. I'm calling from the hospital, and I have to go right back upstairs. One of our agents, a man named Andrei Bulgakov, is upstairs visiting Mr Wallingford. He's on his way to Chicago and he's going to meet Peachy.'

'What? Are you sure? Where is he supposed to meet her?'

'I don't know. He's going there on some other assignment, and I heard him mention to Mr Wallingford that he had picked up a pouch in Washington to be dropped off with an agent named Peachy in Chicago.'

'But didn't you hear anything else?'

'I believe I heard him say that he was going to stay at a place called the Blackstone Hotel.'

'Can't you find out somehow where they're meeting? Maybe you could ask Mr Wallingford under some kind of pretext.'

'I have to be careful, Jay. If I start getting too inquisitive, I won't hear anything.'

'All right. Maybe I can find out something at the Blackstone. How do you spell "Bulgakov"?'

'I don't know. Listen, I'm running an errand for Wallingford, and I have to get back up there.'

'All right. Damn it. I wish you knew more. How is Mr Wallingford?'

'Fine. He's going home soon. Just hold out for another week or so, and things will be back to normal. Take care, Jay.'

'Righto, Ted. Thanks for the information.'

'A disciplinary to Butte, a grade cut, and two weeks on the beach, wait and see.'

'Never! How the hell can they knock him down a grade? He's only grade ten now. I say he gets off with a letter of censure.'

'The hell he will. Hastings's been dismissed with prejudice, right? Or he's been suspended, and everyone knows he'll be dismissed with prejudice. Let's face it, you can't tell Henry O'Connor to go fuck himself and come out of it. So they've got to come back strong on Von Vlack here. I say *at least* two weeks on the beach, maybe more.'

'Nope, disagree. As long as Hastings didn't cop out, Jay's all right. Everybody stuck to their story, didn't they? Von Vlack left the apartment early, right? He had no responsibility. He comes out of it with a letter of censure, and a lecture from O'Connor on the evils of women and booze.'

Jay sat in the rear of the Bureau car dejectedly listening to the two agents in the front seat evaluating his fate in connection with the 'Flamingo Caper', as it was now referred to in the office. But although he was vaguely tuned in on their conversation, his mind was more on an impending surveillance in connection with one of his cases. The case had developed as a result of a pretext telephone call to the Blackstone Hotel that had identified the man Ted Summers had mentioned. After identifying himself to the hotel manager, he had arranged to have the subject discreetly pointed out as he stepped off an elevator into the lobby—a common practice by the large hotels that assisted the Bureau regularly in identifying subjects of security cases. He then had prevailed on the two agents who now sat in the car with him to assist on what was purportedly a surveillance lead on one of Jay's cases. It was Jay's intention to stay with the subject until he had his meet with Peachy.

'I'm amazed Hastings lasted as long as he did,' continued Dick Perkins, the agent behind the wheel. 'He was the wildest bastard I ever saw in the Bureau. I was on a satellite subject with him one night, and he wants to see the strip show down at the Silver Bells. So what's he do? He walks into this lunchroom where the subject's eating, sits down on a stool near him, and starts telling the counterman what a tremendous girlie show they got down at the Bells, how the

187

strippers take everything off and all that. So what happens? The subject walks out of the diner, grabs a cab, and we all spend the night at the Silver Bells.'

'Yeah, Ken was pretty cool,' agreed the other agent, a pleasant-looking, fair-complexioned man named Steve Nichols. 'Still, you never know. Maybe he'll beat the rap. He's a veteran, and he can ask for a civil service hearing on his case.'

'I doubt it,' said Dick. 'I've heard of agents going that route, but they never win. You can't buck the Bureau. It has too much influence. You can be right as rain, but the Bureau is never wrong. Take a pal of mine. He's an agent in the New York office. Remember the insurance forms the Bureau sent out a few months ago that we had to fill out and send back? Well, my pal's name is R.B. Yablanski. He's a Southerner. No first name, no middle name—just "R.B.," that's it. Anyway, he prints "R.B. Yablanski' on the form and sends it back to the Bureau. The same day the Bureau comes back with a teletype: "The agent must print his *full* name on the forms!" So R.B. writes on the form "R *only*, B *only* Yablanski." So is the Bureau wrong? Never! All the forms come back to "Ronly Bonly Yablanski". Now the poor bastard can't shake the name. Everybody, including the Bureau, calls him "Ronly

'Sorry to interrupt,' said Jay, leaning forward in his seat, 'but that looks like our subject.'

The three agents peered through the windshield down the street where a tall, dark-haired man with a military bearing left the hotel. The man paused, looked briefly up the street, and then started walking at a rapid clip in the opposite direction.

'See you later,' said Jay, getting out of the car.

Jay started up the opposite side of the street from which the subject was walking, giving the man plenty of leeway and barely keeping his head in sight.

'Subject entering subway station,' said Jay, speaking into the tiny transistor, shaped like a lapel button, in his suit coat.

'Right, we see him. Steve's on him.' A small receiver under Jay's coat picked up the message from the Bureau car and fed it silently to him through a small instrument resembling a hearing aid in his ear.

Jay was almost a hundred yards behind the subject, and he knew he would have difficulty reaching the train should one come immediately. He was unable to hurry, however, since any unusual movements on his part might easily be picked up by a countersurveillance.

He walked down the steps of the subway just as the train was pulling into the station. The subject of the surveillance was moving toward one of the doors as the cars slowed to a stop. Several yards farther down the platform he saw Steve. The agent gave a sign indicating he would board the train with the subject. It would be Jay's job to wait off the platform ready to surveil the subject in the event he should not take the train. Keeping the subject in view, he fished a dollar bill from his wallet and walked up to the change booth.

'Preparing to board southbound train,' he said, inclining his head slightly and speaking into the lapel button.

'Well, bully for you,' said the man in the change booth, reaching for the bill. 'Only you won't make that one, pal.'

Jay watched the Russian step onto the train, and farther down the ramp he saw Steve boarding one of the other cars. Just as the doors were closing, however, the subject quickly stepped back off the train. He stood looking up and down the length of the ramp to see if anyone followed him off. The platform was empty.

'Say, buddy, you want tokens?' asked the man in the booth, holding one end of the bill, which Jay had refused to relinquish.

'Hold it! Not going!' said Jay, speaking into the button. 'Heading back up to the street.'

'Whatever you say, mister,' said the man in the booth, eyeing Jay closely and letting go of the bill. Jay continued to stand in front of the cage, extending the dollar bill through the window, as the subject walked past him toward the stairs.

'Did Steve catch the subway?' came Dick's voice through the hearing aid.

'Right!' said Jay.

'OK, I've got our boy,' said Dick. 'Grab the wheels at the

189

northwest corner and pick up Steve at the next stop.'

'Right!' said Jay, still staring at the man and extending the bill toward him through the window. 'I'll wait here a few seconds.'

'Sure. Right, pal,' said the man in the booth, becoming increasingly uncomfortable. 'Wait as long as you'd like, only you can't block this window.' Jay turned abruptly and ran toward the stairs. The man in the booth shook his head slightly as he watched him go.

Steve was waiting impatiently at the next subway stop.

'The son of a bitch, I figured him for that move,' said Steve, climbing into the car. 'Is Dick on him?'

Jay had started to answer when Dick's voice came over the car radio. 'Things are picking up. We're at State and Monroe heading west and he's really taking off. You guys better hustle.'

Jay gunned the engine and made a drastic U turn in the face of oncoming traffic. He made it, but the manœuvre earned a chorus of irate blasts.

'That was close,' said Steve.

Jay was about to reply when Dick's voice crackled over the radio. 'You guys better get here pretty quick, or you can forget about it. I can't stay with him much longer without blowing this thing.'

The traffic, pedestrians, and shops lining Michigan Avenue became little more than a blur of movement and colour through the windshield as Jay raced the Bureau car down the street and made a screeching turn onto West Monroe.

'Hey, Von Vlack!' protested Steve. 'You've got 190 pounds of valuable cargo here.'

But the complaint might just as well not have been uttered, for Jay was not listening. His mind was on the impending meeting between Bulgakov and Peachy, and he was determined not to miss it. He had been able to think of little else since talking to Ted Summers. Peachy and Cricket Kent were one and the same. They had to be. He was more convinced than ever, now that he had had time to think about it. In retrospect it all seemed clear. Cricket's evasive manner. The mysterious trips. The fact that she was surveilling him

190

made her no less attractive. She had only drawn an assignment—just like he had. And she had liked him. He was certain of it. He had to see her again. It was a compelling urge that had reached obsessive proportions.

But the most disturbing aspect of it all was the remote possibility that she might appear as a man. It was preposterous, of course. He was certain she was a woman. Everything about her was feminine. Some mistake had been made at Dean Sutton Hall. It had to have been a mistake. Still, the one nagging thought that surfaced repeatedly was that he had never observed any hard core evidence—no decolletage or any feature that would establish positively that she was a woman. However remote, however absurd, however repugnant the idea, it was possible. Cricket Kent could be a man.

The emotional impact of these deliberations had been considerable. Just the remote possibility that he had been in love with a man had required a good deal of rationalising on his part. If Cricket was a man, she had still existed as a woman, if only in his imagination—an exquisite phantom composed of all those things he had ever wanted in a woman—a lovely apparition that had vanished just as he had taken her into his arms.

But he would see her again. Today. Maybe within the next hour. Even if she was a man, he wanted to see her. But was this normal? Was something the matter with him? Could his love for the person be taking him across the sex barrier? Did he love Cricket Kent even though she was a *man*? It was an unnerving thought. That would make him a homosexual—a queer. God! Maybe he was cracking up. The strain, the uncertainty, it was all getting to him. He had to keep things in perspective. The people at Dean Sutton Hall had been mistaken. He had considered calling the Albuquerque Police Department. The housemother indicated that the matter had been reported. Bill Dolan would remember him. He had checked enough records there. He would ask him to read the report from the dormitory.

'This must be a meet,' said Steve, interrupting Jay's thoughts. 'It seems as though it always works out this way. We

191

do a great job tailing a subject until it comes time for the meet and then we blow the thing.'

'How about calling for some assistance?' said Jay quickly. 'Maybe there'd be another Bureau car in the vicinity that could—'

'Are you serious?' said Steve. 'Today's Friday, man. This is bank-robbery day. The only cars in service are guys like us who have no choice. You couldn't raise an answer on a car radio if your life depended on it.'

'What do you mean bank-robbery day?'

'Friday's payday for most businesses, right? All the banks got a load of dough on hand to cash the pay checks. People in the bank-robbery business know this, so they pull their jobs on Friday. Why pull a job on Tuesday when you can make twice as much on Friday? Apparently nobody has told you, but if you're in the vicinity where a bank robbery is pulled, and you answer the radio, then it's your case, pal. You gotta go straight to the bank, and you can kiss off any plans you had for the weekend. You spend the next few days dusting for latent prints and showing mug shots to bank tellers. On top of that you probably end up with a letter of censure for screwing up the investigation some way. Christ almighty, I'm glad you asked. You might have put us all in a real bind before the day—'

'Subject turned and heading south on Dearborn,' broke in Dick's voice. 'I've gotta let him go. He's all yours.'

Within a few seconds the Bureau car was edging its way through the Monroe Street traffic onto Dearborn Street. They had no sooner completed the turn than Steve spotted the subject. 'There he is on the next block on the east side. Looks like he may be going into Picky's Bar. Here, I'll take the wheels. You better get on him quick.'

'You think I should go in the bar?' asked Jay. Cricket could be inside. It would be better to observe her without her knowing. 'Don't you think I should wait till he comes out?'

'No, you can't. There's another door to Picky's that opens out on Monroe Street. He may go out the other way. Besides, he may be making a contact in there. Anyway, he hasn't seen you. Better not get a drink, though. O'Connor's liable to be tailing us, trying to make a case on you because of the party. Order a pot of tea or something.'

'In a bar?' asked Jay. Steve pulled away without answering.

Picky's was a small pub the likes of which could be seen all over Chicago. It consisted of a large rectangular room that housed a long bar, a dozen or so stools, and a few tables and chairs against the opposite wall. A large mirror ran the length of the room behind the bar. In a corner, mounted above the bar, was a television set.

No one appeared to notice Jay as he entered the establishment. Several men were seated at the bar drinking and watching the television. A few men and women sat at scattered tables. The subject, seated on a stool near the door, was ordering from the bartender. It was not a good surveillance situation. Only three stools were unoccupied and two were right next to the subject. He was tempted to take the one farther down the bar, but decided instead on the seat closest to the subject. The gutsy approach was always the best one on a surveillance, according to the older agents.

After pouring a glass of wine for the subject, the bartender turned to Jay. 'What'll it be?'

'Uh, uh . . . glass of ginger ale, please.'

Jay looked down the bar past the subject, feigning an interest in the television show. The subject also was watching the show, and Jay was able to get a good look at him. He was a lean, handsome man with strong features.

He glanced about the room again. There was no one there who resembled Cricket or a male version of Cricket even remotely. He was considering his position, wondering if the man had any idea that an FBI agent was sitting beside him, when a humming noise emanated from the television, interrupting the audio portion of the programme. 'Where you at, Dick?' came Steve's voice loud and clear through the room. Jay was astonished. Again there was the humming noise, and the interference on the television coincided with a garbled transmission in Jay's hearing aid. Immediately he realised that the radio signals from the Bureau car were being picked up by the television receiver.

'We're on him,' continued Steve relentlessly, his voice

distinctly coming over the TV. 'We just followed him into Picky's Bar.' The transmission faded near the end, but it was sufficient. A heavy silence fell over Picky's Bar as a score of eyeballs shifted toward the two recent arrivals.

Jay glanced toward the subject, who was now wearing an amused expression. Bulgakov coolly raised his glass of wine toward Jay, nodded slightly, and gave a most agreeable smile.

Jay sat pensively with his chin in his hand as the bartender brought his ginger ale. 'Would you mind changing that for a Scotch and soda?' he said.

After a few minutes Andrei Bulgakov finished his wine and turned on his stool to leave. Pausing, he turned back toward Jay and, with the same splendid smile, said, 'Ve go?'

Larry Mullins eased his enormous frame into the seat, and the Bureau car settled appreciably on his side.

'Wow! You'd make tremendous ballast, Larry,' said Jay. The man shot him a dark look but said nothing.

'Only kidding, Larry,' added Jay hurriedly. He had not intended to offend his associate. Things were going poorly enough for Larry. His weight was up, his overtime down, and generally, his spirits rock bottom. Of late O'Connor had been applying pressure on him, and if there was one thing that did not bring out the best in Larry Mullins it was pressure. Introversive even during good times, the recent criticism had driven him further within himself. Never having been exactly a joy to be with, he now was like a disgruntled gorilla and was avoided by most agents. Sitting in a Bureau car for nine or ten hours on an inactive surveillance could be tedious enough without compounding the dreariness with 260 pounds of sulking gloom in the adjoining seat.

Larry had been with the government for over ten years, and, considering some of the incidents in which the large man had been involved, his longevity was regarded by the agents as miraculous. Many attributed his survival to a meeting he had had with the Director some five years previously. Larry had requested to visit the Director during one of the agent's trips to Washington for training. At best, such ventures were calculated risks, since one could never be sure what the black

194

ink would reflect after the meeting. A man's fortunes, of course, rode with the results.

Following the interview, Larry's personnel file emerged from the Director's office with the words scratched on top, 'Why is this man still an agent???'

The question caused an immediate flurry among those in charge of deciphering the black ink. While they suspected what the Director had in mind, they could not be sure, and there was always the possibility he meant that Larry should have been promoted. At any rate, no one relished the idea of implying to the Director that the black ink was not clear. Rather, Larry had been packed off to Chicago, where he enjoyed a remarkable anonymity lest any of his activities come to the attention of the Director.

'Lucky Mully' they called him after that—although never to his face. Lucky did not have a disposition that lent itself to much joking.

As they drove down Wabash Street the silence hung heavy in the Bureau car. Jay was glad the day was drawing to a close. After the fiasco in the bar the previous day, Bulgakov had returned to the hotel, and they had called off the surveillance. The man would never attempt a contact after that. Jay had been bitterly disappointed. He felt certain that he had been on the verge of seeing Peachy. He had tried to contact Bill Dolan at the Albuquerque Police Department, but the man was on vacation and would not be back for a few days. Larry's sphinxian personality had contributed to the cheerless atmosphere, and things seemed bleak.

Jay had eased the Bureau car to a stop at the corner of Wabash and Randolph to wait for a red light when from somewhere outside an angry voice started shouting. He looked past Larry out the side window and saw a large tractor-trailer in the process of backing out of an alley. So enrapt in his problems had he become that he had failed to see the truck and had stopped directly behind it, blocking it in the alley. The driver, his head sticking from the cab, was in an agitated state.

'What are you, a couple of wise guys? Can't you see I was backing out, you stupid bastard!'

195

'Take it easy,' said Jay. 'I didn't even see you there.'

'I'll take it easy. I'll back this thing right over that goddamn tootsie toy.'

Jay started to back up, but it was too late. Lucky Mully, having taken the driver's comments personally, was on his feet stalking toward the truck. The driver watched uneasily as the immense figure strode toward him. Larry opened the door of the cab and stared up at the man forebodingly.

'Well, I can't move this thing with you guys there,' offered the man, his bellicose manner considerably repressed.

Larry reached up under the dashboard and grabbed a fistful of wires. With one short tug he wrenched them free. 'No problem,' grunted Larry, uttering his first words of the day. 'You're not going anywhere.' He stood waiting to see if the driver had any comments. There were none. Turning, he walked back to the Bureau car. As soon as Jay felt the vehicle settle he drove rapidly away.

'You probably shouldn't have done that, Larry,' he murmured in mild admonishment. 'It's things like that that embarrass the Bureau, you know.' He knew he sounded like Henry O'Connor, but he had enough trouble.

At the Bureau garage he took leave of the car and Lucky Mully, and with a sense of relief at having unloaded two liabilities, he boarded the elevated for the Near Northside.

Home was now a rooming house just beyond the Gold Coast across from Lincoln Park. In addition to the landlady, the establishment accommodated a dozen boarders, a dog, a parrot, and a host of cockroaches which waged a continuous, indeed promising, battle with the occupants for control of the premises.

'Good evening, Mr Von Vlack,' croaked a voice from the living room as he closed the door.

He could not see the speaker, but assumed from the modulation that it was either the landlady or the parrot. Playing it safe, he answered merely, 'Good evening.'

'Your office called a few minutes ago, Mr Von Vlack,' continued the voice. 'They said for you to call soon's you got in.'

'Thank you, m'am.' Without breaking stride Jay hooked his

196

hat over the end of the bannister at the foot of the stairs and proceeded down the linoleum-covered hallway to a pay phone located on the wall under the staircase. He dialled the office number and within a few minutes was talking to Barney Deneen.

'What's the good word, Barney?'

'It's not good. O'Connor wants to see you first thing in the morning.'

'God, what a way to start off a morning. Any idea what he—'

'Yes, but you gotta act surprised when he tells you, OK?'

'Right, don't worry. So what's up?'

'A teletype came in about a half hour ago from the B. You been transferred to the New York Office.'

'New York? Am I suspended?'

'Nope, you're damn lucky. You came out of the thing pretty clean. You got a rabbi down the Bureau?'

'I wish I had. Did O'Connor say anything about it?'

'Yeah, mad as hell. He thinks you should've been put on the beach at least. He says he should've put you under oath when he questioned you about the party. He's done it before, you know. Malfeasance-of-government-employees statute. Then he's got a perjury case on you if he proves you were lying to him. Nice guy!'

'OK, Barney, thanks for the info.'

'You bet. Just remember—'

'I know, act surprised. Don't worry, Barney.'

Jay hung the receiver on the hook. New York... Lindenwald!

The New York office was the big leagues of the Bureau. More happened there in two weeks than in two years any place else. To cope with it, the Bureau had amassed an organisation larger and more complicated than any other five offices combined.

Heading up this complex operation when Jay arrived was an individual named Sidney Granville Cabot, or just 'Slippery Sidney', as he was referred to by the agents. As did Elston Doolittle and Henry O'Connor, Sidney Cabot had most of the

197

qualifications that enabled him to make his job as enduring an assignment as possible under the Bureau system, but unlike these contemporaries, Sidney was neither nervous nor overtly worried about his role. Rather, he was cold, analytical, and precise. On one occasion during his tenure in the New York Office he had fired 12 agents for inflating their overtime figures and had done so in the same dispassionate way that he handled routine administrative matters. Of course, the firing had reverberations that shook the office. The fired agents were referred to in somewhat awesome terms as 'The Twelve'. But it all had been just another personnel matter to Sidney. Probably the best description of the man is illustrated by an observation made by the Director. He wondered if possibly Sidney were not a trifle *too* severe with the agents.

If any soft spots did exist in Sidney Cabot's personnel policy, it was more than compensated for by his choice of Assistant Special Agents in Charge. Of these there were four. Joseph B Jackson, more appropriately labelled 'Tap Jackson', handled the internal security division. Besides several older agents who fed him information on a regular basis, Tap kept tabs on his men through a repertoire of tricks he had developed over the years. These included a variety of bugs and listening devices.

But for the immediate news, or the quick big one he needed for Cabot, he still utilised the old stand-by on which he had relied prior to the introduction of the more sophisticated eavesdropping equipment—the men's room. There, astride a commode, behind closed doors, he had been known to sit half a morning waiting for the one slip, the one unguarded comment that would give him the lead he needed. As far as Cabot was concerned, Tap Jackson was the best-informed administrator in the office.

Heading up the espionage division was Louis V Markovich, a man who spoke several languages, including one for the agents and another for the Bureau. Markovich had held his post for over two years, much to the amazement of those close to him. Most had given him only three months at the outside before the Bureau became aware of how inept he really was—a prognosis that eventually earned for him the name

'Lingering Louie.'

But unquestionably Cabot's most feared hatchet man was Horace Potter. A Southern gentleman, Potter was the administrative head—sort of a number one man to Cabot—and it is doubtful if there was a single person in the New York Office who trusted him, including his superior. Probably his forte was ferreting out misrepresentations in the agents' number three cards—the record of each agent's daily activities. Just a week or so prior to Jay's arrival Potter had successfully trapped one of the agents' wives into acknowledging that her husband was home almost every night before seven o'clock—a damning admission in view of the overtime requirements.

But if Cabot had a vulnerable spot in his administrative organisation, it was the agent in charge of the criminal division, Charles Patrick O'Rourke, who was known among the agents, for good reason, as 'Cabaret Charlie'. O'Rourke's health was not up to snuff. He suffered from, among other things, an ailing liver. As a result, he was known to avail himself of sick leave on occasion—like five afternoons a week. This was all right by Cabot, however, since when Cabaret Charlie did return from lunch the office took on the smell of a training room. It was generally agreed that O'Rourke must have the goods on Cabot or Cabot would have dumped him long ago.

With such a dedicated and able staff Slippery Sidney was quite able to keep his fingers on the capricious pulse of the New York operations. He knew where to find his agents when he needed them. One Friday afternoon he created a mild civil disturbance when he walked into Central Park, a spot regularly frequented by the agents. Between agents ducking and pigeons flying, it was a memorable afternoon for the elderly ladies who fed the birds. While his track record against crime and subversion was only so-so, his success at containing 'the enemy from within', as he referred to his agents, had been remarkable. By virtue of his staff, particularly Potter and Tap Jackson, as well as his own ingenuity, he was the personification of Cervantes' man with an oar in every boat.

It was into this sensitive world that Jay Von Vlack walked

199

one morning, a few days after receiving word of his transfer in Chicago.

Having arrived in New York late the preceding night, he had gone directly to Lindenwald. It was wonderful to be home. The fresh neat quarters over the garage, the faint odour of his father's pipe, his small room with the comforting relics from earlier days, the endless serenity of Lindenwald. It was therapy desperately needed for a double agent with frazzled nerves. His father had told him that Mr Wallingford had come home and seemed fully recovered. It was good news. Presumably Mr Wallingford was regaining control of things. Possibly that was the reason for his transfer to New York. There was less chance of Hawkins taking some unilateral action against him now that he was living at Lindenwald. His two-year contract would expire before long. Maybe they had decided to retire him a bit early. It was a wonderful feeling. Before long possibly he could be back in the law office—commuting to New York City, briefing his cases, renewing old associations.

Within a short time it could be all over. A bad dream to be laid away in a corner of his mind and referred to only as a basis for a better appreciation of the good things in life. Yet he could never forget Cricket. That was a part of the dream that would never fade. It had been good to sleep in his own bed that night. It almost seemed that none of it had ever happened.

Jay felt refreshed as he walked into the New York Office. He was referred by the receptionist to the office of Mr Charles O'Rourke, where he sat and waited for almost two hours until O'Rourke finally reported for duty.

'How long you been in the Bureau, Von Vlack?'

'About a year and a half now, sir.'

'You know the system then. Keep your cases current and watch your overtime. The last I heard the average daily overtime was headed somewhere around two hours a day. And a couple of more hours for commuting, and you can see you're probably better off bringing your bed in here.' O'Rourke paused and reached for a paper on his desk. 'There was a note job pulled at the National Commercial yesterday.

200

You can handle a few leads on that to begin with. Contact Tim Clancy on the third floor. He'll fill you in on procedure for working with the police department.' O'Rourke stood up abruptly, indicating that Jay's indoctrination into the New York Office had been completed.

Tim Clancy had been a Bureau agent for over 25 years. Under normal conditions he never would have received an appointment in the first place, but in the early forties, what with the war creating a scarcity in manpower, even the likes of Clancy was acceptable.

He was a product of the Bronx from start to finish—Fordham Prep, Fordham University, and Fordham Law School. About the only Bureau requirement he had was his LLB and this by the narrowest of margins—again, the manpower shortage was prevalent even in law schools. He was shorter than the minimum Bureau height requirement, heavier than the maximum weight for his build, nearsighted, asthmatic, inclined to hypochondria and 4-F! One of the instructors probably summed it up best when Clancy first reported to the FBI Academy. 'If this is what's left, it's time we went coed.'

As an embryo agent Clancy had thoughts of making it big in the outfit. When he finally became a relief supervisor he pursued Bureau policy so avidly that it caused concern even among his superiors lest he gain a foothold on the rung of Bureau management.

But fate had intervened shortly after his promotion. It had come in the form of a truck driver Clancy had outfoxed for a parking spot. During the ensuing argument the agent had seen fit to draw his revolver. While prudence might have dictated the fast draw to preserve his pudgy frame, the Bureau had felt the manœuvre contributed little to the manly reputation of the organisation, and Clancy was back on the street as a rock-bottom agent with a letter of censure to boot.

Not all of the agents were so disposed to forget the incident as was Clancy. Those who had served under the supervisor during his brief tenure were particularly remindful. ('Say, Clance, there's a truck driver outside who wants to see you.')

And so the subsequent years had been bitter ones for the agent. Rejected by the Bureau and rebuffed by his fellow agents, he had lived a limbo existence counting the months till his retirement. Now, assigned to the 'farm' (the name given to that squad composed of older agents nearing retirement who conducted mostly record checks), he did little more each day than peruse files at the various precincts.

There appeared little chance to change this bleak outlook when he looked up from his desk at the tall, blond-haired man standing in front of him.

'Are you Tim Clancy?' asked the man.

'You're looking at him.'

'I'm Jay Von Vlack. O'Rourke gave me a lead on that note job pulled at the National Commercial Bank on the West Side yesterday. He told me you would take me over to the twentieth precinct so I could talk to the detectives handling the case.'

'Yeah, yeah,' answered Clancy gruffly, with a look that suggested his morning was being complicated. 'Why don't you give a guy a little notice on these things? I got my own cases, you know.'

Jay arched his brows slightly and the grey eyes took a fix on the bridge of Clancy's nose. 'Sorry, but they didn't give them much notice at the bank yesterday.'

'All right, all right,' said Clancy, puffing a bit faster on his cigar. Years of imitating the office 'heavies', who were all cigar smokers, had brought him to the point where he actually enjoyed smoking. Now on the farm, which was also referred to as the 'cigar squad', the cigar was as much a part of the job as were the various files that were kept strewn on top of the desks for their effect. 'I'll fix you up, only it's gonna take a while. I got a lead down at the Immigration Office first. Then we'll have lunch and head over to the twentieth.'

'Well, I don't know,' said Jay. 'I was hoping I could cover this lead and then take some annual leave this afternoon. I was just transferred here yesterday, and I wanted to take care of some personal things.' He planned to go to Nayraville that afternoon to see Ted Summers. He wanted to compare notes with him as soon as possible. Also, he was anxious to call Bill

202

Dolan at the Albuquerque Police Department, who was supposed to return from vacation that morning.

'You young guys are all alike,' said Clancy, talking around the stogey, which now angled belligerently from the side of his mouth. 'Everything's gotta be done quick. Now, let me tell you something, pally. The quicker you do something around here, the quicker you're in trouble.'

'Yes, you're probably right.' Jay slumped into a nearby chair. 'Tomorrow's Saturday, anyway.'

'Listen, you seem like a nice kid,' said Clancy after a pause, apparently feeling he was now receiving the deference that should be accorded an older agent. 'You're just in from Chicago, you say? Well, I'll try to set you straight on a few things around here. C'mon, get your hat and coat.' He picked up some memos and stuffed them into a battered folder.

'I'll have to fill out a number three card. I'll meet you at the register,' said Jay.

'Here's one,' said Clancy, reaching into a drawer and dropping the pink card on the desk. Jay began to fill in the card with the day's planned activities.

'Hey, wait a second. Here, let me show you something,' said the older agent. 'You don't want to write plain like that on a number three so an inspector can read the thing. Make it as tough to read as possible. Particularly the times in and out. Here, see this?' He held up his card proudly. 'What you think of that, huh?'

'I can't read it.'

'Well, that's the whole point. Don't you understand? That's part of the game. See how I make the figures on the time in and out? This way I can make my one a four and my three an eight, see?' Clancy went on to demonstrate several tricks for altering his card.

'Now go get your hat and coat,' said Clancy, concluding the lesson. 'I'll see if I can't show you a few things in the field.'

They arrived at the twentieth before lunch. The precinct was a dusty old red brick building located in Central Park. There was an unkempt look about the exterior common among New York City's public buildings.

'Was this place ever part of the zoo?' asked Jay as they

203

approached the entrance. 'It looks like the same kind of buildings they have over there.'

'Hah!' snorted Clancy. 'If you think it looks like the zoo from the outside, wait till you see some of these detectives.' Chuckling over his comment, the agent pushed through the front door.

Once inside, Clancy affected a tough personality. 'Danahy and Flanagan in?' he said gruffly to the desk sergeant.

The sergeant glanced up briefly and, without answering, gestured with his thumb over his shoulder toward the rear. Clancy stalked toward a door leading to the detectives' squad room. Inside, two large, puffy-looking individuals in shirt sleeves were seated at desks. Both were smoking cigars and were wearing round porkpie hats with the brims turned up in front.

'You guys Flanagan and Danahy?' asked Clancy.

'Yeah,' said one, in a who-wants-to-know tone. 'I'm Danahy.'

'I'm Clancy. This is Von Vlack, FBI.'

'We got your call. What's on your mind?' asked the detective. There was a brusqueness to the man's manner that indicated he was not interested in prolonging the discussion.

'Von Vlack's got the note job pulled at the National Commercial yesterday. He wants to check a few leads with you.'

'We ain't got nuttin!' said the other detective, rising from his desk and walking toward a file cabinet at the other side of the room.

'Yeah, we been drawing blanks on that fucking thing,' said Danahy. 'You guys got anything?'

'Naw, nothing,' said Clancy, giving Jay a half wink. 'Von Vlack here can fill you in.'

Jay proceeded to outline in detail what information the Bureau had developed in the case. Both detectives listened apathetically and when the agent had finished, Danahy said, 'First time I ever got anything from an agent.'

'Yeah,' said the other man, who was presumably Flanagan. 'You guys had a change of policy over there?'

'What are you talking about?' said Clancy. 'We cooperate.

204

What about the kidnapping last month?'

'What about the kidnapping?' answered Danahy defiantly. 'We bust the case and your chief over there ends up with his puss in the newspaper holding the baby as though the FBI made the whole thing.'

'Yeah,' chimed in Flanagan, 'the way he looked you'd think he gave birth to the thing instead of taking credit for the recovery.'

'Listen, that's a lot of crap and you know it,' said Clancy. 'We gave you guys everything we had. You're just sore 'cause you blew the publicity on it. You held up busting the case for a full day so you wouldn't have to compete with the election returns for publicity, and you know it. It was your own fault. C'mon, Von Vlack, let's get out of here!'

Once outside, Clancy reprimanded Jay. 'You gave them everything you had. You shouldn't a done that. They'll be out shaking down those suspects before you ever get near them.'

'What do you mean?'

'Like I been trying to tell you, kid, it's not for real. Those guys will use that information for their own advantage.'

'Really? You mean they won't cooperate?'

'Cooperate! Hell, why do you think I winked at you in there? I figured you had more sense than that. These guys are a bunch of bandits. You worked in Chicago. You should know better than that.'

'Aren't any of these people honest?'

'There's a few here and there. It's the system though. It's tough for a cop to stay completely honest. If he isn't on the take, everybody in the outfit's scared of him. He's a liability to the rest of the guys. It's like an agent who won't phoney his overtime. Sooner or later he starts playing the game or he gets out. It's a way of life. These guys don't think they're doing anything wrong. They think it's part of the job.'

As they drove out of the park onto Central Park West, Clancy looked at his watch. 'It's almost twelve o'clock. Let's go over to Lila's for a sandwich.'

'Is that one of those restaurants on Broadway?'

'It's no restaurant. It's a cathouse. Lila's one of my informants. She's a madam.'

205

'You mean we're going to a whorehouse?' Jay shifted a bit uncomfortably. 'Doesn't the, ah . . .Bureau frown on that?'

'Why should they? Christ, they put enough pressure on for informants, don't they? Where the hell you going to develop informants if you don't go where the action is?' Clancy fell silent for almost a minute and then, 'Besides, wait till you see Lila. Real religious. Goes to church every Sunday. Serves her girls fish on Friday. Just like an old Irish mother.'

'Well, I don't know, I've got some things to do.' Jay looked at his watch. 'Do you mind if I make a phone call? It's kind of important.'

'All right. Make it quick, though, will you?'

Clancy stopped in front of a drugstore and Jay went inside. After getting change at the register, he walked to a phone at the rear of the store.

'Operator, I'd like to call person to person to Officer Dolan at the Albuquerque Police Department, Albuquerque, New Mexico.'

The call took an inordinately long time to place, and Jay shifted several times from one foot to the other. He changed hands with the receiver and noticed the perspiration marks on the phone. He was tempted to ask the operator why it was taking so long but restrained himself.

Finally the operator came back on the line. 'Go ahead, please.'

'Officer Dolan, speaking.'

'Hello, Bill. This is Jay Von Vlack, FBI.'

'Hello, Jay. How are you? How are you adjusting to Chicago?'

'I've already adjusted and left, Bill. I got transferred to New York.'

'They really move you guys around. What can I do for you?'

'I want to get a record check. It's personal. Can you help me out?'

'Sure. What have you got?'

'Kent. First name Gertrude. Also known as Cricket. Residence, Dean Sutton Hall, University of New Mexico. White, Female. Age, mid to late twenties. Hair, blonde. Eyes, blue. Height, five feet nine inches. Weight approximately

140. Employment, Registrar's Office. UNM.'

'That should do it if we got her,' said Dolan. 'Want me to call you back? This might take a few minutes.'

'No. I'd better wait, Bill. I'm calling from a pay station. I don't want to give it up.'

'That sounds like New York. I'll try to hurry.'

Jay leaned back against the wall and cradled the phone between his shoulder and ear. Several minutes passed and the operator came back on to ask for overtime charges.

'Hello, Jay'.

'Yes Bill.'

'We got her. It's a 10-27 Female Impersonator. What do you want to know?'

Jay swallowed hard and shifted the phone to the other hand. 'There must be a report from Dean Sutton Hall there. What does it say?'

Several seconds elapsed and Jay could hear the officer rifling through paper.

'Yeah, here it is. It's several pages. Santos conducted the interview at the dormitory. He's a long-winded bastard. Do you want me to read it all? There must be five pages here.'

'No, I guess not,' said Jay, eyeing the two quarters on the stand that was all that was left of the change. 'All I'm interested in is how they knew it was a man.'

'Let's see . . . oh, here it is. One of the girls saw him in the shower.'

Jay felt his heart plummet. So, it was true. Prima facie evidence. It had been a man.

'Wait a minute. I'm sorry.' It was Dolan's voice again. 'That's wrong. She didn't actually see him in the shower. She saw some identification in his wallet while he was taking a shower. Apparently the guy had been acting suspiciously so this broad went through his wallet while he was in the shower. She saw some identification with his picture, and all that.'

'But how could she tell it was a man?'

'From his identification, I guess. It says here that the guy had only been there a couple of months, and that he acted very suspicious. Never had anything to do with anybody, and only lived there now and then. This broad got suspicious of

207

him so she pulled a bag job on him when he was in the shower.'

'How could they tell it was a man, though? Is there anything there that actually proves that it was a man?'

'No, not that I can see. Only his identification here. It looks like she copied the stuff of his driver's licence.'

'What does it say?'

'Let's see. Avery Hawkins, 2635 Northern Boulevard, Washington, D.C.—'

'Avery Hawkins!' interrupted Jay. 'Are you positive? Isn't there anything else there? Did they check the thing out?'

'Hey, Jay. This is a female-impersonation case, remember? What did you expect, a full field investigation? We get several of these every week. Soon as the guy knew they were wise, he took off. So that's the end of it. Case closed.'

'Sure, I understand—'

There was a click and the operator came on the line. 'Please deposit another—'

'OK, Bill. Thanks very much. I appreciate your help.'

'Right, Jay. Take it easy. Don't get mugged up there.'

Avery Hawkins! Jay stood several seconds with his hand resting on the phone, trying to organise his thoughts. Cricket Kent? An Assistant Director of the FBI? Avery Hawkins a woman?

A blast from a horn outside signified a wearing patience. Pocketing the change, he went outside. A cloud of heavy cigar smoke hung over the front seat of the Bureau car, suggesting Clancy had been getting nervous.

But Jay cared little. Cricket Kent was Avery Hawkins! It was a paralysing revelation. The effeminate Assistant Director. Now it made sense why no one ever got to see him. It was because Avery Hawkins could not carry it off as a man. Anyone exposed to him for any extent would immediately see he was a woman. But why would she try to impersonate a man? The Director would have to be aware of it. Unless . . . of course! That was probably the reason. The Director! There had never been a woman in his life—either in the Bureau or out of it. It was the unwritten code—No Dickless Tracys! It was an astonishing thought. Could that be it? Could the iron will and uncompromising character of the man even transcend sexual barriers? Had he insisted a woman turn into a man in order to aspire in the organisation?

They were weird speculations, but to Jay anything was possible now. But of the conglomeration of thoughts that tumbled confusedly through his mind one stood out clearly. Cricket Kent was a girl. The fact that she was Hawkins in no way diminished her appeal. If anything, it enhanced her. She was not only a girl. She was a brilliant girl.

'Clancy, I think I'll forgo lunch today. Would you mind dropping me at a subway?'

'What? Take it easy, take it easy.' Clancy reached for the brown manila folder on the seat next to him. 'Here, check through these memos. See if you can find a lead on Robert York—escaped federal prisoner. I've got to do a criminal check on him over here at the fourteenth. We'll have a quick bite at Lila's and then make the check. Then you can drop me off at a subway stop and dump this car back in the garage.'

Jay looked at his watch. He had to have lunch, anyway. Another hour would make no difference. He took the folder and proceeded to leaf through the memos. Suddenly he stopped. 'Say, what's this case?' He held up a serial on which the title read 'Disappearance federal officer—SA Harvey Tucker.'

'Oh, that's on the new agent who disappeared out of training school a year or so ago. I get a dozen leads a month on that thing. It's top secret. Not supposed to talk about it. It's tied in with the Who Case. Apparently the Ruskies managed to infiltrate some areas of the Bureau, and they think Tucker got mixed up in it some way.'

Jay glanced at the sheet of paper. So the Bureau was honing in. They would have to be if they were tying in Tucker with the Who Case.

'I wonder how they were able to infiltrate the Bureau,' said Jay.

'The communists have been trying for years to get in the outfit. They know if they could ever get control of the Bureau, then the rest would be easy. Whoever controls the Bureau controls the country.'

209

'Well, I don't know about that,' said Jay, considering a course of calculated agitation. 'I can see where the communists would certainly have a leg up on things, but I think it's more the administration that controls the country. It's the politicians who—'

'Buddy boy, what do you think I'm trying to tell you?' A look of condescension spread over the Clancy features. 'The Bureau has them all intimidated. There's not a politician down there worth his salt who's going to take on the Director. I don't care if it's the President or some committee in the legislature. They just can't win. Sure, a few tried. Where are they now? As soon as some committee starts breathing down his throat the Director is unavailable for comment, or else he can't tell them what they want to know because it's a confidential matter which has to do with the internal security. How many times have you heard that? It stops them all cold. The only committee that ever even gets to talk to him is the appropriations Committee. And what a laugh that is. Once a year he goes over, trots out a few statistics, and they roll over and play dead. Did you ever read the transcript of one of those things? It's the closest thing to an interview of Jesus Christ that we've got on this planet.'

Jay paused to consider his strategy. He would have liked to channel Clancy's conversation back to the Who Case, but the matter of the Bureau's power had struck a responsive chord.

'Just the files alone are enough to scare most prominent people.' Clancy was off again. 'Most everybody has done something wrong at one time or another, and everybody wonders how much of the book the FBI has on them.'

'Don't other agencies have access to the files? What about the Central Intelligence Agency?'

'The Director gives the CIA only what he wants them to have, and I understand that's goddamn little. I hear the little we do give them they manage to screw up. No, sir. Nobody has access to those files unless the Director says so.'

'I'm sure there are a lot of people who don't have to worry about their backgrounds—'

'Well, I never met any of those people,' interrupted Clancy. 'Besides, it's not what's in the files, it's what people think *might* be in the files. Add to that the Su-tech, the informants, the bugs, the authority to conduct an undercover investigation on anyone at all in this country and you got yourself quite a formula. I don't care if you're the President. You'd have to be nuts to take him on. Who needs it? If you're a politician, there's plenty of things to crusade on. Why not pick a fight that you might be able to win?'

'What about this Who Case, how were they—'

'Now, there's a guy who might be able to bear the Director,' interrupted Clancy. ''Cause he's playing the Director's game. Money, informants, surveillances, infiltration, organisation, the technical know-how. That's the guy who keeps the Man awake nights. That's the guy who can put the Director in mothballs.'

'How about this Tucker chap? How was he involved?'

'I don't really know. We'll know pretty soon, though. It's pretty hot right now. They got a witness. They found some airline ticket agent he'd been talking to. She saw him leave the terminal with a couple of guys. We've been sending the Washington field office pictures of everyone Tucker ever knew. He's from upstate New York, you know.'

'Did they ever find out what happened to him?'

'Naw, but he's got to be dead, though. Why, the heat that's been on that thing—if he were alive, they would've turned him up by now. They liquidated him—that's for sure.'

There was a long pause and then Jay said, 'I guess they'll break the Who Case eventually.'

'Oh, they'll bust it all right,' retorted Clancy. 'They always do. They've had a special blue-ribbon squad working the case for over a year. They way I get it, they're getting closer to the thing. Some agents involved, too, I guess. No, you can say what you want about this outfit, but it's sure relentless. They'll solve that Tucker thing there, too. Just a question of time. Probably pretty quick, too—now that they got that ticket agent as a witness.'

Jay shifted his body into four different positions, found none of them comfortable, and finally hunched forward in his seat, drumming the fingers of his right hand against the dashboard as he gazed through the windshield at the traffic sifting its way through the Avenue of the Americas.

Within a few minutes Clancy was backing the Bureau car into a snug parking place in front of a long row of brownstones. After locking the car, they mounted the steps to one of the buildings and Clancy rang the bell. There was a long pause and Clancy finally said, 'Lila's checking us out. She's got a periscope in the rear of the building—looks like something that came off a submarine. She checks out all—'

He was interrupted as the door opened and a kind elderly face appeared in the opening. 'Timothy darling, how are you? I haven't seen you for weeks.'

'Hi, Lila. We in time for lunch?'

'You certainly are. Just let me grab something to put on. None of the girls are here, Timothy. We were closed down, you know.'

'No kidding?' said Clancy, removing the cigar. 'What happened?'

'Oh, you know the detectives, Timothy, always wanting their cut. They're not like you boys, you know. They expect the girls to perform for them for nothing. It was getting so there were more detectives here than down at the precinct. I finally had to tell them that they'd have to pay like everyone else. Well, it wasn't two weeks after that before we were raided. Knocked the door right down and came in snapping pictures like it was a show at the Coliseum.'

'Gee, that's rough, Lila,' said Clancy with genuine sympathy. 'When do you think you'll be back in business?'

'Oh, I'm not sure,' said Lila dolorously. 'Maybe in about two weeks . . . God willing.'

Ping!

It was a light, euphonic sound like the clinking of two Martini glasses which came from the small delicate bell attached to the top of the front door. Jay had just opened the door of the Nayraville Drugstore when a heavy voice called from across the street.

'Hello, Jay.'

Jay turned and saw the head and torso of Ted Summers projecting from the doorway of the Tudor House. He was

212

delighted to see him, having just looked for him at Lindenwald.

Inside the Tudor House he shook Ted's hand warmly as they exchanged amenities.

'Care for something, Jay?' asked Ted, nodding at the bar.

'No, nothing, thank you.'

After securing Ted's drink from the bar, they moved to a corner of the cocktail lounge.

'How is Mr Wallingford?' asked Jay as they sat down.

'Fine, fine. He's just like his old self again. You'd think he'd never been sick. He walks all over, spends half the day on the phone—just like always. It was a very mild coronary, you know. You should have seen him at the hospital. They couldn't keep him in bed...' He proceeded to describe the activities at the hospital and the goings-on about the estate.

It was soon evident that Ted had been in the Tudor House for some time. His face was slightly flushed and he was more talkative than usual. Jay recalled that sometimes on Fridays, business permitting, Ted would leave for the Tudor House a bit early.

As he listened, Jay followed the flights of the Martini glass between the table and Ted's lips. An unwavering red eye in the form of a stuffed olive gazed at him intently through the side of the frosty glass. It made him uncomfortable for some reason, and he was not at all displeased when the bulging orb finally disappeared at the end of a toothpick into Ted Summers' mouth.

'Well, now that you've been in the FBI for a while, Jay, do you think you'd like to make a career of it?'

'I rather think you know the answer to that,' Jay replied dryly.

'Why not? I could see you as a top Bureau official some day.'

'It'd be possible,' Jay said. 'None of the really good agents seem to want the job. You know, that's probably the greatest weakness in the organisation—its concept of management development. It's really absurd.'

'I've heard Mr Wallingford say that, too,' said Ted. 'Is the Director really that much of a tyrant?'

'That's part of it, but the Bureau system actually discourages agents from seeking advancement. In most organisations there's always compettiton for the key positions, but in the Bureau the best jobs are in the field. If an agent does have aspirations, there's this incredible procedure he must go through. First, he asks to see the Director and appeals directly to his vanity, telling him what an outstanding leader he is and that sort of thing. Then, if the Director is sufficiently impressed, he jots down on the personnel file that the agent should be considered for administrative advancement. This starts things in motion and the agent is on his way. But most of the agents don't bother.'

'Why is that?'

'Because there's no real inducement. There's very little monetary reward, and the road to the top is just awful. First, the agent becomes a supervisor in the field office, where he sits in a cage all day proofreading the other agents' reports. The big thing here is not to let anything through that's going to embarrass the Bureau. If he survives this he's called to Washington as a Bureau supervisor where he sits in another cage and proofreads the proofreaders in the field. This is even worse since he's that much closer to the flak from the Director's office. His only hope is to get one of the S-A-C jobs, but to qualify for this he has to join an inspection team—they call them goon squads. Then he spends a few years travelling around the country, rarely getting a chance to be home, waiting for some vacancy to occur in the S-A-C positions. Now the S-A-C are the most vulnerable of all. They're trying to keep their jobs by appeasing the Bureau with an endless supply of statistics. And believe me the job is to get the statistics first and worry about the facts later. But still, it's better to be a nervous S-A-C than travelling forever on the goon squad, so the goons see to it that S-A-C vacancies occur pretty regularly.'

'Oh, I don't know. There must be more to it than that. That smatters a bit of the disgruntled employee—the agent who never made it—'

'It's the truth,' interrupted Jay. 'You probably think I'm exaggerating. It's like the agents say. "Don't ever bother

214

telling anyone about the Bureau because no one will ever believe you." But that's basically the way it works. I'm generalising, of course, but essentially that's management development in the Bureau. An agent is regarded by his associates as a fool to ask for administrative advancement. In some instances S-A-C have had to order agents to take supervisory assignments against their will. You can imagine the calibre of management that exists under such a situation.'

'It does kind of bear out a comment that Mr Wallingford made recently,' said Ted.

'What's that?'

'He said the Director didn't want to retire because he didn't think there was anyone on his staff capable of taking over his position.'

'I'm going to ask Mr Wallingford if I can see him tomorrow,' said Jay, following a pause in the conversation. 'I heard some disturbing things this morning from one of the older agents.' He told about his discussion with Tom Clancy concerning the Who Case.

'I'm sure Mr Wallingford knows a good deal more about the Who Case than this Clancy chap,' said Ted. 'Hawkins supposedly heads up that blue-ribbon squad.'

'I'm sure he does, too. I can tell just from what I've heard that Hawkins and his group are diverting the leads. But if the Bureau has this witness who can identify Hawkins' men as the ones who left that terminal with Tucker, then the rest shouldn't be too hard. And you know what I'm thinking, Ted? Where does that leave you and me? I don't know what position the government will take on Harvey Tucker, but after listening to that agent this morning, it isn't very encouraging. To listen to him, you'd think we were all going to end up in the electric chair.'

Jay paused and looked into the dark eyes across the table. It was apparent the man was concerned. The eyes wavered, blinked, looked into the Martini glass, and, with no place left it seemed, returned to Jay's face.

'I found out some other things this morning,' continued Jay. He related the information he had received from Bill Dolan, watching the older man carefully for his reaction. 'So

215

you see, Cricket Kent, Peachy, and Avery Hawkins are one person—*a woman*. Did you know Hawkins was a woman, Ted?'

'Of course not. Jay, have you been on the pipe?' Ted regarded him with a wry look. 'How in blazes could Hawkins be a woman? I admit he looks a little fruity, but a woman? Impossible!'

'What proof do you have that he isn't? said Jay defensively, wondering again if it was indeed possible.

'I'm sure you've got it all confused. Maybe this Kent person *was* Peachy, and maybe Peachy had some of Hawkins' identification. Who knows? But if Hawkins were a woman, Mr Wallingford would certainly know it, and I would have heard something.'

'I'm sure Mr Wallingford doesn't tell you everything,' said Jay quietly.

'No, he doesn't,' acknowledged Ted. 'And to be honest, I know very little about Hawkins. As I told you, Mr Wallingford has great confidence in him and has delegated considerable authority to him. Hawkins runs his own show—even more so since Mr Wallingford's heart attack. But what you say doesn't sound logical. For example, why would Hawkins be working at that university?'

Jay shrugged his shoulders. 'According to Mr Wallingford, New Mexico is the centre of much of the espionage activity in this country because of all the key facilities. Hawkins had to be there a good deal of the time, and he needed a base of operation—a cover. Some place near the airport where he could get in and out fast. What could be better than the university office where he had a token job he could perform a couple of days a month. Hawkins probably developed the Comptroller, or whoever heads up the office, as a contact so that he could use the job as a front when he needed it. As a woman working at the university he had the perfect cover to observe me as well as handle his other activities out there.'

'Well, even if he were a woman—which I don't think he is—why would he be masquerading as a man—as Avery Hawkins?'

'Obviously I don't know everything, Ted, but I can

216

theorise. You said that Mr Wallingford started Hawkins with us right out of law school, right? Why didn't he have him apply to the Bureau at the beginning? He would have been much more valuable there. Maybe it was because Hawkins, being a woman, couldn't qualify as an agent. There are no female agents. That's the Director's rule. All Hawkins could hope to qualify for in the Bureau was a clerk or a stenographer with absolutely no chance of promotion to a level where he could be effective.'

'But haven't you answered your own question, Jay? Hawkins *is* in the Bureau—an Assistant Director. He would have to be a man. You just said so yourself.'

'Yes, but remember, you told me that it was the Director himself who was impressed by Hawkins and brought him into the Bureau.' Jay leaned over the table and looked at the man earnestly. 'Why couldn't the Director have quietly set Hawkins up with an office, and represented him as a man? Hawkins of course is delighted to cooperate. No one ever sees Hawkins so who knows the difference? That way the Director has a brilliant assistant who, incidentally, is a perfect submarine when he's not dressed as a man. Think of the special assignments he can handle.

'There are all kinds of ways it could have happened,' continued Jay after a slight pause. 'For all we know the Director might have heard about Hawkins and issued instructions for him to be made an agent. Then after Hawkins was in the Bureau no one had the courage to go in and tell the Director that he'd made a woman an agent. I've heard a hundred stories about the Director just like that.'

Ted Summers shook his head in disbelief. 'They must really brainwash you people in that organisation. You don't honestly think anything like that could actually happen, do you?'

'Listen, Ted, you don't know the Director. You could be a hermaphrodite, but if he says you're a man, then as far as the Bureau is concerned you're a man.' Jay paused and leaned back in his chair. 'Look, Ted, I know I'm grasping at straws. I don't know how it happened. I'm only guessing. But you did say once that Mr Wallingford thought it was the miracle that

217

Hawkins ever got into the Bureau. Maybe that was the miracle—a female agent. . . Anyway, that was no man I kissed out there.'

Ted Summers remained unconvinced. He looked into his Martini glass and shook his head resignedly. 'I don't think so, Jay. It's just too . . .Well, it's all too improbable. But I know how you must feel. You've been subject to a lot. It's been a great strain. You can imagine all sorts of things in this business. You're just a little shaken because you made love to a man. Psychologically that's bad, and—'

'For God's sake, don't make it worse than it is! I didn't make *love* to him—or her, that is. I only kissed her.'

'See, Jay, you're hedging. You're not really sure yourself. Oh, well, the whole thing is so confusing. Sometimes it's all beyond me. Anyway, Hawkins may be up here tomorrow. I'm going to—'

'Really? Why didn't you tell me?' interrupted Jay. 'You mean he's coming to Lindenwald?'

Ted nodded. 'I just heard it this afternoon.'

'Well, what's it all about? Can't you see how important this is to me, Ted? How long's he going to be here?'

'I don't really know that much about it. I think he's staying overnight. Wallingford ordered a guest room made up, and I don't know of anyone else who's coming.'

'Maybe I could get to see him,' said Jay. He leaned back in his chair, the thought beginning to crystallise in his mind. The thought of seeing Cricket was overwhelming. But what would she be like as Avery Hawkins? What would she say to him? Would she be courteous? Abrupt? Embarrassed? She would have to be uncomfortable. It would be difficult for her, pretending to be a man. She would have to be on the defensive. But would she be? Avery Hawkins' reputation was a formidable one. Brilliant, vicious—the Barracuda! No, she was hardly that. A barracuda never could have kissed so tenderly.

'I wish you could see yourself,' said Ted, interrupting his thoughts. 'Even if Hawkins were this Kent person, I don't understand how you could fall for her. Hawkins was ready to have you dismissed just a short while back—maybe to have you liquidated.'

'That was before we ever knew each other.'

Ted shrugged his shoulders and looked away. 'I hope you're right. Oh, well, if you can believe what that agent told you this morning about their cracking the Who Case, then I suppose none of it makes any difference anyway.'

'I'm not worried about the FBI.' Ted drained the last bit of liquid from the glass and loosened his tie with his other hand. 'Let them solve this Tucker thing, and the espionage, too, for that matter.'

Jay wondered how many Martinis he had had.

'Even if they do, I doubt if they can bother that man on the hill very much,' continued Ted. 'He covers himself on everything—almost everything, that is.'

'What do you mean "almost"?' said Jay, piqued by the man's comment.

'Yes, he's pretty slick,' continued Ted, ignoring the question. He was quiet for several seconds as though pondering his next words. Finally he glanced toward the bartender and Jay perceived he was considering another Martini.

'I've always liked you and your dad, Jay. You've been like my own family—the only family I've ever had, for that matter.'

There was another long silence, and then Ted Summers spoke. 'Harold!' The bartender nodded and moved toward the line of bottles behind the bar.

It was not until he had taken a substantial swallow from the fresh vodka Martini that the older man spoke again, and then the words came barely audibly from lips that scarcely moved. 'I've known you all your life, Jay. Your father is probably one of the finest men who ever lived, and he was very kind to me those days when I worked for him on the grounds. So was your mother. She was a beautiful woman. It's been over 25 years since that night she disappeared, but I remember her. I remember her like it was yesterday. . .'

Ted Summers fell silent and Jay was about to speak when the man continued.

'I'm not worried about the FBI or any of these things. I

219

know a lot about Wallingford's activities, but I've never done anything wrong. And I really don't know where I'd be if it weren't for him all these years. But . . . there is something that's always bothered me. I don't know anything about these agencies, and when it's right to dismiss someone with extreme prejudice. . .'

Ted paused to take another drink and then looked long and hard at the bar across the room. He took another sip from his glass, and to Jay it seemed the man's eyes had moistened ever so slightly.

'Many strange things have happened up there on that hill. I can tell you that, Jay. Many years ago, when you were . . . not much more than a baby.' Ted Summers averted his eyes, paused momentarily, and then said, 'I'm not sure just what it was, but . . . you know that cherry tree by Mr Wallingford's study? Your father and I never even realised it was there till it suddenly blossomed out of all those shrubs. We never planted it.'

Early the following morning, even before Jay had opened his eyes, somewhere in the dawning stages of his consciousness a sense of excitement took root. It grew steadily as it travelled with him through the vacuous grey wall into wakefulness. When finally he opened his eyes, the reason for it burst on his consciousness—a star-spangled realisation that today Cricket Kent was coming to Lindenwald.

He rose and walked to the open window near his bed which looked out over a small pond behind the servants' quarters. A slender edge of the sun peeking above the tops of distant trees gave promise of a clear June day. A dense, almost jungle-like foliage on the far side of the pond was filled with ornithic song. Jay loved the morning sounds. It signalled the start of the day for millions of other creatures, all every bit as important to themselves as was Jay Von Vlack. It helped keep things in perspective.

From the time he had had to stand on his toes to see over the window sill he had been intrigued by the pond and its inhabitants. Whether it had been a wild duck beating its wings against the water or a bullfrog lamenting from a moss-covered

220

rock, they had all been greeted with the same wide-eyed wonder. They had been the only companions in a young world filled with grown-ups.

One creature had been a particular friend. It was a large brown snapping turtle which surfaced in the murky pool beneath his window to which he threw morsels of food. One morning, not knowing why, he had taken careful aim with his slingshot and scored a perfect bull's-eye. It had been an astonishing shot. He had never expected to come even close. The turtle had disappeared and had never returned. The thought that he might have killed it had caused him days of anguish.

On this particular morning the pond was very still. The only movement at all was from a few lily pads that floated near the bank occasionally transmitting tiny eddies, quickly suppressed by the viscosity of the water.

As he stood looking from the window his mind wandered to the cherry tree at the rear of the main house. He had thought about it considerably since Ted Summers had mentioned it the previous day. The suspicion had begun to grow. It was a terrible thought, without any substance really. But, nevertheless, he was determined to look under the tree at the first opportunity.

He turned from the window and walked from the bedroom, through a small sitting room, into the kitchen. His father had already gone, leaving behind a pot of coffee and some bacon warming in the oven. Two eggs rested on the stove near a pan. Jay poured a cup of black coffee and walked back to the bedroom, where he started to dress.

He had called Mr Wallingford the night before, and a meeting had been arranged for nine o'clock that morning. Mr Wallingford had sounded a bit gruff, and Jay had hung up with the feeling that it would be very unpleasant.

Regardless, he had to see him. Many things had to be clarified—matters of enormous significance. The most important thing was their relationship. How did he now stand? His two-year contract would soon expire. Would he be permitted to return to the law practice? What about Hawkins' plan to have him dismissed from the Bureau? Had it been

221

rescinded? He felt certain it had. Possibly he could in some way suggest a meeting between Hawkins and himself.

Following breakfast he called the New York Office and requested a day's annual leave. He then left the apartment. After glancing at his watch and noting that he was still a few minutes early, he decided to take the longer route, down the road to the main entrance of the house, rather than the path.

As he walked golden shafts of sunbeams streaked through the trees and bounced off the pink and red rhododendron lining the road. The whistle of a cardinal followed by the squawk of a blue jay came from back among the trees. He picked up a slender stick he saw lying on the grass. Passing a white birch tree, he slapped the trunk gently with the switch.

He had reached a point in the road where it started bending into a circular drive in front of the house when he noticed a long grey limousine come to a stop near the front gate. He watched curiously as the car started moving again slowly up the road toward him. There was something about the vehicle that had an official look to it. He wondered if it carried Avery Hawkins.

He altered his course, moving back among the trees. He arrived near the front entrance a few seconds before the limousine and took a position near some dogwood trees where he could observe the visitors without being noticed.

The car eased to a stop, and a tall, swarthy man quickly alighted. It was the individual who had met him on the street corner one night during training school and taken him to the car. The man opened a rear door of the vehicle. From the back seat emerged a blond, rather frizzy-haired man with a round, pleasant face. Jay believed it to be the other man he had seen that night. The man glanced in Jay's direction, and Jay moved farther back among the trees. From the new position he could not see, but was within earshot.

'Here, let me take that, Avery,' said a heavy, masculine voice.

'I'm certainly getting royal treatment today. Gotty opens the door, you take my briefcase.'

It was Cricket's voice, light and friendly. A thrill shot through Jay's body.

'Well, we don't come to Lindenwald very often,' responded the other voice. 'We have to be at our best, right, Gotty? The tone was light but respectful.

Jay carefully eased his head out beyond the trees. He saw the driver, but Hawkins and the other man had moved up toward the entranceway out of sight.

'Everett, will you make sure Gotty gets that package I brought for Mr Wallingford out of the trunk?'

'OK, Avery.'

Jay thought he recognised the voice of the man, and with the mention of the name Everett, he realised the tall blond man was Everett Reeves. Also, he was surprised at the relaxed exchange. From his reputation he had assumed Assistant Director Avery Hawkins would be cavalier in his manner, commanding a good deal more subservience from his subordinates. Instead, it appeared there was a friendliness between them, almost a camaraderie.

'Hello, Avery, Everett.' It was Mr Wallingford's voice. 'Come right in. Why don't you just leave the bags there? I understand you stayed in the city last night. . .' The voices were lost as the group moved on inside.

Jay looked at his watch. It was five after nine. He wondered if he should go in, but decided against it. It would be best to see Hawkins under a more relaxed situation if possible.

After waiting several minutes, he walked to the door and entered. The foyer was empty. He walked to the study, where Mr Wallingford had said he would meet him, and went in to wait. He had been sitting only a short while when David Wallingford entered and closed the door quietly behind him. He was looking fit, and other than a slight loss of weight, it was hard to tell that he had been ill.

'Good morning, Jay.' He crossed the room and shook hands briskly. He gave Jay only the briefest glance, but in the flashing exchange Jay caught the anger of the grey eyes. It was an ungracious welcome that jarred the younger man.

Mr Wallingford wasted little time getting to the point. 'I was extremely displeased with that White Sands affair. That agent who was killed—Ostermeyer—was being groomed for a very important assignment. What happened?'

Rattled by the man's abruptness, Jay launched into a disjointed description of the incident. Before he had finished, Wallingford interrupted him. 'That slide rule was invaluable. It contained, among other things, a list of Soviet agents active within the East German espionage apparatus which took years to secure. Why didn't you just reach over and take the damn thing away from him? You knew it had explosives in it, didn't you?'

'I had no chance, sir. The Major was very excited. I figured Ostermeyer could do anything I could, and everything had deteriorated so I thought it just best to get out of there.'

'You've only been asked to handle two assignments since you started, Jay. Both were simple courier missions, and you've managed to fail on both occasions.'

Jay felt very warm as he sat staring at the floor. There was little he could say. He had anticipated it would be unpleasant, but Wallingford's anger exceeded what he had expected. 'I honestly don't know what to say, Mr Wallingford,' he said quietly. 'It will be two years next month since I went to that training camp in Virginia, and it's been a very confusing two years for me, to say the least.'

'I should say your performance bears out that observation rather well,' said Wallingford acrimoniously. 'I might add that your two years have been a bit confusing to all of us. What is it the Director says, "Don't embarrass the Bureau"? Well, I don't know the extent to which you've done that, but you certainly have embarrassed me. The supervisor of the operation has done an outstanding job, and here I went and imposed you on him. . .'

Jay kept his eyes trained on the floor as Wallingford went on to deprecate his performance. As he listened, Jay knew that their relationship had changed. It was not only Wallingford's anger. Somehow things were different. The spell seemed broken.

Mr Wallingford had not talked long before he seemed to tire. Also, his anger seemed to subside. 'Millions of lives will be affected by the success or failure of this project,' he said, leaning back in his chair. 'The infiltration of the FBI is the most important undertaking in the western hemisphere. The

Bureau is a base of power in this country. Do you realise the significance of that?' He waited for Jay to answer, but Jay said nothing.

'Maybe that's been part of our problem,' continued Wallingford. 'It's probably hard for you to realise the importance of controlling this agency.'

'Truthfully I've never understood it, Mr Wallingford,' said Jay softly. He knew Wallingford's temper was still steaming beneath the surface, a hot geyser that would spout if provoked. Yet he had to express his feelings on the subject. 'After having spent a year and a half in the organisation I sometimes wonder if the FBI is all that powerful. From what I've seen, it's a terribly inept organisation. If it weren't such a serious thing it would be funny. I could tell you stories that would be hard for you to believe.'

'It may appear that way, but its power base is incredible.' Wallingford's voice was softer and his manner more restrained. 'It touches everything, the presidency, Congress, everything. The Bureau technology, the unlimited budget, the broad investigative authority—it's an awesome combination.

'Let me give you an example. Let's take the House Appropriations Committee. This is one of the most powerful committees in Congress. It examines all budget requests throughout the federal government, including the FBI. This committee has several FBI agents on its staff. The implications are obvious.'

David Wallingford paused and the grey eyes searched Jay's face appraisingly.

'You've been a lawyer long enough to understand the effects of influence within the legislative process. The FBI's influence is felt throughout the system. Just look at the Director himself. The man who occupies one of the most sensitive positions in the whole jungle of Washington politics has retained his position from one administration to the next for over 45 years. They restrict Presidents to 8 consecutive years. Think of it. Do you know who was President when the Director took office? Calvin Coolidge! That should signify something to the most blunted observer. But do you know the

225

most important part of it all? Everyone—the people, the government leaders—almost all of them are unaware of the extent of the Bureau power.

David Wallingford paused for a second and then added, 'Of course, they're going to wake up eventually and start to enact some restrictive legislation. There are already some indications of this in the wake of all the publicity the FBI got recently from their wire-tapping activities. But right now, it's wide open for whoever can get control.'

When it appeared the man was through talking, Jay said, 'I'm sure you're aware of this, sir, but I thought I should mention it. I've heard some rumours to the effect that the Bureau expects to break the Tucker case and that they think it may be related in some way to the Who Case.'

'I wouldn't worry too much about those rumours. We feel we have things under control.'

Encouraged by Mr Wallingford's mood, which seemed to be improving progressively, Jay decided to push on to more sensitive areas. 'There are some matters which I've been very anxious to discuss with you, sir.' He related the incident that took place at the dormitory and the information he had developed at the Albuquerque Police Department. As he had planned, the explanation enabled him to broach the subject of Cricket Kent without jeopardising Ted Summers' confidence. 'I guess you understand how I'd wonder about all this, sir.'

David Wallingford looked at Jay intently for several seconds without speaking. Then he said, 'I presume you know Hawkins is here?'

'Yes, sir, I do.'

'Maybe it would be just as well if you two had a talk. He could just as well explain things to you as I. Possibly better. Are you going to be home today?'

'Yes, sir. All day. I took annual leave.'

'Very well.' Mr Wallingford stood up abruptly. 'I have some meetings to get over, and then I have to go south for a few days. Now that you're home we shall have more time to chat. I realise you're probably anxious to talk about the future, but I think we can hold that in abeyance for a few days.' They shook hands.

226

'Yes, I think that may be very good for you to talk to Hawkins,' said Mr Wallingford musingly, as though he had been considering the matter as he spoke. 'So they got on to him out there, huh?' He smiled slightly. 'I didn't think Hawkins ever made mistakes.'

The rest of the morning Jay spent at his apartment. Following lunch, he called the main house and left word where he would be, and then went to the swimming pool. Selecting a chaise close to the dressing room where he could easily hear the telephone, he pulled off his robe and lay down in the sun.

It was a lazy June day, of the kind to which people look forward during the stormy days of February and March. The sky was deep and still. The only movement was an occasional jet leaving a thin vapour trail like the stroke of an artist's brush or a stray cloud that now and then sailed past in the form of a puffy white spinnaker. It was the kind of day for one to relax and think pleasant things.

As he lay on the chaise looking up at the sky, Jay's thoughts were mostly on Cricket. Mr Wallingford must have seen her by this time. He expected the phone to ring any second. It was nerve-wracking just lying there waiting for it to ring.

Finally he rose and put on his robe and slippers and walked to a corner of the pool area that looked out over the meadow. There he sat on a railing and lit a cigarette. A small breeze rustled through the leaves of a row of poplar trees that stood like a small guard near the entrance to the pool. It swept down ruffling the surface of the water lightly and then brushed refreshingly past.

He had been sitting for several minutes when he noticed a figure wearing what appeared to be shirt and slacks emerge from behind the corner of the main house and start down a path toward the formal gardens. Because of the distance, he could not see clearly, but almost immediately he knew from the graceful movement that it was Cricket.

The sight of the girl, even from the distance, intensified the longing he had felt during the preceding weeks. He was tempted to go down to see her. It would be a wonderful place to talk, walking among the flowers. But he was not dressed. It

227

could be awkward. Besides, Mr Wallingford had said that he would handle things. It would not be proper for him to force himself on the guest at this stage.

He watched every gesture closely as the person moved about in the gardens. They were graceful, feminine movements. After several minutes, the figure walked back to the house and disappeared. It had been an emotional experience that left Jay frustrated.

He walked back to the chaise and lay down, but before long, unable to relax, he picked up his robe and went back to the apartment.

It was late in the afternoon. Jay was sitting in a chair, smoking a cigarette, when the phone rang.

'Hello, Jay. This is Avery Hawkins.' The voice of Cricket Kent came over the line. 'Mr Wallingford just left for the city. He suggested that I give you a call to see if you'd care to join me for a cocktail.'

'I would like to . . . very much.'

'All right. Why don't I meet you in that large room just off the foyer as you come in the front door? Does 5:30 sound OK?'

'Yes, that's fine. Thank you.'

Jay felt cold as he replaced the phone. It was almost as though he had a chill. He walked quickly into the bedroom and started to dress.

At precisely 5:30 Jay stood inside the door of the downstairs study staring at the face before him. It was mal-formed—almost hideous really. It was oblong, but twisted near one cheek in a way that was grotesque. One eye was normal enough, but the other, a trifle lower and as though designed for an altogether different body, appeared to be peering off in another direction. It was a face seemingly assembled from various parts and pieced together in a do-it-yourself fashion. Rather than the face of a human, to Jay it seemed it should be on some poor creature that slithered out of the pond behind the house.

Looking at his wavering reflection in the antique mirror, Jay questioned the merits of the piece. It was several centuries old and its patrimonial qualities, like everything at Lindenwald, were impeccable. But a mirror served one's vanity, and Jay wondered how anyone could ever have used it even hundreds of years ago without being repelled. Yet like so many ungraceful things it had endured, its deficiencies made attractive with the passing of time.

Jay moved his head several times endeavouring to focus on the part in his hair. But the reflection was a crooked line that defied straightening and he gave up.

He glanced at his watch and started winding it nervously. Turning, he walked toward a liquor cabinet in a far corner of the room. He poured himself a substantial shot of Scotch and took a long swallow. The whiskey scorched its way down his throat.

Several minutes passed and there was still no sign of Cricket. They were anxious moments. He walked to a window that looked out from the side of the house. He could see the servants' apartments and wondered if someday he might stand at the window as the owner of Lindenwald, looking over at his previous quarters.

The shrubs in the flower bed beneath the window caught his eye, and his thoughts turned again to the cherry tree at the rear of the house. The flower bed was soft. It should be easy to dig down under the tree. A pick and shovel would do the job. He would start a few feet out from the base, go down a couple of feet at an angle, and then come in underneath. That way he would avoid killing some of the roots. It would not be too difficult. And there was no alternative—no other way to find out what was underneath. He would do it soon—maybe that evening if Karlo was right about Mr Wallingford's leaving town.

It was then that he noticed the silent figure standing near the dogwood tree at the corner of the building. The figure startled him. It was the man who had chauffeured the grey limousine, the man they called Gotty. He was very still as though hardly more human than the trees among which he was standing. That is, all but the eyes. These were focused directly on Jay.

Jay quickly shifted his gaze back to the flower bed. It had

229

not been the kind of look that one would acknowledge.

He turned and walked toward another window farther down. He was standing, gazing at the view, when a soft voice broke the stillness of the room.

'Hello, Special Agent.'

Avery Hawkins stood in the doorway. It was an extraordinarily handsome figure, if somewhat pretty, with light brown hair streaked blond by the summer sun. The hair was long by Bureau standards, but neatly trimmed around small, almost dainty ears. A pair of striking blue eyes peered from a face that, although delicate, seemed cast from a perfect mould. A navy-blue blazer and light-blue denim slacks covered a frame that seemed to be that of a trim, average-sized male. A shirt was open at the neck displaying a light blue ascot. But undoubtedly the smile was the most dazzling aspect of the appearance. It was relaxed and confident—a smile that only one who was the proprietor of such splendid features could deliver.

It was not at all what Jay had anticipated. He had conjured a picture of Cricket Kent, beautiful but a bit comical in male clothes, a bit embarrassed trying to carry off her masculine role. It was not the case. The trim figure who strode toward him smiling was a poised, confident individual. While beautiful as Cricket Kent, the person was every bit as handsome in the role of Avery Hawkins. Immediately Jay was gripped by uncertainty

'Mr Hawkins . . . I presume,' said Jay, with a slight shrug of his shoulders.

Avery Hawkins laughed as they shook hands. 'You can't call me "Mr Hawkins," Jay. Not after what we've been through together.' The person continued to smile, exuding a relaxed self-assurance. 'Just call me "Avery".'

'Avery?' said Jay in a facetious tone. He did little to conceal his scepticism.

Again the laugh. It was a refreshing, almost adolescent laugh that rolled out easily.

'Well, I'm sure you understand, Jay. Sometimes one's duty must prevail over—'

'That was well beyond the call of duty up on that ledge . . .

Avery.'

'Maybe I shall join you in one of those.' Avery walked to the liquor cabinet and poured some vodka and tonic into a tall glass. 'Yes, Mr Wallingford told me that you got on to me out there. I think he rather enjoyed that you found out.'

'What's it all about?' said Jay abruptly. He had planned to force a recognition of the facts early, and the congenial tone of the meeting encouraged him to ask the question. 'Why were you surveilling me?'

Avery turned away with a glass in hand and said, 'First, let's have a drink. Intelligence work doesn't often present a time when two spies can join for a drink in such pleasant surroundings. Here's to your health, Jay. It's good to see you again.'

They drank, and Avery walked toward a chair. 'I love this place. I don't think there's another spot like it anywhere.'

'You've been here before, have you?' asked Jay.

'Oh yes. Many times. In fact, once I saw you here.'

'You did?' said Jay, surprised.

'Yes, quite a few years ago. It was just from a distance. Mr Wallingford and I were leaving and we saw you walking up toward the swimming pool. He told me all about you. So you see, I've known you for some time.' Again, the relaxed, self-assured smile.

'How long have you known Mr Wallingford?' asked Jay.

'Oh . . . I don't know. Probably not as long as you. That's lovely, isn't it.' Avery nodded toward the painting over the fireplace.

'Supposedly it resembles my mother,' said Jay, turning.

'Yes, I know,' said Avery. 'Mr Wallingford told me. I understand she disappeared many years ago.'

'Yes, she left our apartment one night, and that's the last she was heard of.'

'That's tragic.' A look of concern showed in the eyes.

'I never saw my mother or my father,' said Avery, after a pause. 'Mr Wallingford is the closest thing to a parent that I've ever had. He's been very good to me. . .' And then as though to change the subject, 'This is a magnificent room, isn't it?'

231

For the next several minutes they sat discussing the works of art in the room and Jay realised that Avery Hawkins was every bit as familiar with the downstairs study as was he. It made him increasingly uncomfortable.

It was soon apparent that Avery was not going to discuss any business. Any efforts by Jay to get on the subject were channelled into other areas. Time was passing. Finally he knew that if he was to elicit anything at all, it would have to be in some form of confrontation.

'Avery . . . I've been absolutely baffled by our relationship. In view of things that have happened I don't feel it's unreasonable to ask for some sort of explanation.'

Avery Hawkins gazed at him thoughtfully for several seconds without replying. It reminded Jay of the times when Cricket Kent would pause, milling over her answers. 'I'm sure Mr Wallingford has told you, Jay, that we discuss business only on a need-to-know basis. I know it may be difficult for you to understand, being relatively new, but tight security is imperative when it comes to intelligence work. It comes ahead of everything else—even certain moral considerations. An agent who talks, or even one who is threatened with exposure and may be forced to talk, is a liability to the entire organisation. That's why, as cruel as it may seem, it's far better to remove such an agent. You should keep that in mind. "Intelligence", as they call it, is nothing more than an extensive group of agents contacting each other in an effort to transmit information. It's rather like a string of beads. If one breaks, then the others follow quickly.'

As he listened a sense of euphoria came over Jay. How much was due to the Scotch he did not know, but somehow just sitting there in the room with Avery engendered a feeling of well-being.

Jay swallowed what was left of his drink, and when a pause occurred in the conversation, he stood up. 'Will you join me in another?'

'Yes, thank you.' Before handing it to Jay, Avery took a last swallow from the glass and, then rising, walked to the window from which Jay had been looking previously. 'Is that where you live, over there?'

'That's right,' answered Jay from the liquor cabinet. He poured a substantial amount of vodka into Avery's glass. He started to put the bottle down, and then added a touch more. 'That's home,' he said, carrying the glasses toward the window.

They stood at the window, holding their glasses while looking across the drive toward the servants' quarters. The sun had moved down beyond a cluster of maple trees off to the left, but a few rays still reflected off the windowpane. It was the closest they had been since the afternoon on the ledge.

As though sensing Jay's feeling, Avery left the window and walked to the fireplace, placing the drink on the mantel. Jay turned from the window, and as he did his eye caught the silent figure outside standing in the precise spot among the trees where he had been before. It gave Jay an uneasy feeling.

Avery was lighting a cigarette as Jay walked to a chair near the fireplace and sat down. The flame reflected briefly in Avery's face, giving a wavering golden cast, and Jay was suddenly struck by an odd almost weird percipience. But what was it? A likeness perhaps? Something from the past? A familiarity in the features? He raised his eyes to the portrait. The unwavering green eyes looked down at him intently. The lips seemed to part as though to speak, but then it was gone. Irrevocable.

'Anything wrong, Jay?' asked Avery, glancing at him curiously while he shook out the match.

'No, nothing,' answered Jay. As he sat drinking and exchanging remarks a sense of hopelessness settled over him. It was obvious Avery Hawkins was determined to keep Cricket Kent a thing of the past. Jay was pursuing the same illusive phantom—a girl from another world who apparently was gone and would not be permitted to return.

'Well, I suppose I should be going on,' said Avery. 'I've enjoyed this, Jay, very much.'

Jay felt the sinking feeling he invariably experienced when Cricket Kent was leaving. Emboldened by the Scotch and experiencing a sense of futility and frustration, he rose and walked to where Avery stood leaning against the mantel. 'I want to ask only one question. I'm sure I know the answer, but I want to hear you say.'

Avery looked at him uneasily and forced a grin. 'Remember what I said? It's a need-to-know policy.'

'Please. Just answer yes or no,' said Jay. 'It is Cricket, isn't it?'

Avery paused in the usual meditative manner, and then again came the confident smile. 'I don't think you need to know that now. But if you ever do, I don't think I shall have to tell you.'

Jay shrugged hopelessly and smiled. 'Very well . . . Avery. Goodbye.'

'Goodbye, Jay.' There was a trace of sadness in the eyes.

Jay turned and walked toward the door. At the door he stopped and looked back again at the figure, and smiled. 'You know, Avery, now that I've seen your road uniforms, I can't help wondering what you wear for home games.'

Avery Hawkins dissolved in boyish laughter.

The scene from Jay's bedroom window could evoke a variety of emotions. The pond could be a gay and happy place, or sad at times, or, as it was at this particular moment, forlorn and a bit frightening. It was twilight. A few crows flitting among the treetops were indistinguishable from bats. From across the pond the cheerful sounds so prevalent during the day were slowly muted, and a dull, dead, intermittent bleat began, beating louder and faster as the creatures of the darkness took over. There was enough light left on the far bank to reflect a grey upside-down scene, but soon this, too, died away, dissolving into the slick ebony pool. The vivid colours of the wild flowers and the green tones of moss and algae faded into shadows and the world of sunshine was lost in a preview of death.

In the window of his bedroom Jay sat looking out at the scene, feeling the irrecoverability of the parting day. It had been a lovely day. One that had been so promising when he stood there at the window early that morning. But it had come and gone and his hopes had been largely unfulfilled.

The meeting with Cricket had been a frustrating

234

experience. He knew little more than he had before. Indeed, he wondered if there would ever be anything more. She was like one of the wild flowers on the side of the pond that suddenly appeared gloriously from nowhere only to disappear without a trace.

The meeting with Mr Wallingford had been no more productive; he had communicated little of his intentions. Jay wondered again about the relationship between Avery Hawkins and Mr Wallingford. It was strange. In some ways it was similar to his own. But Hawkins was unquestionably the fair-haired one right now.

His thoughts turned to the cherry tree, once again arousing his curiosity. Soon the big house would be dark and virtually empty. If Avery Hawkins was still there, he would be in one of the guest rooms in the other wing. He would be able to dig undisturbed, and in a matter of minutes he would know. Of course, maybe Ted Summers had been imagining things. But what if he had? No harm would be done. All Jay had invested was an hour or so of his time.

But it was the other possibility that was disturbing—the fact that something might actually be there.

He continued to sit at the window as darkness covered Lindenwald. A sense of foreboding seemed to descend on the estate. His father came, wished him goodnight, and went to bed. It was almost midnight when he finally rose and, taking a flashlight, started for his father's tool shed at the rear of the greenhouse. After securing a shovel and pick, he started for the main house.

It was cool for a June night. While there was no moon, the skies were clear and the rolling land behind Lindenwald was clearly visible. It was only in the deep shadows of the shrubbery near the base of the house that it was truly dark. It was here that Jay moved cautiously among the bushes.

Rounding the corner at the rear of the dwelling, he glanced up once again at the garrison windows that enclosed David Wallingford's study. They were dark, affirming the report he had received earlier that Mr Wallingford was gone.

At the rear of the house he pushed his way through the foliage to the perimeter of the shrubbery and paused when he first glimpsed the cherry tree. It was a magnificent tree. His father had commented in the past on its beauty. When it was blooming, it was a particularly lovely sight, its branches bending low toward the ground, where the soft petals collected underneath. His father never raked under the tree during these times, but rather let the blossoms collect on the shrubs and spread out from the base like a soft white gown.

Jay glanced up once again toward the study. He rested the pickaxe against the side of the house and taking the shovel moved quietly beneath the tree. Immediately he experienced a great sense of relief, of comfort almost, beneath the full leaves overhead. It was an odd sensation—particularly in view of the excitement the mission had engendered.

Carefully he placed the tip of the spade against the soft flower bed a few feet from the base of the tree. After placing his foot on top of the shovel he paused, once again considering the advisability of his undertaking.

Steeling himself for what lay ahead, he thrust the metal blade deep into the ground, unaware of the silent figure with the emotionless eyes in the shadows who reached for the pickaxe that leaned against the building.

'Good morning, *former* Special Agent Holloway.'

Jumping Joe's face blanched the colour of the dull buckskin jacket he was wearing. He had just been summoned by Elston Doolittle via car radio from El Paso, where he had undertaken a host of fresh leads in connection with the Leopard Boulevard case. The buckskin jacket together with a large flopping sombrero wwas part of his ensemble to blend in with the local gentry while endeavouring to develop the leads among the Mexicans who inhabited the area.

Partly out of deference to his boss, but mostly from self-consciousness, he had removed the hat before entering Doolittle's office. Now he stood nervously ringing the hat between his hands as he regarded the large man sitting in front of him. It was not only the greeting, but the icy, courteous manner with which it had been delivered that was so totally unnerving to Joe. The appearance of his boss sitting rigidly behind the desk wearing a courteous, if paper-thin,

236

smile was a sight simply beyond the subordinate's comprehension.

'I beg your pardon . . . sir?'

'You heard me, *Mr* Holloway.' It was still the same restrained tone, but behind it Joe sensed the rage of a thousand ages. And the *Mr* part. The boss hadn't called him *Mr* since he had introduced Joe to Mrs Doolittle over five years previously.

'I have here before me your resignation all duly witnessed and ready for you to sign,' continued Doolittle. He patted a sheet of paper that rested neatly before him on the centre of his desk.

'My—my what, sir?' murmured Joe twisting the sombrero into a gigantic bow tie. 'I don't think I understand, sir. I'm not resigning. I still have six years to go, remember? You just said last week you only had to put up with me for another six—'

'You stupid, blundering idiot!' The plans for restraint erupted into a wild bellow that reverberated through the outer offices, the force of the blast lifting Miss Quinby a full three inches from her chair. 'You don't have six *minutes* left in this outfit. I should have dumped you when I first came here. Do you know where I've been these past three days?' Two red-rimmed eyes glared ferociously out of the haggard face at Jumping Joe. 'Answer me! Do you?'

'Yes, yes. Of course, sir. You,' stammered Joe, 'You've been to the seat of government. Ah . . . nice to have you back, Chief.'

'That's right!' boomed Doolittle. 'I spent two whole days with the Director, and I had my ass chewed out 480 minutes each day. Do you know what it's like, Holloway, to have your ass chewed out for *two whole days?*'

Joe knew. He nodded his head solemnly.

'Yes, Mr Holloway, with our Director for two days.' Doolittle had suddenly regained control and was biting the words off with frigid equanimity. 'And this afternoon, do you know where I'm going?'

Joe shook his head numbly.

'To San Juan, Puerto Rico.' Doolittle shifted his eyes to the large elm tree just beyond the open window of his office. 'I've

237

been transferred . . . to another country.'

For a moment Joe was afraid Doolittle was about to break down. He shifted from one leg to another several times. 'Anything I can do?' asked Joe with genuine sympathy.

'Yes,' replied Elston Doolittle, turning once again to the matter at hand. 'Just sign here above your name.'

'But, Chief, what's it all about? I still have six years—'

'You've got two minutes, Holloway,' interrupted Doolittle, firing a savage look at his subordinate. 'You're through. The sands have run out. They've finally caught up with you, Holloway. You remember that new agent Von Flake or whoever he was who was in *your* charge—that *you* were responsible for? Do you remember him, Holloway?' Doolittle's voice was rising again, trembling with rage.

'Yes, sir. I think so, sir. Blond-haired, nice-looking kid—'

'Well, it just so happens, Holloway, that he was a sleeper agent.'

'A what, sir?'

'A *sleeper* agent, damn you!' Doolittle slammed the top of his desk, and a small bird which had come to rest on a branch of the elm tree fluttered quickly away through the leaves. Doolittle stood up abruptly and began pacing the well-worn path between the desk and the window. 'A sleeper agent. Like you, only he was getting paid for it by the Russians. And here he was right under *your* very nose—for a whole goddamn year. A double agent working for the communists and here you are *training* him—for *them*.' Doolittle paused before the open window, weighing, it seemed, the advantages of bringing it all to an end with one leap.

'My God, Chief! How . . . I mean . . . really . . .'

'It's all in the file there,' said Doolittle, still looking out the window, the voice coming from one whose thoughts were far off in some distant clime. 'The Director released the information to the field this morning.'

Joe Holloway gingerly picked up a thick file whose cover contained in large block letters the words '*TOP SECRET*.' Slowly he turned to the synopsis—the passage of Bureau reports appearing on the first page containing a synoptic review of all the salient facts that appear later in the details.

Joe read the synopsis as he read everything—slowly.

James J Von Vlack
INTERNAL SECURITY—R

SYNOPSIS

VON VLACK believed recruited by KGB sometime late 1960s and assigned USA as sleeper agent until Oct. 1969 when reactivated in Bureau as double agent pursuant to Soviet programme for infiltration of FBI. Disappearance of VON VLACK's former roommate SA HARVEY TUCKER (Missing Federal Officer 57–651) spring 1970 believed possibly linked to subject organisation. Physical and technical surveillances maintained on VON VLACK since TUCKER'S disappearance in effort to develop leads relative to identity of TOPLEV KGB agent Western Hemisphere (code name MR WHO 75–284) unsuccessful to date. VON VLACK assigned Albaquerque June 1970. Transferred to Chicago May 1971. Transferred to NYO June 1971 and kept under loose surveillance until his disappearance July 1, 1971. VON VLACK'S present whereabouts unknown. Investigation continuing.

PENDING

Joe Holloway didn't bother with the details of the report. He knew a prima facie case when he saw one. Carefully he replaced the file in its original position on the desk. Then, with the barest sigh, he reached for the typewritten piece of paper bearing his name. It was an inartistic resignation, brief and to the point:

I, Joseph T Holloway, hereby submit my resignation as Special Agent of the Federal Bureau of Investigation effective close of business this date.

Very truly yours,
Joseph T. Holloway

Witnessed:
Elston P Doolittle
Special Agent in Charge

Joe slowly and precisely inscribed his name. Then, rubbing a tiny globule of moisture from his eye, he turned solemnly toward his boss and made his final contribution to the Bureau scene. 'Chief, you know that synopsis there on Von Vlack? I'm not sure, but I think someone misspelled the word "Albuquerque".'

PART THREE

Mr Who

It was twilight and the vibrant patches of colour that covered the rolling meadows of Lindenwald by day were fading into the dull landscape of evening. Darkness was hurried by tumbling black storm clouds gathering on the horizon. Dusk quickly settled over the grounds, and the tapering rays of light that drifted through the garrison windows formed grid patterns on the far wall. The Lord of Lindenwald sat blanketed in shadows in a wine-coloured leather chair watching the remnants of the fading day.

He picked up his pipe from a nearby stand. Then, fumbling for a lighter in his dark satin smoking jacket, he stood and walked toward a framed photograph that occupied an important position on the panelled wall. It was a small picture bearing the achromatic hue characteristic of very old photographs. It showed Johan Von Vlack, the head gardener of Lindenwald, as a young man standing near the servants' quarters. On his arm was a beautiful blond-haired woman, and it was on her that David Wallingford focused his attention.

Casually, in the languid fashion of one for whom time held ever decreasing significance, he lit his pipe and then again rested his eyes on the lovely face. A coil of smoke curling from the pipe caused the figure to shimmer slightly in the subdued light. It was a momentary vision but the infusion of movement in the exquisite smile pierced 30 years of blunted memories, and for one rare instant Werta Von Vlack was with him—the delicate features, the superior bearing, the incomparable style that would have been the perfect complement for

Lindenwald had he been able to control the indomitable spirit.

A light breeze floated into the room through the partially opened window and ruffled the crown of the white head. It was soft, feminine hand from long ago, tousling butter-coloured hair, stimulating thoughts from a happier time. For a few brief seconds they were with him—the lovely face, the light laughter, the tiny hands—a parade of memories that passed quickly, muted by the years.

From somewhere beyond the estate there was the sound of a meadowlark. And then, as always, on the wind came the Byronic lines that had haunted him through the years, ' . . . and whispering she'd ne'er consent, she consented.'

Two long, sharp rings from a telephone interrupted his reverie. Rising quickly, he walked to a far corner, where he picked up one of two telephones resting on a table.

'Hello. . . Yes, Mr President. . . No, I didn't go to Langley. I had to attend to a matter here. . . Yes, sir. Everything is quite in order. Our men occupy all the key positions. . . Yes, we have all the dossiers under our control. . . Yes, of course, sir. We shall see that you receive yours the first thing in the morning . . . Yes, I can assure you everything is under control. You can appoint a new Director tomorrow . . . No, sir. He doesn't know. He still thinks it's a communist conspiracy. . . That's quite all right, Mr President. The power of the Bureau was an awesome threat and no one feels better about bringing it under control than we in the CIA . . . Thank you, sir.'

After hanging up the phone he turned and walked to the window and assumed the position from which he had observed a century of seasons. A thread of lightning, an irregular cardiogram in the billowing dark clouds, lit up the sky, and for an instant Lindenwald was suspended in a grey gothic world.

From the distance came a long sustained thunderclap like millions of hands erupting in spontaneous applause. It hung on the night air for a few brief seconds and then expired, reverting to a low ominous grumble which reverberated across the sky.

The first few raindrops came, beating against the

244

windowpane. Again the breeze, only stronger now, and the thundercloud cherry tree swayed in the wind, its gloomy lavender leaves fluttering and bending to shield the stripling by its side.